Lynn Knight has edited the Virago Modern Classics series at Virago Press since 1988. She has written introductions, contributed to the *Oxford Companion to Twentieth Century Literature* and reviewed for the *Observer*. She lives in South London.

Infinite Riches

Classic Stories by
Twentieth-Century Women Writers

Edited by
LYNN KNIGHT

Faber and Faber
BOSTON · LONDON

First published in the United States in 1993 by
Faber and Faber, Inc., 50 Cross Street, Winchester, MA 01890.
Originally published in the United Kingdom in 1993 by
Virago Press Limited, 20–23 Mandela Street, Camden Town,
London NW1 0HQ.

Library of Congress Cataloguing-in-Publication Data

Infinite riches : classic stories by twentieth-century women writers /
[edited by] Lynn Knight.
p.   cm.
ISBN 0-571-19824-4
1. Short stories, English.   2. Short stories, American—Women
authors.   3. English fiction—Women authors.   4. Women—
Fiction.   I. Knight, Lynn.
PR1309.S5154   1993
823'.01089287—dc20   93-14355

The cover shows a detail from *Sonja in Green* by Sir James Gunn.
Photograph © Christies Color Library.
Cover design by the Senate

Printed in the United States of America

Contents

Acknowledgements

Permission to reproduce the following stories is gratefully acknowledged: 'An Act of Reparation' by Sylvia Townsend Warner from *Selected Stories*, Chatto & Windus, 1989, Copyright © Susanna Pinney, William Maxwell 1989, by permission of the Executors of the Sylvia Townsend Warner Estate and *The New Yorker*; 'Living on the Box' by Penelope Gilliatt, from *What's It Like Out?*, Martin Secker and Warburg Ltd., 1968, Copyright © Penelope Gilliatt 1968, by permission of the author; 'Plain Pleasures' by Jane Bowles from *The Collected Works of Jane Bowles*, Peter Owen, 1984, Copyright © Paul Bowles, reprinted by permission of Peter Owen Publishers; 'The Secret Woman' by Colette from *The Other Woman*, Peter Owen, 1971, English language Copyright © Peter Owen 1971, by permission of Peter Owen Publishers; 'I Stand Here Ironing' by Tillie Olsen, from *Tell Me a Riddle*, Faber & Faber Ltd., 1964, Copyright © 1964, by permission of the author and Abner Stein; 'Flesh' by Elizabeth Taylor from *The Devastating Boys*, Chatto & Windus 1972, Copyright © Elizabeth Taylor 1972, by permission of Virago Press Ltd. and A. M. Heath; 'The Sentimentality of William Tavener' by Willa Cather, from *Collected Short Fiction 1892–1912*, edited by Virginia Faulkener, introduced by Mildred R. Bennett, Copyright © 1965, 1970 by the University of Nebraska Press, by permission of the University of Nebraska Press; 'A Dream of Winter' by Rosamond Lehmann, from *The Gypsy's Baby*, William Collins 1946, Copyright © Rosamond Lehmann 1946, by permission of The Society of Authors as the literary representative of the Estate of Rosamond Lehmann; 'The Jest of Jests' by Djuna Barnes from *Smoke and Other Early Stories*, Sun and Moon Press,

ACKNOWLEDGEMENTS

1982, Copyright © Sun and Moon Press 1982, by permission of the Maggie Noach Literary Agency; 'The House of Clouds' by Antonia White, from *Strangers*, The Harvill Press, 1954, Copyright © Antonia White 1954, by permission of Curtis Brown & John Farquharson on behalf of the Estate of Antonia White; 'Out with the Girls' by Nell Dunn, from *Up the Junction*, MacGibbon & Kee Limited 1963, Copyright © Nell Dunn 1963, by permission of the author and Virago Press; 'Until Such Times' by Jessie Kesson from *Where the Apple Ripens*, Chatto & Windus, 1985, Copyright © Jessie Kesson 1985, by permission of Chatto & Windus; 'As They Rode Along the Edge' by Leonora Carrington, from *The Seventh Horse and Other Tales*, Dutton, 1988, Copyright © Leonora Carrington 1988, translated from the French by Kathrine Talbot, by permission of Dutton, an imprint of New American Library, a divison of Penguin Books USA Inc. and Virago Press; 'Time is Unredeemable' by Attia Hosain, from *Phoenix Fled*, Chatto & Windus, 1953, Copyright © Attia Hosain 1953, by permission of the author and Virago Press; 'Distance' by Grace Paley from *Enormous Changes at the Last Minute*, André Deutsch, 1975, Copyright © 1956, Farrar, Straus & Giroux, 1974, N.Y., by permission of Grace Paley and André Deutsch; 'Seen from Paradise' by Dorothy Richardson from *Journey to Paradise*, selected and introduced by Trudi Tate, Virago Press, 1989, Copyright © The Estate of Dorothy Richardson 1989, by permission of Virago Press; 'The Salt of the Earth' by Rebecca West from *The Harsh Voice*, Jonathan Cape 1935, Copyright © Rebecca West 1935, by permission of the Peters, Fraser and Dunlop Group Ltd.

Every effort has been made to trace copyright holders in all copyright material in this book. The editor regrets if there has been any oversight and suggests the publisher is contacted in any such event.

Introduction

These stories travel from the decorum of an Anglo-American hotel, to a masked French ball, via postwar India and a village in the Scottish highlands, and from the middle classes of England between the wars, to the vitality of the 1960's inner city. The concerns they explore are as varied as their terrain, casting light on the lives and experiences of a host of women and, obliquely or overtly, the codes and assumptions of their particular time and place.

Infinite Riches features some of the most accomplished women writers of this century. *Grande dames* of the short story, such as Sylvia Townsend Warner and Elizabeth Taylor, whose work is frequently anthologized (and from whom it was agony to choose only one story), mingle with authors who are less widely known. That the choice of individual stories brought its own enjoyable difficulties is a mark of the authors' considerable talent and the enormous pleasure their work has given me. The selection is as personal as that in any anthology. There are stories I've loved for years, fresh delights discovered among old loves and others that held new attractions. I looked for stories that replay themselves, whose moods and undertones strike an insistent note; that reveal what Willa Cather described as:

> the double life: the group life, which is the one we can observe in our neighbor's household, and underneath, another – secret and passionate and intense – which is the real life that stamps the faces and gives character to the voices of our friends . . . and which more than any other outward event make[s] our lives happy or unhappy.[1]

This 'real life' is integral to an anthology in which interior dramas are frequently employed to reach into the hidden corners of otherwise unsung lives. The crux of Penelope Gilliatt's story is an event where 'real life' unintentionally collides with well-rehearsed lines and is all too vividly and publicly exposed. Her evocation of a marriage that has degenerated into an emotional war of attrition and whose participants no longer know one another is economically crafted. She creates *and* dismantles the relationship within single sentences of wounding clarity and then wraps them in the gestures and idiosyncrasies upon which the relationship has snagged itself. The result is a lingering portrait of a woman wrung out by love and 'insufficiency'.

The finest short stories bring to the revelation of a given moment an elliptical past that enlarges it. So, in her lean yet abundant tale, 'The Sentimentality of William Tavener', Willa Cather seems to do no more than glance backwards, but in doing so recreates a whole community of farmsteading, with all its privations, as well as the essence of a marriage, from courtship to middle age: a complete cycle, with loss and replenishment, within only a few pages.

Many of the stories build upon the minutiae of dailiness to convey more than is stated. Part of Elizabeth Taylor's skill is her fusion of conversational nuance and tone with layer upon layer of small details that render the seemingly incidental crucial. Whatever her subject, she writes from within it, character and situation are never forced, but moulded. Phyl of 'Flesh', 'massive and glittering and sunburnt', with her kindliness and her small talk perfected by years behind a bar, is one of Elizabeth Taylor's most glorious creations. 'Flesh' tells of a holiday assignation but, as with all her work, this intricate blend of wit and poignancy speaks of fundamental hopes and aspirations.

In 'The House of Clouds', drawn from Antonia White's experience of Bedlam, details are focused to oppressive effect, triggering one nightmarish fantasy after another. Sylvia Townsend Warner's uplifting comedy uses kitchen utensils, and some violently clashing wallpapers, to categorize two women and two marriages. She offers a recipe, too, for good measure and some tantalizing smells along route. 'An Act of Reparation' makes you hungry as you smile (unlike the dreadful meal served to Elizabeth Taylor's hopeful lovers). Food – and alcohol – albeit plainer fare, is equally significant to Jane Bowles' story, and served with an offbeat wit.

Humour, in many shades, is an important feature of *Infinite Riches*. Leonora Carrington's surrealist tale, trouncing 'the odour of sanctity', proceeds with a wicked glint and Nell Dunn's women, out on the town with the zestful optimism of youth, are refreshingly cheeky. Elsewhere, a rueful humour lightens uncomfortable realizations, and wit abounds. Djuna Barnes brings an impressively salty tone to her dissection of lovers' rites, while Grace Paley's foot-tapping New York rhythms underpin each phrase of 'Distance'. Her narrator, with an armoury of received opinions and slack language, may seem to take life as it comes, but asks the biggest question: 'What the devil is it all about?'

It's a question that many of the women here could ask as they pursue the marriages and love affairs that form a considerable part of this anthology. For some stories, relationships – in various stages of contentment and disarray – are the focal point, in others they are simply part of life's upholstery. Two are rooted in the social and cultural benefits and expectations that marriage confers. Attia Hosain's 'Time is Unredeemable' constructs a painful mockery of a 'wedding night' and in 'Souls Belated' Edith Wharton examines the theme she made her own:

the brutality of Old American Society in ostracizing those who transgress its rules. 'Souls Belated' is double-edged, ironically exposing the effect of those rules on two lovers who have fled the country, and supposedly rejected its mores. In contrast, the women in stories by Colette and Dorothy Richardson slip the leash of conventional behaviour: one finds liberation by stalking a party wearing disguise, the other expresses sheer joy at being alone, in a tale whose structure is as freewheeling as her thoughts.

Class is the backbone of Rebecca West's novella, 'The Salt of the Earth'. The setting is England between the wars and its interest lies as much in the precise location of an era — with maids and calling-cards — as in the actions of Alice Pember-ton. The worst embodiment of middle-class leisure, she has sharpened self-righteous interference to the point of tyranny, and is the only woman in this collection whom I wouldn't care to meet. 'The Salt of the Earth' teases with suspense and is guided by the increasing despair of Alice's husband Jimmy. Like the couple in 'Souls Belated', though separated by time and a continent, he is imprisoned by convention. However, in America middle-class divorce was possible — if unforgivable — in England, it was simply unthinkable.[2]

Rosamond Lehmann looks at the same world of servants and plenty in the moment heralding its disintegration: the cusp of the Second World War. The narrator of 'A Dream of Winter' has 'friends with revolutionary ideas and belonged to the Left Bookclub' and, with a nice touch for a story that also unravels class guilt, her young son chastizes his sister for picking up the local dialect. Children punctuate 'A Dream of Winter', drifting in and out, yet demanding our whole attention. Their natural curiosity, so swiftly satisfied, their grasshopper minds, are caught to perfection. The children in Rosamond Lehmann's fiction are always alive on the page. So, too, is the child of Jessie Kesson's story, with her partial knowledge of the adult world, her vulnerability and inadequate defences. But the most haunting perspective on childhood is Tillie Olsen's 'I Stand Here Ironing', in which a mother looks back to an age of 'depression, war and fear' and a relationship with her first-born daughter that was hampered by poverty and anxiety. Part lament, part incantation, its honesty bruises. Each word has been honed and is clean, in a story of want and struggle that completely avoids sentimentality.

Although the majority of the stories in this collection were written in the first half of this century, the yearnings and contrivings they express have a contemporary resonance. The women who inhabit *Infinite Riches* (with the exception, hopefully, of Alice Pemberton) are just as bold, buffeted and blinkered as the rest of us.

1. Willa Cather, *Not Under Forty*, Alfred A. Knopf, USA, 1936
2. Introduction to *The Harsh Voice*, Rebecca West, Virago Press, London, 1982

Sylvia Townsend Warner

An Act of Reparation

Lapsang sooshang – must smell like tar.
Liver salts in *blue* bottle.
Strumpshaw's bill – why 6*d*?
Crumpets.
Waistcoat buttons.
Something for weekend – not a chicken.

So much of the list had been scratched off that this remainder would have made cheerful reading if it had not been for the last item.

Valerie Hardcastle knew where she was with a chicken. You thawed it, put a lump of marg inside, and roasted it. While it was in the oven you could give your mind to mashed potatoes (Fenton couldn't endure packet crisps), bread sauce and the vegetable of the season – which latterly had been sprouts. A chicken was calm and straightforward: you ate it hot, then you ate it cold; and it was a further advantage that one chicken is pretty much like another. Chicken is reliable – there is no apple-pie-bed side to its character. With so much in married life proving apple-pie-beddish, the weekend chicken had been as soothing as going to church might be if you were that sort of person. But now Fenton had turned – like any worm, she thought, though conscious that the comparison was inadequate – declaring that he was surfeited with roast chicken, that never again

1

was she to put one of those wretched commercialized birds before him.

'Think of their hideous lives, child! Penned up, regimented, stultified. They never see a blade of grass, they never feel the fresh air, all they know is chicken, chicken, chicken – just like us at weekends. Where is that appalling draught coming from? You must have left a window open somewhere.'

'What do you think I ought to get instead? I could do liver-and-bacon. But that doesn't go on to the next day.'

'Can't you get a joint?'

A joint. What joint? She had never cooked a joint. At home, Mum made stews. At the Secretarial College there was mince and shepherd's pie. No doubt a joint loomed in the background of these – but distantly, like mountains in Wales. When she and Olive Petty broke away from the college to share a bed-sitting room and work as dancing partners at the town's new skating rink their meals mainly consisted of chips and salami, varied by the largesse of admirers who took them to restaurants. Fenton, as an admirer, had expressed himself in *scampi* and *crêpes Suzette* – pronounced 'crapes', not 'creeps' – with never a mention of joints. Grey-haired, though with lots of it, he was the educated type, and theirs was an ideal relationship till Mrs Fenton, whom he had not mentioned either – not to speak of – burst out like a tiger, demanding divorce. The case was undefended. Six months later to the day, Fenton made an honest woman of her. Brought her down to earth, so to speak.

Marriage, said the registrar, was a matter of give-and-take. Marriage, thought Valerie, was one thing after another. Now it was joints. Sunk in marriage, she sat at a small polished table in the bank, waiting for Fenton's queries about his statement sheets to be thoroughly gone into, meanwhile enjoying the orderliness and impersonality of an establishment so unlike a kitchen or a bedroom.

And at an adjoining table sat the previous Mrs Hardcastle who for her part had come to withdraw a silver teapot from the bank's strong room, examining with a curiosity she tried to keep purely abstract the young person who had supplanted her in Fenton's affections. Try as she might, abstraction was not possible. Conscience intervened, compunction and stirrings of guilt. It was all very well for Isaac; he had not drawn Abraham's attention to the ram in the thicket. It was all very well for Iphigenia, who had not suggested to the goddess that a hind could replace her at the sacrificial altar. Isaac and Iphigenia could walk off with minds untroubled by any shade of responsibility for the substituted victim. But she, Lois Hardcastle, writhing in the boredom of being married to Fenton, had snatched at Miss Valerie Fry, who had done her no harm whatever, and got away at her expense. And this, this careworn, deflated little chit staring blankly at a shopping list, was what Fenton had made of her in less than six months' matrimony.

'Oh, dear!' said Lois, and sighed feelingly.

Hearing the exclamation and the sigh, Valerie glanced up to discover who was taking on so. She could see nothing to account for it. The woman was definitely middle-aged, long past having anything to sound tragic about. Indeed, she looked uncommonly healthy and prosperous, was expensively made up, wore a wedding ring, had no shopping bags – so why should she jar the polish and repose of a bank by sighing and exclaiming 'Oh dear'? Leg of lamb, leg of pork, leg of . . . did nothing else have legs? A bank clerk came up with a sealed parcel, saying 'Here it is, Mrs Hardcastle. If you'll just sign for it.'

'Here, you've made a mistake! Those aren't Mr Hardcastle's – ' As Valerie spoke, she saw the parcel set down in front of the other woman. Fenton's other one. For it was she, though so smartened up as to be almost unrecognizable. What an awkward situation! And what a pity she had drawn attention to herself by saying that about the parcel. Fortunately, Fenton's other one did not appear to have noticed anything. She read the form carefully through, took her time over signing it, exchanged a few words with the clerk about the time of year before he carried it away. Of course, at her age she was probably a bit deaf, so she would not have heard those give-away words. The give-away words sounded on in Valerie's head. She was still blushing vehemently when the other Mrs Hardcastle looked her full in the face and said, cool as a cucumber, 'Mrs Lois Hardcastle, now. What an odd place we've chosen to meet in.'

Pulling herself together, Valerie replied, 'Quite a co-incidence.'

'Such a small world. I've come to collect a teapot. And you, I gather, are waiting for Fenton's statement sheets, just as I used to do. And it's taking a long time, just as it always did.'

'There were some things Mr Hardcastle wanted looked into.'

Not to be put down, Mr Hardcastle's earlier wife continued, 'Now that the bank has brought us together, I hope you'll come and have coffee with me. I'm going back to London tonight, so it's my only chance to hear how you both are.'

'I don't know that I can spare the time, thank you all the same, I'm behindhand as it is, and I've got to buy a joint for the weekend.'

'Harvey's or Ensten's?'

'Well, I don't really know. I'd rather thought of the Co-op.'

'Excellent for pork.'

'To tell the truth, I've not bought a joint before. We've always had a chicken. But now he's got tired of chicken.'

Five months of love and chicken . . .

'I'm afraid you've been spoiling him,' said Lois. 'Keep him on cold veal for a few weeks and he'll be thankful for chicken.'

'I hadn't thought of veal. Would veal be a good idea?'

'Here come your statement sheets. Now we can go and have some coffee and think about the veal.'

'Well, I must say, I'd be glad of it. Shopping gets me down.'

Tottering on stiletto heels and still a head shorter than Lois, the replacement preceded her from the bank, jostling the swinging doors with her two bulging, ill-assembled shopping bags. Lois took one from her. It was the bag whose handle Fenton, in a rush of husbandry, had mended with string. The string ground into her fingers – as fatal, as familiar, as ever.

The grey downs grew into lumps of sin to Guenevere in William Morris's poem, and as Fenton's wives sat drinking coffee the shopping bags humped on the third chair grew into lumps of sin to Lois. They were her bags, her burden; and she had cast them onto the shoulders of this hapless child and gone flourishing off, a free woman. It might be said, too, though she made less of it, that she had cast the child on Fenton's ageing shoulders and hung twenty-one consecutive frozen chickens round his neck ... a clammy garland. Apparently it was impossible to commit the simplest act of selfishness, of self-defence even, without paining and inconveniencing others. Lost in these reflections, Lois forgot to keep the conversation going. It was Valerie who revived it. 'Where would one be without one's cup of coffee?'

For, considering how handicapped she was with middle age and morality, Fenton's other one had been putting up a creditable show of sophisticated broadmindedness, and deserved a helping hand – the more so since that sigh in the bank was now so clearly explainable as a sigh of regret for the days when she had a husband to cook for. Lois agreed that one would be quite lost without one's cup of coffee. 'And I always think it's such a mistake to put milk in,' continued Valerie, who with presence of mind had refused milk, black coffee being more sophisticated. Two sophisticated women, keeping their poise on the rather skiddy surface of a serial husband, was how she saw the situation. For a while, she managed to keep conversation on a black-coffee level: foreign

5

travel, television, the guitar. But you could see the poor thing's heart wasn't really in it; grieving for what could never again be hers, she just tagged along. Yes, she had been to Spain, but it was a long time ago. No, unfortunately, she had missed that programme. 'I never seem to have enough time. Do have another cake.' She seemed to have time enough now. The cake lay on her plate, the coffee cooled in her cup; still she sat brooding, and frowned as though she were calculating some odds, hatching some resolution. Could it be that she was going to turn nasty? All of a sudden, she looked up and exclaimed, 'I know. Oxtail.'

'I beg your pardon?'

'Oxtail. Instead of a joint. Come on.'

Well, if it made her happy . . .

It certainly did. A wife Fenton hadn't given her an idea of, a wife as animated and compelling as a scenic railway, swept Valerie to the butcher's, summoned old Mr Ensten himself, made him produce a series of outlandish objects totally unlike Valerie's conception of what could be called a joint, chose out the most intimidating of the lot, stiff as a poker and a great deal longer, watched with a critical eye as he smote it into coilability, swept on to a greengrocer to buy carrots, garlic, celery and button mushrooms, then to a grocer's shop, bafflingly small, dusky and undisplaying, where she bought peppercorns, bay leaves and a jar of anchovies, finally to a wine merchant where she bought half a bottle of claret. Whirled on in this career, consulted and assenting over God knew what next, abandoning all thought of the rest of her shopping list, Valerie fell from gasps to giggles. Why peppercorns, when pepper could be got ready ground? Why anchovies, when there was no thought of fish? And garlic? Now it was claret.

'And a taxi, please.'

As though it were perfectly normal for wine merchants to supply taxis, the taxi was fetched. Valerie was put into it; the parcels and shopping bags were put in after her.

'Seventeen Windermere Gardens,' said Lois.

Once, escaping from the Secretarial College, Valerie and Olive Petty bought half-crown tickets for a Mystery Drive. The bus, thundering through a maze of small streets, had taken them past the Corporation Gas Works into the unknown. It had dived into woods, skirted past villages with spires and villages with towers, shown them an obelisk on a hill-top, a reservoir, a bandstand, an Isolation Hospital, a glimpse of the sea, a waterfall, a ruined castle. Then, with a twirl through some unidentifiable suburbs, it set them down by the War Memorial, a stone's throw from the Secretarial College. Now it was to be the same thing. The Mystery Shopping Excursion would end at 17 Windermere Gardens. All that remained was to say something calm and suitable.

'Such an unexpected pleasure to meet you. You've quite changed the day for me.'

'But I'm coming, too. I'm coming to cook the oxtail. I hope you don't mind.'

'Mind? My God, I'd be thankful! And more.'

The ring of sincerity transformed the poor girl's voice. To say 'transfigured' would, however, be going too far. Transformed it. Unmuzzled it.

No act of reparation, thought Lois, sitting in the taxi, can be an exact fit. Circumstances are like seaweed: a moment's exposure to the air, an hour's relegation to the past tense, stiffens, warps, shrivels the one and the other. The impulse to ease even a fraction of the burden she had imposed on that very different Miss Valerie Fry of the divorce proceedings – an impulse first felt in the bank as an amused acknowledgement of a faint sense of guilt, which at the word 'joint' had fleshed itself in the possibility of a deed, and a compassion against which she had soon ceased to struggle – for only someone in a state of utter dejection could have eaten three of those appalling little cakes – would fit neither the offence nor the moment. Probably even the medium was ill chosen. She happened to like oxtail herself, but very likely the girl would have preferred rolled ribs. Only one static element would resist the flux of time: Fenton's planet-like, unconjectural course. The Borough Offices where he worked as an architect closed at midday on Saturday. The planet-like course then took him to lunch at the Red Lion, and then to a healthful swim in the public baths, and then to his club; and he would be home at six.

'I'm afraid, as I wasn't expecting you, there won't be more than bread and cheese,' said the voice, now back in its muzzle.

'Nothing I should like better. It will give us more time to cook in. When does Fenton usually get home?'

'Four, or thereabouts.'

Even Fenton wasn't the same. She glanced with admiration at the young person whose society was two hours more alluring than hers had been; then at her wristwatch.

'Well, if I don't dawdle over my bread and cheese, that should be long enough. At any rate, it should be well on its way by then.'

'By then? All that time to cook a tail? You *must* be fond of cooking!'

The tone of spontaneous contempt, thought Lois, was just what anyone trying to apply an act of reparation might expect, and therefore what she deserved.

The taxi turned down Windermere Terrace. Seeing the iteration of small houses, each carefully designed to be slightly at variance with the others, each with a small identical garage and small front gardens for demonstrations of individuality, Lois observed that in some of the gardens the ornamental shrubs had grown larger, in others had died. They entered the house.

'I should think it must feel a bit queer to you, coming back like this,' Valerie said.

'No. Rather homelike. What a pretty new wallpaper – new wallpapers, that is.' A pink wall with squiggles, a blue wall with stripes, a yellow wall with poodles, kiosks and the Eiffel

8

Tower, a black wall with marbling. And did Fenton come home two hours earlier to gaze on these?

'I put them all on myself. And one with fishes in the bathroom. I expect you know your way to the bathroom?'

'I must not, will not, be censorious,' said Lois to herself. And Valerie, arranging ready-sliced bread and processed cheese for two, muttered to her four walls, when she was left alone with them, 'If she goes on being a condescending old ray of sunlight, I'll murder her.'

There was no time to expect that Lois knew her way to the kitchen. She was in it in a flash.

'I haven't got around to decorating this yet. To tell the truth, I'm not all that struck on cooking.'

'Where do you keep the large stewpan?'

The large stewpan was traced to the cupboard under the stairs, where it held jam pots and spiders. But at some time it must have been used, for Lois had left it clean. The cooking knives were rusty, the wooden spoons had been used to stir paint. Moths and skewers were in every drawer she opened. Without a flutter of pity, of compunction, of remorse, of any of the feelings that should accompany an act of reparation as parsley and lemon accompany fried plaice or red-currant jelly jugged hare, Lois searched, and cleaned, and sharpened, and by quarter to three the oxtail was in the large stewpan, together with the garlic, carrots, bay leaves, peppercorns and celery.

'What about the mushrooms?' Valerie inquired. She had rubbed the mushrooms and did not intend to see them slighted.

'They go in later on.'

'Well, as you seem to be managing all right, perhaps I'll . . .'

'Yes, do.'

One of the things Fenton particularly liked about Valerie was her habit of awaiting him. A man likes to be awaited. At the end of a dull day's architecture, to find a wife quietly sitting, undistracted by any form of employment, not even

9

reading a book, but just sitting and waiting and ready to look pleased is very agreeable. Today he happened to be forty minutes later than usual, a conversation with a man called Renshaw having delayed him. His expectations were forty minutes livelier, and as he closed the garage and walked towards his door he said to himself that there was really quite a dash of the Oriental in him. The discovery of this dash – he had not been aware of till Valerie – had even reconciled him to the prospect of baked beans or scrambled eggs on cold toast, if such was the price of being awaited. Besides, he always had a good substantial lunch at the Red Lion. But today Valerie was awaiting him amid a most exhilarating smell of cooking. It would be gross to comment on it immediately: to mulct her of the caresses of reunion, to fob off her proper desire to hear what he had been doing all day. And though she did not comment on his unpunctuality, he was at pains to tell her of his unforeseen encounter with Renshaw – not the Renshaw who skated and had been instrumental in bringing them together but his cousin E. B. Renshaw; to recount what E. B. Renshaw had said and to give a brief account of his character, career and accomplishments as a slow bowler. Only then did he say, 'No need to ask what you've been doing. What a wonderful smell! What is it?'

'Oxtail.'

'Of course! Oxtail! I thought I knew it.'

'Do you like oxtail?'

'Immensely – when it's not out of the tin. I can smell that this isn't.'

'Oh, no!'

He snuffed again. Lois had added the mushrooms and the anchovies and was now administering claret.

'Delicious! What's in it?'

'All sorts of things. Button mushrooms.'

Her smile struck him as secretive – no wonder, with this talent up her sleeve. And all performed so casually, too, so

10

unobtrusively; for there she sat, reposeful, not a hair out of place, none of the usual cook's airs of flurry and inattention, not a single 'Just wait one moment' while he was relating his day and the meeting with E. B. Renshaw.

'When will it be ready?' he said with ardour.

'Not just yet. Do you like my nail varnish? It's new. I bought it today.'

'Very pretty. Do you think you ought to go and stir it?'

'Oh, no! She'll do that.'

'She?' Had Valerie gone and got a cook? A cook from whom such odours proceeded would demand enormous wages, yet might almost be worth it. 'She? What she?'

'Your other wife. She's in there. She's been doing it all the afternoon.'

'Do you mean Lois?'

'Of course I mean Lois. You haven't any other wives, have you?'

This pertness when referring to his previous marriage was customary, and did not altogether displease. Now he didn't even notice it. He had a situation to grapple with, and the better to do so removed part of it off his knee.

'How did this happen?'

'We met at the bank – she'd gone there for some teapot or other. We couldn't sit there glaring at each other, so we began to talk.'

About him, of course. What confidences had been exchanged? What invidious –

'She told me you liked cold veal.'

A total misrepresentation. Lois had always been malicious, seizing on some casually expressed liking to throw in his teeth. 'What else did she say?'

'Nothing much. I had to do most of the talking. And before I knew where I was, she was wanting to come and cook you an oxtail. I couldn't very well stop her, could I? Of course I paid for it. The worst of it is, she was in such a rush to get here that I hadn't a chance to ask Strumpshaw about

11

that sixpence, or to get the waistcoat buttons or the right liver salts or your China tea. She isn't what I'd call considerate.'

'I shall have to go and see her.'

He would have to open the kitchen door, take the full assault of that witching smell, see Lois cooking as of old – an unassimilable answer to prayer. For of course she mustn't come again, she mustn't go on doing this sort of thing; nor was he a man to be won back by fleshpots. Yet he knew himself moved. Poor Lois, making her way back almost like an animal, forgetting her jealousy, her prejudice, all the awful things she had said at the time of the divorce, trampling on convention and *amour-propre*, just to cook him a favourite dish. What had impelled her to do this? Remorse, loneliness, an instinctive longing to foster and nourish? For many years her feeling for him had been almost wholly maternal – which made her insistence on the divorce even more uncalled for. What had set it off? Seeing the teapot, perhaps. They had both been fond of the teapot. It was Georgian.

Or was it all a deliberate scheme to lure him back?

He sprang to his feet, straightened his waistcoat, left the sitting room, entered the kitchen. It was empty. She had gone. Tied to the handle of the stewpan was a visiting card, on the back of which she had written: 'This will be ready by seven. It should simmer till then. *Don't let it boil.*'

Penelope Gilliatt

Living on the Box

The poet, feeling stale, thought the world stale and began to abuse it. Since he lived in isolation, being a nature poet and finding contact with people a digression from his work, the only object of abuse that was readily available to him was his wife.

During the twelve years of their life together, he had tutored her carefully in monkishness. As part of the training he spoke to her rarely. To rail at her meant opening a conversation, and this involved preposterous changes in his day.

Generally he rose at five-thirty, before she was awake. She got up later than he did because she went to sleep later, tossing and sometimes weeping, and in the end usually fumbling her way downstairs to get herself a drink. Until noon he stayed out of the cottage, walking across the Northumbrian moors with a knob-headed stick and humming Anglican hymns, whose verbal schemes he admired for their metrical embodiment of depression. At twelve he had a simple meal, cooked with natural foods and sea salt, which she hacked with a chisel from a damp sackful in the yard. At one he slept, and at three he worked in a shed at the bottom of the garden. In the evenings they read together, keeping silent because he believed that silence was more real than chatter, and at half past nine they went to bed. Sometimes she sat on the end of his divan if she couldn't sleep and tried to wake him up to talk, but he slept with the heaviness of the very thin, and her weight on the divan made it sag and creak in a way that embarrassed her.

In the earlier years of living with her he had sometimes left her a note speared on the kitchen tap before he went out for his walk – stirred and perhaps even drawn by the sight of her plain, flushed face in bed, which had begun to acquire in sleep a look of distress and disappointment. Lately the notes had not been written. She thought the zest of her replies probably struck him as crude. In his mordant presence she always felt vulgar and self-indulgent. When he made one of his rare, shapely jokes, they gave her a flash of great pleasure – a passing reassurance that life was good after all – and then an experience of despair and palsy. He was the only person she had ever known whose humour seemed entirely immobile. It expressed no wish, no venom, no energy in any direction. But to complain that its effect was therefore paralysingly glum would no more have occurred to her as fair than to complain that it made her feel fat. It did both, but this only drove home to her the grossness and subjectivity of her own temperament. On an evening when he had broken the silence with one of his quietist cracks she would feel a sense of remorse and insufficiency descending on her, and hours later find herself in the larder, eating the remains of whatever was under the meat sieve and weeping that she should do something so self-defeating and stupid.

On the days when he used to leave her a note in the morning she knew well enough that there was no good to be hoped for in replying to it. She understood that her excitement upset his sense of style. At the same time she was so ravenous to talk to him that it was quite impossible to stop herself. She would write her first reply in the bathroom, turning on the geyser to pretend she was having a bath and writing joyfully on a breadboard balanced on the small wooden basin (they used a breadboard as a bathmat on the freezing floor, because he liked the genuineness of natural wood). And then, after putting the note on his bed for him to read when he came back for his rest and covering it with the undyed hessian bedspread in case their child saw it, she would sit down and try to wring words out of the sleepy little boy at breakfast before he went off to school, and find that she had an empty morning in which to worry about what she had written. She would make the poet's lunch, starting with the radio playing but switching it off after a time because he believed that people should be able to do without background noise. And as she was moving about she would realize that her letter communicated nothing of her pleasure and love, so she would get the paper back and add a postscript and a laborious drawing. Then she would do housework, but it was such an austere cottage that there was hardly anything to do. And while she was having a whisky and eating a piece of cake at eleven o'clock, in a hapless impulse to demonstrate and somehow fix her freebooting mood – though she saw the irrationality of it on a day that had begun with a clear insight that at least she would try to equal his thinness even if she could never hope to achieve the frugality of his expectations – just as she was leaving the last part of the cake, she would think of a better way to write the note. By the time she had done it several times, and copied out the postscript, and redone the drawing, it sounded false to her and she lost her nerve completely. At lunchtime, when he read the note, he would always thank her as warmly as he could, but her mistake of taste was plainly defined in his face.

She had a vision of him sometimes, struggling for breath beneath the crassness of her impulses, in the same way that she sometimes imagined her fattening body to be asphyxiating his small fine frame in bed. Shy and unhappy, she one day went to sleep in the spare room, hoping that he would come in to find her, but he credited her with his own temperament and thought only that she wished to be alone. Indeed, he was quite unaware of her frenzy and mildly loved her.

The absurd fact was that he had married her for her gaiety. But in his grey presence her larks had soon seemed shameful, and she had disciplined herself as though she were entering an order. He observed the ebbing of her vivacity with thoughtless disappointment. Occasionally he hated her for it, because he took it to be a reproach of himself. Their life was one for which she was very unfitted, and her gigantic effort to enjoy it struck him as a piece of self-deception. He knew, when he considered the point, that she did not even really like his poetry. His visions of moral order in biology and of the superior integrity of sap, expressed in a thin, precise style like the print of a hopping bird in snow, struck her as impossible to live with. But, on the face of it, the perfect little couplets about twigs and foxes that he wrung out of his gargantuan walks justified the form of their lives as fully in her eyes as in his. She knew everything he had written by heart. The sound of her repeating a line back at him drove him mad.

'Have some more stew,' she said one evening.

'No thank you.'

'Is anything the matter?'

'No.'

'Is work all right?'

He didn't reply, and filled his pipe. She came round to his chair and put her big arms around his neck, aware of what her flesh would feel like on his skin and at the same time ashamed to be self-conscious. 'I was thinking today about "Frost",' she said. Unable to see his face, she recited 'Frost' to him. Her voice was pretty, but she made 'Frost' sound a thin dirge, and he looked murderous. He decided at that moment to make a victim of her.

One morning, he stayed at home and dropped his gum boots hard beside her bed to wake her up.

'You'd rather I wrote sea shanties,' he said in her ear.

She looked alarmed. 'What time is it?'

'Or hornpipes.'

'Why haven't you gone out today? Have you got a cold?'

'You'd like it better if I tried to make people happy, wouldn't you? What obligation have I to do that? Or to you, to make you happy? Doesn't it ever strike you as faintly ludicrous – the pursuit of happiness by a species that is less equipped for it than anything in nature?' He did a short angry dance by the bed. It was like the rollicking of a Desert Father.

'I don't understand a word you're saying.'

'Naturally.'

'I've just woken up.'

'I wish you wouldn't deceive yourself.'

'What about?'

'How unhappy you are. How much you hate my poetry.'

'I don't. I love it. You . . . I don't understand.'

'You aren't asked to.'

'But we live together.'

'We might be on other planets.'

'I thought you liked being left on your own.'

'On my own? I'm about as much on my own here as a man with a dog that wants to be taken for a walk. Your forbearance is a weapon that you know how to use all too well.'

She started to weep, with her long brown hair falling over her face.

'Don't. You look like Elizabeth Barrett Browning's spaniel with a cold,' he said thinly.

Later there was a letter from the BBC about doing a long television interview. Out of waywardness, because she had assumed he wouldn't want to, he decided to accept.

'It'll certainly be a coup for them,' she said helplessly. In extremity, she kept trying to be pleasant. 'I expect you'd like me out of the road. Though perhaps they'll want lunch.'

'They'll be here all day. They're sure to want the poet's wife,' he said tartly. 'You can tell them how much you love the work, can't you?' He always spoke about his poetry as 'the work'; it was this sort of dispassion that so excited the BBC.

'We must get all this!' cried the young producer to his assistant, driving his Rover over the moors from Newcastle and pointing to the horizon. 'Somehow the sky seems bigger up here. I think one feels that in his poetry.'

'We mustn't force the domestic part of it in this one,' the assistant said. 'I'm not sure we shouldn't do it all outside. What do you think? He's such an abrasive spirit, isn't he? Nothing . . . upholstered – do you know what I mean? That's what's so remarkable about him.'

'I suppose he's one of the few classicists writing. Is that the line, do you think? One could say that he was the dissenter in an age of . . . romantic anarchy. Anarchic romanticism. No. Megalopolitan romanticism, perhaps. Anyway, an age with an intense admiration for disorder. Whereas he sees *order* in things, doesn't he? In a very unfashionable way.'

The poet's wife was told when they arrived that they would want to film her. She had spent too long getting dressed, changing again and again, because her thighs looked bigger in every pair of trousers that she put on. The exertion and self-scrutiny had made her flush, and she began to turn purple under layers of powder. This made her late with the lunch, and at the table she found the young men impossible to talk to because she was trying to retain the lines of what she had prepared to say. In the afternoon, they went out on the moors with the cameras, and she sat crouched over the plates while the logic of the sentences fell apart completely. She wanted to talk about his poetry. All she could think of was the two of them, and her suspicion that he was right about her. She knew that she had never been an intellectual, but she thought that she had probably once been capable of insight. At the beginning she had known clearly enough that he was an irrevocably solitary man, and it had seemed to her fortunate to live with him at all. He would say, 'People need air round them,' and she would pretend she agreed. Or perhaps she had felt it then herself.

When the young men came back and started to film her in the kitchen, she forgot every word she had learned.

The poet had no television. To watch the programme, a month later, they went with their child to Newcastle and took a room at the Station Hotel. The poet's wife tried to avoid going, by saying that it was late for the child and that she would have expected her husband not to be curious. While they waited in the room, which was furnished like a nursing home, with the child reading a comic on the bed and eating a bag of shortbread biscuits, she thought that it was as well to be next door to the railway station in case she had to get away quickly.

At the sight of his big-nosed face slanted across the screen, like a pale and captious parrot, the poet detested his sufficiency and looked across at her to ward off its effect. He had a powerful impression that the programme was happening in a vault. When the film used some footage of his wife moving about the cottage, he felt as if he had been given a reprieve. She used this moment to light a cigarette.

'What's "Muse"?' the child asked suddenly.

'Shut up,' his mother said.

'Father keeps saying it.'

'It's what I hang around for all day,' said the poet, 'when your mother is doing something useful.'

'Useful! You could do without any of it. And what do you mean, that you hang around? You write on the dot. Nothing stops you. It's like the bloody crops.'

19

'I can't hear,' the child said.

'If some people think that I live in a void, as you put it,' said the poet on television, 'perhaps that tells us more about them than about me. I can't think of a thousand acres of natural activity as a void. I agree that it's not a particularly easy life for most people to support. I don't suppose my wife finds it easy, for example. But for me it's the condition of working. I find most company the opposite of useful because it's conducted at a feverish level. The high temperature of the modern is what I suspect most about it. Art now romanticizes chaos. We have developed an aesthetic of inconsequence and accident. I mistrust a literature that finds suicide more significant than death, and a man's inability to communicate more sorry than the frenzy of his need to. By celebrating the clamorous, we celebrate the bomb.'

The poet's wife turned away her head and tried to grow absorbed in their child.

'Twentieth-century art glamorizes the act of flying apart,' the poet on television continued. 'No one seems to face the fact that this is bound to reduce the tragic to the simply catastrophic. There's nothing tragic about a man flying off course like a burst tyre and exploding in a ditch. We now have a colossal documentation of what it feels like to be in the margin. The sensibility of the centrifugal can't go any further, can it? It can only become more heated. Or as I see it, more sentimental. It seems to me that there is something finally maudlin and trivial about seeing neurosis as Nemesis.'

The camera shifted angle: white face against white wall, a head picked clean of expression, like a skull. The poet felt indifferent toward it; the poet's wife felt suddenly free of it.

'Not that I find it easy to deny what everyone else in Europe apparently finds truthful. But I should like to make poems that are about space and órder, in the same sense as some modern sculpture. Not poems that make you feel on the *edge* of space but poems that make you feel you contain space *inside yourself*. I've seen abstracts that do this. With the verbal arts I think it can only be done for the moment by writing about nature. In an age that sees all human behaviour and motive as finally hectic, and finds an art that says so rather glorious, the humanist is driven to the vegetable.'

The poet's wife unexpectedly laughed. 'You never said all this.'

'I thought it was implicit.'

'I hadn't any idea you would call yourself a humanist.'

'. . . not a *void*, anyway. Simply to contain space,' said the television in the poet's voice, over a shot of him half an inch high striding over the moors. 'The word "void" only projects modern people's irritation with anyone outside their own trap. I expect my wife used it.'

The poet hadn't expected the programme to leave this in, and he was shocked.

'He doesn't live in a void,' said the poet's wife on television, in a cut that shook her with its glibness.

They had photographed her sitting on a kitchen stool in a white passage, with her back against a long stretch of wall, like someone at a dance. '"Void" is the wrong word. He lives in a sort of gavotte where no one is ever going to drop a glove. But he calls it a world, and he's such a good writer that he can make it seem like one. I think he feels that the most difficult thing in a man's life is to find some sort of balance between longing for company and longing for isolation. Some of us don't think of that till we're dying. My husband has been practising dying for years. I never know whether the death wish is a wish to get out of activity or out of existence. My husband said once that he wanted to be dead but still to be. I don't understand that. I'm a poor person to talk about his work really, because I don't understand the open air. But looking for the truth in nature walks? Hips and haws don't *mean* anything. They're just hips and haws. He thinks a tide chart is a sort of hymn sheet. The only difference between the significance of a tide chart and the significance of a railway timetable is that a railway timetable can be altered, isn't it? I don't believe that the sort of intractability there is in nature has very much to teach us. I think it just excites people now because it's remote, like the idea of four days of lemon juice to men who have business lunches every day. I mean . . . I suppose I mean that I don't think my husband would be a nature poet if he didn't live now, here, in England. Some other time, he might have been a hymn writer, perhaps. Or a theologian. He just has a monkish temperament. I make it sound as if he finds it easy . . . He doesn't really dislike people. He used to love girls. I think his poetry is an effort to be stoic. Being married is probably a hindrance.'

'You shouldn't have said that,' said the poet.

She watched her big face fade into a still of his Savonarola profile while an actorish voice spoke more of his verse.

'Did you expect them to leave all that in?' he said.

'I suppose so.'

'You talked as if I were dead. Or deaf.'

'No. I'd never, never have said such things if you were dead.' She wondered how she could explain this to him if he didn't see it already. The little boy had lost interest and started pulling open the drawers of the dressing-table. She put her coat on.

'You looked beautiful,' he said after a pause that agonized them both. He was suddenly moved by her physically, as he had been by the sight of her in the film. 'Like a Bonnard.'

She thought he was throwing her a sop and it steeled her.

'I'm sorry,' she said stiffly.

'You should have said it all before.'

'I didn't know it before.'

'Other people would call it treacherous, I suppose. I don't. It's rather a relief. Where are you going?'

'London.' She packed the child into his gum boots.

'Oh, no. Not now. It'll be all right. I'm not angry. It's absurd to go because you think I'm angry. Is that it?'

'I can't do anything else now. It's happened in the wrong order. Most things about us have. Not like botany at all.'

She kept her face turned away as she moved about the

room, and looked stony. At the door she suddenly grinned at him, and when she had gone the grin seemed to him still to be hanging in the air, like the Cheshire cat's. He wept.

That night he took a midnight train to London, searched for her all day, and had his first demanding quarrel with her in a Chinese restaurant at five o'clock in the afternoon, blue-jowled with fear and tiredness, and smelling of the stale smells of travellers. She came back to the north with him after that and they lived together again for a time.

Jane Bowles

Plain Pleasures

Alva Perry was a dignified and reserved woman of Scotch and Spanish descent, in her early forties. She was still handsome, although her cheeks were too thin. Her eyes particularly were of an extraordinary clarity and beauty. She lived in her uncle's house, which had been converted into apartments, or tenements, as they were still called in her section of the country. The house stood on the side of a steep, wooded hill overlooking the main highway. A long cement staircase climbed halfway up the hill and stopped some distance below the house. It had originally led to a power station, which had since been destroyed. Mrs Perry had lived alone in her tenement since the death of her husband eleven years ago; however, she found small things to do all day long and she had somehow remained as industrious in her solitude as a woman who lives in the service of her family.

John Drake, an equally reserved person, occupied the tenement below hers. He owned a truck and engaged in freelance work for lumber companies, as well as in the collection and delivery of milk cans for a dairy.

Mr Drake and Mrs Perry had never exchanged more than the simplest greeting in all the years that they had lived here in the hillside house.

One night Mr Drake, who was standing in the hall, heard Mrs Perry's heavy footsteps, which he had unconsciously learned to recognize. He looked up and saw her coming downstairs. She was dressed in a brown overcoat that had belonged to her dead husband, and she was hugging a paper bag to her bosom. Mr Drake offered to help her with the bag and she faltered, undecided, on the landing.

'They are only potatoes,' she said to him, 'but thank you very much. I am going to bake them out in the back yard. I have been meaning to for a long time.'

Mr Drake took the potatoes and walked with a stiff-jointed gait through the back door and down the hill to a short stretch of level land in the back of the house which served as a yard. Here he put the paper bag on the ground. There was a big new incinerator smoking near the back stoop and in the center of the yard Mrs Perry's uncle had built a roofed-in pigpen faced in vivid artificial brick. Mrs Perry followed.

She thanked Mr Drake and began to gather twigs, scuttling rapidly between the edge of the woods and the pigpen, near which she was laying her fire. Mr Drake, without any further conversation, helped her to gather the twigs, so that when the fire was laid, she quite naturally invited him to wait and share the potatoes with her. He accepted and they sat in front of the fire on an overturned box.

Mr Drake kept his face averted from the fire and turned in the direction of the woods, hoping in this way to conceal somewhat his flaming red cheeks from Mrs Perry. He was a very shy person and though his skin was naturally red all the time it turned to such deep crimson when he was in the presence of a strange woman that the change was distinctly noticeable. Mrs Perry wondered why he kept looking behind him, but she did not feel she knew him well enough to question him. She waited in vain for him to speak and then, realizing that he was not going to, she searched her own mind for something to say.

'Do you like plain ordinary pleasures?' she finally asked him gravely.

Mr Drake felt very much relieved that she had spoken and his color subsided. 'You had better first give me a clearer notion of what you mean by ordinary pleasures, and then I'll tell you how I feel about them,' he answered soberly, halting after every few words, for he was as conscientious as he was shy.

Mrs Perry hesitated. 'Plain pleasures,' she began, 'like the ones that come without crowds or fancy food.' She searched her brain for more examples. 'Plain pleasures like this potato bake instead of dancing and whisky and bands ... Like a picnic but not the kind with a thousand extra things that get thrown out in a ditch because they don't get eaten up. I've seen grown people throw cakes away because they were too lazy to wrap them up and take them back home. Have you seen that go on?'

'No, I don't think so,' said Mr Drake.

'They waste a lot,' she remarked.

'Well, I do like plain pleasures,' put in Mr Drake, anxious that she should not lose the thread of the conversation.

'Don't you think that plain pleasures are closer to the heart of God?' she asked him.

He was a little embarrassed at her mentioning anything so solemn and so intimate on such short acquaintance, and he could not bring himself to answer her. Mrs Perry, who was ordinarily shut-mouthed, felt a stream of words swelling in her throat.

'My sister, Dorothy Alvarez,' she began without further introduction, 'goes to all gala affairs downtown. She has invited me to go and raise the dickens with her, but I won't go. She's the merriest one in her group and separated from her husband. They take her all the places with them. She can eat dinner in a restaurant every night if she wants to. She's crazy about fried fish and all kinds of things. I don't pay much mind to what I eat unless it's a potato bake like this. We each have only one single life which is our real life, starting at the cradle and ending at the grave. I warn Dorothy every time I see her that if she doesn't watch out her life is going to be left aching and starving on the side of the road and she's going to get to her grave without it. The farther a man follows the rainbow, the harder it is for him to get back to the life which he left starving like an old dog. Sometimes when a man gets older he has a revelation and wants awfully bad to get back to the place where he left his life, but he can't get to that place − not often. It's always better to stay alongside of your life. I told Dorothy that life was not a tree with a million different blossoms on it.' She reflected upon this for a moment in silence and then continued. 'She has a box that she puts pennies and nickles in when she thinks she's running around too much and she uses the money in the box to buy candles with for church. But that's all she'll do for her spirit, which is not enough for a grown woman.'

Mr Drake's face was strained because he was trying terribly hard to follow closely what she was saying, but he was so fearful lest she reveal some intimate secret of her sister's and later regret it that his mind was almost completely closed to everything else. He was fully prepared to stop her if she went too far.

The potatoes were done and Mrs Perry offered him two of them.

'Have some potatoes?' she said to him. The wind was colder now than when they had first sat down, and it blew around the pigpen.

'How do you feel about these cold howling nights that we have? Do you mind them?' Mrs Perry asked.

'I surely do,' said John Drake.

She looked intently at his face. 'He is as red as a cherry,' she said to herself.

'I might have preferred to live in a warm climate maybe,' Mr Drake was saying very slowly with a dreamy look in his eye, 'if I happened to believe in a lot of unnecessary changing around. A lot of going forth and back, I mean.' He blushed because he was approaching a subject that was close to his heart.

'Yes, yes, yes,' said Mrs Perry. 'A lot of switching around is no good.'

'When I was a younger man I had a chance to go way down south to Florida,' he continued. 'I had an offer to join forces with an alligator-farm project, but there was no security in the alligators. It might not have been a successful farm; it was not the risk that I minded so much, because I always yearned to see palm trees and coconuts and the like. But I also believed that a man has to have a pretty good reason for moving around. I think that is what finally stopped me from going down to Florida and raising alligators. It was not the money, because I was not raised to give money first place. It was just that I felt then the way I do now, that if a man leaves home he must leave for some very good reason – like the boys who went to construct the Panama Canal or for any other decent reason. Otherwise I think he ought to stay in his own home town, so that nobody can say about him, 'What does he think he can do here that we can't?' At least that is what I think people in a strange town would say about a man like myself if I landed there with some doubtful venture as my only excuse for leaving home. My brother don't feel that way. He never stays in one place more than three months.' He ate his potato with a woeful look in his eye, shaking his head from side to side.

Mrs Perry's mind was wandering, so that she was very much startled when he suddenly stood up and extended his hand to her.

'I'll leave now,' he said, 'but in return for the potatoes, will you come and have supper with me at a restaurant tomorrow night?'

She had not received an invitation of this kind in many years, having deliberately withdrawn from life in town, and she did not know how to answer him. 'Do you think I should do that?' she asked.

Mr Drake assured her that she should do it and she accepted his invitation. On the following afternoon, Mrs Perry waited for the bus at the foot of the short cement bridge below the house. She needed help and advice from her sister about a lavender dress which no longer fitted her. She herself had never been able to sew well and she knew little about altering women's garments. She intended to wear her dress to the restaurant where she was to meet John Drake, and she was carrying it tucked under her arm.

Dorothy Alvarez lived on a side street in one half of a two-family house. She was seated in her parlor entertaining a man when Mrs Perry rang the bell. The parlor was immaculate but difficult to rest in because of the many bright and complicated patterns of the window curtains and the furniture covers, not the least disquieting of which was an enormous orange and black flowerpot design repeated a dozen times on the linoleum floor covering.

Dorothy pulled the curtain aside and peeked out to see who was ringing her bell. She was a curly-headed little person, with thick, unequal cheeks that were painted bright pink.

She was very much startled when she looked out and saw her sister, as she had not been expecting to see her until the following week.

'Oh!' Dorothy exclaimed.

'Who is it?' her guest asked.

'It's my sister. You better get out of here, because she must have something serious to talk to me about. You better go out the back door. She don't like bumping up against strangers.'

The man was vexed, and left without bidding Dorothy goodbye. She ran to the door and let Mrs Perry in.

'Sit down,' she said, pulling her into the parlor. 'Sit down and tell me what's new.' She poured some hard candy from a paper bag into a glass dish.

'I wish you would alter this dress for me or help me do it,' said Mrs Perry. 'I want it for tonight. I'm meeting Mr Drake, my neighbor, at the restaurant down the street, so I thought I could dress in your house and leave from here. If you did the alteration yourself, I'd pay you for it.'

Dorothy's face fell. 'Why do you offer to pay me for it when I'm your sister?'

Mrs Perry looked at her in silence. She did not answer, because she did not know why herself. Dorothy tried the dress on her sister and pinned it here and there. 'I'm glad you're going out at last,' she said. 'Don't you want some beads?'

'I'll take some beads if you've got a spare string.'

'Well I hope this is the right guy for you,' said Dorothy, with her customary lack of tact. 'I would give anything for you to be in love, so you would quit living in that ugly house and come and live on some street nearby. Think how different everything would be for me. You'd be jollier too if you had a husband who was dear to you. Not like the last one . . . I suppose I'll never stop dreaming and hoping,' she added nervously because she realized, but, as always, a little too late, that her sister hated to discuss such matters. 'Don't think,' she began weakly, 'that I'm so happy here all the time. I'm not so serious and solemn as you, of course . . .'

'I don't know what you've been talking about,' said Alva Perry, twisting impatiently. 'I'm going out to have a dinner.'

'I wish you were closer to me,' whined Dorothy. 'I get blue in this parlor some nights.'

'I don't think you get very blue,' Mrs Perry remarked briefly.

'Well, as long as you're going out, why don't you pep up?'

'I am pepped up,' replied Mrs Perry.

*

Mrs Perry closed the restaurant door behind her and walked the full length of the room, peering into each booth in search of her escort. He had apparently not yet arrived, so she chose an empty booth and seated herself inside on the wooden bench. After fifteen minutes she decided that he was not coming and, repressing the deep hurt that this caused her, she focused her full attention on the menu and succeeded in shutting Mr Drake from her mind. While she was reading the menu, she unhooked her string of beads and tucked them away in her purse. She had called the waitress and was ordering pork when Mr Drake arrived. He greeted her with a timid smile.

'I see that you are ordering your dinner,' he said, squeezing into his side of the booth. He looked with admiration at her lavender dress, which exposed her pale chest. He would have preferred that she be bareheaded because he loved women's hair. She had on an ungainly black felt hat which she always wore in every kind of weather. Mr Drake remembered with intense pleasure the potato bake in front of the fire and he was much more excited than he had imagined he would be to see her once again.

Unfortunately she did not seem to have any impulse to communicate with him and his own tongue was silenced in a very short time. They ate the first half of their meal without saying anything at all to each other. Mr Drake had ordered a bottle of sweet wine and after Mrs Perry had finished her second glass she finally spoke. 'I think they cheat you in restaurants.'

He was pleased she had made any remark at all, even though it was of an ungracious nature.

'Well, it is usually to be among the crowd that we pay large prices for small portions,' he said, much to his own surprise, for he had always considered himself a lone wolf, and his behavior had never belied this. He sensed this same quality in Mrs Perry, but he was moved by a strange desire to mingle with her among the flock.

'Well, don't you think what I say is true?' he asked hesitantly. There appeared on his face a curious, dislocated smile and he held his head in an outlandishly erect position which betrayed his state of tension.

Mrs Perry wiped her plate clean with a piece of bread. Since she was not in the habit of drinking more than once every few years, the wine was going very quickly to her head.

'What time does the bus go by the door here?' she asked in a voice that was getting remarkably loud.

'I can find out for you if you really want to know. Is there any reason why you want to know now?'

'I've got to get home some time so I can get up tomorrow morning.'

'Well, naturally I will take you home in my truck when you want to go, but I hope you won't go yet.' He leaned forward and studied her face anxiously.

'I can get home all right,' she answered him glumly, 'and it's just as good now as later.'

'Well, no, it isn't,' he said, deeply touched, because there was no longer any mistaking her distinctly inimical attitude. He felt that he must at any cost keep her with him and enlist her sympathies. The wine was contributing to this sudden aggressiveness, for it was not usually in his nature to make any effort to try to get what he wanted. He now began speaking to her earnestly and quickly.

'I want to share a full evening's entertainment with you, or even a week of entertainment,' he said, twisting nervously on his bench. 'I know where all the roadside restaurants and dance houses are situated all through the county. I am master of my truck, and no one can stop me from taking a vacation if I want to. It's a long time since I took a vacation – not since I was handed out my yearly summer vacation when I went to school. I never spent any real time in any of these roadside houses, but I know the proprietors, nearly all of them, because I have lived here all of my life. There is one dance hall that is built on a lake. I know the proprietor. If we went there, we

32

could stray off and walk around the water, if that was agreeable to you.' His face was a brighter red than ever and he appeared to be temporarily stripped of the reserved and cautious demeanor that had so characterized him the evening before. Some quality in Mrs Perry's nature which he had only dimly perceived at first now sounded like a deep bell within himself because of her anger and he was flung backward into a forgotten and weaker state of being. His yearning for a word of kindness from her increased every minute.

Mrs Perry sat drinking her wine more and more quickly and her resentment mounted with each new glass.

'I know all the proprietors of dance houses in the county also,' she said. 'My sister Dorothy Alvarez has them up to her house for beer when they take a holiday. I've got no need to meet anybody new or see any new places. I even know this place we are eating in from a long time ago. I had dinner here with my husband a few times.' She looked around her. 'I remember *him*,' she said, pointing a long arm at the proprietor, who had just stepped out of the kitchen.

'How are you after these many years?' she called to him.

Mr Drake was hesitant about what to do. He had not realized that Mrs Perry was getting as drunk as she seemed to be now. Ordinarily he would have felt embarrassed and would have hastened to lead her out of the restaurant, but he thought that she might be more approachable drunk and nothing else mattered to him. 'I'll stay with you for as long as you like,' he said.

His words spun around in Mrs Perry's mind. 'What are you making a bid for, anyway?' she asked him, leaning back heavily against the bench.

'Nothing dishonorable,' he said. 'On the contrary, something extremely honorable if you will accept.' Mr Drake was so distraught that he did not know exactly what he was saying, but Mrs Perry took his words to mean a proposal of marriage, which was unconsciously what he had hoped she

33

would do. Mrs Perry looked at even this exciting offer through the smoke of her resentment.

'I suppose,' she said, smiling joylessly, 'that you would like a lady to mash your potatoes for you three times a day. But I am not a mashed-potato masher and I never have been. I would prefer,' she added, raising her voice, 'I would prefer to have *him* mash my potatoes for *me* in a big restaurant kitchen.' She nodded in the direction of the proprietor, who had remained standing in front of the kitchen door so that he could watch Mrs Perry. This time he grinned and winked his eye.

Mrs Perry fumbled through the contents of her purse in search of a handkerchief and, coming upon her sister's string of beads, she pulled them out and laid them in her gravy. 'I am not a mashed-potato masher,' she repeated, and then without warning she clambered out of the booth and lumbered down the aisle. She disappeared up a dark brown staircase at the back of the restaurant. Both Mr Drake and the proprietor assumed that she was going to the ladies' toilet.

Actually Mrs Perry was not specifically in search of the toilet, but rather for any place where she could be alone. She walked down the hall upstairs and jerked open a door on her left, closing it behind her. She stood in total darkness for a minute, and then, feeling a chain brush her forehead, she yanked at it brutally, lighting the room from a naked ceiling bulb, which she almost pulled down together with its fixtures.

She was standing at the foot of a double bed with a high Victorian headboard. She looked around her and, noticing a chair placed underneath a small window, she walked over to it and pushed the window open, securing it with a short stick; then she sat down.

'This is perfection,' she said aloud, glaring at the ugly little room. 'This is surely a gift from the Lord.' She squeezed her hands together until her knuckles were white. 'Oh, how I love it here! How I love it! How I love it!'

She flung one arm out over the window sill in a gesture of

abandon, but she had not noticed that the rain was teeming down, and it soaked her lavender sleeve in a very short time.

'Mercy me!' she remarked, grinning. 'It's raining here. The people at the dinner tables don't get the rain, but I do and I like it!' She smiled benignly at the rain. She sat there half awake and half asleep and then slowly she felt a growing certainty that she could reach her own room from where she was sitting without ever returning to the restaurant. 'I have kept the pathway open all my life,' she muttered in a thick voice, 'so that I could get back.'

A few moments later she said, 'I am sitting there.' An expression of malevolent triumph transformed her face and she made a slight effort to stiffen her back. She remained for a long while in the stronghold of this fantasy, but it gradually faded and in the end dissolved. When she drew her cold shaking arm in out of the rain, the tears were streaming down her cheeks. Without ceasing to cry she crept on to the big double bed and fell asleep, face downward, with her hat on.

Meanwhile the proprietor had come quietly upstairs, hoping that he would bump into her as she came out of the ladies' toilet. He had been flattered by her attention and he judged that in her present drunken state it would be easy to sneak a kiss from her and perhaps even more. When he saw the beam of light shining under his own bedroom door, he stuck his tongue out over his lower lip and smiled. Then he tiptoed down the stairs, plotting on the way what he would tell Mr Drake.

Everyone had left the restaurant, and Mr Drake was walking up and down the aisle when the proprietor reached the bottom of the staircase.

'I am worried about my lady friend,' Mr Drake said, hurrying up to him. 'I am afraid that she may have passed out in the toilet.'

'The truth is,' the proprietor answered, 'that she has passed out in an empty bedroom upstairs. Don't worry about it. My daughter will take care of her if she wakes up feeling sick. I used to know her husband. You can't do nothing about her now.' He put his hands into his pockets and looked solemnly into Mr Drake's eyes.

Mr Drake, not being equal to such a delicate situation, paid his bill and left. Outside he crawled into his freshly painted red truck and sat listening desolately to the rain.

The next morning Mrs Perry awakened a little after sunrise. Thanks to her excellent constitution she did not feel very sick, but she lay motionless on the bed looking around her at the walls for a long time. Slowly she remembered that this room she was lying in was above the restaurant, but she did not know how she had gotten there. She remembered the dinner with Mr Drake, but not much of what she had said to him. It did not occur to her to blame him for her present circumstance. She was not hysterical at finding herself in a strange bed because, although she was a very tense and nervous woman, she possessed great depth of emotion and only certain things concerned her personally.

She felt very happy and she thought of her uncle who had passed out at a convention fifteen years ago. He had walked around the town all the morning without knowing where he was. She smiled.

After resting a little while longer, she got out of bed and clothed herself. She went into the hall and found the staircase and she descended with bated breath and a fast-beating heart, because she was so eager to get back down into the restaurant.

It was flooded with sunshine and still smelled of meat and sauce. She walked a little unsteadily down the aisle between the rows of wooden booths and tables. The tables were all bare and scrubbed clean. She looked anxiously from one to the other, hoping to select the booth they had sat in, but she was unable to choose among them. The tables were all identical. In a moment this anonymity served only to heighten her tenderness.

'John Drake,' she whispered. 'My sweet John Drake.'

Colette

The Secret Woman

He had been looking for a long time at the sea of masks in front of him, suffering vaguely from their mixture of colours and from the synchronization of two orchestras which were too close. His hood constricted his temples; a nervous headache was coming on between his eyes. But he relished, without impatience, a state of malaise and pleasure which permitted the imperceptible passing of the hours. He had wandered along all the corridors of the Opéra, drunk the silvery dust of the dance floor, recognized bored friends and placed round his neck the indifferent arms of a very plump girl who was disguised as though humorously as a sylph.

This hooded doctor was embarrassed by his fancy dress and staggered about like a man in skirts, but he dared not remove either his costume or his hood, because of his schoolboy lie:

'I'll be spending tomorrow night at Nogent,' he had said to his wife the day before. 'They've just telephoned me, and

I'm very much afraid that my patient, you know, the poor old lady . . . Just imagine, I was looking forward to this ball like any kid. Isn't it ridiculous, a man of my age who's never been to the Opéra ball?'

'Utterly ridiculous, darling, utterly! If I'd known, perhaps I wouldn't have married you . . .'

She laughed, and he admired her narrow face, pink, matt and long, like a delicate sugared almond.

'Don't you want to go to the green and purple ball? Even without me, if it amuses you, darling . . .'

She had trembled, there passed through her one of those long shudders of disgust which brought a tremble to her hair, her delicate hands and her bosom beneath her white dress whenever she saw a slug or a filthy passer-by:

'As for me . . . Can you see me in a crowd, at the mercy of all those hands . . . What do you think, I'm not strait-laced, I'm . . . I'm put out! There's nothing to be done about it!'

Leaning against the loggia balustrade, above the great staircase, he thought of this trembling hind, as he contemplated before him two enormous square hands, with black nails, clasped round the bare back of a sultana. Emerging from the braided sleeves of a Venetian lord they dug into the white female flesh as though it were dough . . . Because he was thinking of her he jumped violently as he heard beside him a little uh-hum, a kind of cough typical of his wife . . . He turned round and saw someone sitting astride the balustrade, wearing a long and impenetrable disguise, looking like Pierrot because of the smock with vast sleeves, the loose trousers, the headband and the plaster-white colour which covered the small area of skin visible below the fluffy lace of the mask. The fluid fabric of the costume and the cap, woven of dark purple and silver, shone like the conger eels that you fish for at night with iron hooks from boats lit by lamps burning resin. Overwhelmed with astonishment he awaited the recurrence of the little uh-hum, which did not come . . . The eel-like Pierrot remained seated in nonchalant fashion and its heel tapped against the marble baluster, revealing only two satin slippers, while a black-gloved hand lay folded at one hip. The two oblique slits in the mask, carefully meshed over with tulle, revealed only a subdued glint of indeterminate colour.

He almost called out 'Irène!' And restrained himself, remembering his own lie. Since he was clumsy at play-acting he also rejected the idea of disguising his voice. The Pierrot scratched its thigh, with a free, proletarian gesture, and the anxious husband breathed again.

'Ah! It's not her.'

But the Pierrot pulled out of a pocket a flat gold box, opened it and took out a lipstick, and the anxious husband recognized an antique snuff box fitted with a mirror inside, the last birthday gift ... He placed his left hand over the painful area of his heart with such a brusque and involuntary gesture that the eel-like Pierrot noticed him.

'Is that a declaration, purple Domino?'

He did not reply, for he was half stifled with surprise, waiting and nightmare, and listened for a long moment to the barely disguised voice – the voice of his wife. The Eel looked at him, as it sat in cavalier fashion, its head on one side like a bird; it shrugged its shoulders, jumped to the ground and moved away. Its movement liberated the anxious husband, who, restored to a state of active and normal jealousy, began to think again and rose without haste to follow his wife.

'She's here for someone, with someone. In less than an hour I'll know everything.'

A hundred hoods, purple or green, guaranteed that he would be neither noticed nor recognized. Irène walked in front of him, nonchalantly; he was astonished to find that she rolled her hips softly and dragged her feet a little as though she were wearing Turkish slippers. A Byzantine figure, wearing emerald green, embroidered with gold, seized her as she went by, and her body bent in his arms; she looked thinner, as though the embrace would cut her in two. Her husband ran a few steps and reached the couple just as Irène was crying flatteringly 'You big brute!'

She moved away, with the same relaxed and quiet step, stopping often, musing at the doors to the open boxes, hardly ever looking round. She hesitated at the foot of the steps, turned off to the side, came back towards the entrance of the orchestra stalls, joined a noisy, closely packed crowd with a skilful gliding movement like the blade of a knife fitting neatly into its sheath. Ten arms imprisoned her, an almost naked wrestler pinned her firmly against the edge of the ground-floor boxes and held her there. She gave way beneath the weight of the naked man, threw back her head in laughter that was drowned by other laughter, and the man in the purple hood saw her teeth gleam beneath the lace of the mask. Then she escaped easily and sat down on the steps which led to the dance floor. Her husband, standing two paces behind her, looked at her. She readjusted her mask and her crumpled smock, then tightened the headband. She seemed as calm as if she had been alone, and moved away again after a few moments' rest. She went down the steps, placed her hand on the shoulders of a warrior who asked her, silently, to dance, and she danced, clinging to him.

'That's the man,' the husband said to himself.

But she did not say a word to the dancer encased in iron, whose skin was damp, and left him quietly after the dance. She went off to drink a glass of champagne at the buffet, then a second glass, paid, stood by motionless and curious as two men began to fight among screaming women. She also amused herself by placing her little satanic hands, which were entirely black, on the white bosom of a Dutch woman wearing a gold headdress, who cried out nervously.

At last the anxious man who was following her saw her stop, as though bumping against him on the way, close to a young man who had collapsed on a bench, out of breath, and was fanning himself with his mask. She bent down, disdainfully held the savage, handsome young face, and kissed the panting, half-open mouth . . .

But her husband, instead of rushing forward and forcing the two mouths apart, disappeared into the crowd. In his consternation he no longer feared, no longer hoped for betrayal. He was sure now that Irène did not know the young man, drunk with dancing, whom she was kissing, nor the Hercules; he was sure that she was neither waiting nor looking for anyone, and that abandoning the lips she held beneath her own like an empty grape, she was going to leave again the next moment, wander about once more, collect some other passer-by, forget him, and simply enjoy, until she felt tired and went back home, the monstrous pleasure of being alone, free, honest in her crude, native state, of being the unknown woman, eternally solitary and shameless, restored to her irremediable solitude and immodest innocence by a little mask and a concealing costume.

Translated from the French by Margaret Crosland

Tillie Olsen

I Stand Here Ironing

I stand here ironing, and what you asked me moves tormented back and forth with the iron.

'I wish you would manage the time to come in and talk with me about your daughter. I'm sure you can help me understand her. She's a youngster who needs help and whom I'm deeply interested in helping.'

'Who needs help . . .' Even if I came, what good would it do? You think because I am her mother I have a key, or that in some way you could use me as a key? She has lived for nineteen years. There is all that life that has happened outside of me, beyond me.

And when is there time to remember, to sift, to weigh, to estimate, to total? I will start and there will be an interruption and I will have to gather it all together again. Or I will become engulfed with all I did or did not do, with what should have been and what cannot be helped.

She was a beautiful baby. The first and only one of our five that was beautiful at birth. You do not guess how new and uneasy her tenancy in her now-loveliness. You did not know her all those years she was thought homely, or see her poring over her baby pictures, making me tell her over and over how beautiful she had been – and would be, I would tell her – and was now, to the seeing eye. But the seeing eyes were few or non-existent. Including mine.

I nursed her. They feel that's important nowadays. I nursed all the children, but with her, with all the fierce rigidity of first motherhood, I did like the books then said. Though her cries battered me to trembling and my breasts ached with swollenness, I waited till the clock decreed.

Why do I put that first? I do not even know if it matters, or if it explains anything.

She was a beautiful baby. She blew shining bubbles of sound. She loved motion, loved light, loved colour and music and textures. She would lie on the floor in her blue overalls patting the surface so hard in ecstasy her hands and feet would blur. She was a miracle to me, but when she was eight months old I had to leave her daytimes with the woman downstairs to whom she was no miracle at all, for I worked or looked for work and for Emily's father, who 'could no longer endure' (he wrote in his good-bye note) 'sharing want with us'.

I was nineteen. It was the pre-relief, pre-WPA world of the depression. I would start running as soon as I got off the streetcar, running up the stairs, the place smelling sour, and awake or asleep to startle awake, when she saw me she would break into a clogged weeping that could not be comforted, a weeping I can yet hear.

After a while I found a job hashing at night so I could be with her days, and it was better. But it came to where I had to bring her to his family and leave her.

It took a long time to raise the money for her fare back. Then she got chicken-pox and I had to wait longer. When she finally came, I hardly knew her, walking quick and nervous like her father, looking like her father, thin, and dressed in a shoddy red that yellowed her skin and glared at the pock marks. All the baby loveliness gone.

She was two. Old enough for nursery school they said, and I did not know then what I know now – the fatigue of the long day, and the lacerations of group life in the kinds of nurseries that are only parking places for children.

Except that it would have made no difference if I had known. It was the only place there was. It was the only way we could be together, the only way I could hold a job.

And even without knowing, I knew. I knew the teacher that was evil because all these years it has curdled into my memory, the little boy hunched in the corner, her rasp, 'why aren't you outside, because Alvin hits you? that's no reason, go out, scaredy.' I knew Emily hated it even if she did not clutch and implore 'don't go Mommy' like the other children, mornings.

She always had a reason why we should stay home. Momma, you look sick. Momma, I feel sick. Momma, the teachers aren't there today, they're sick. Momma, we can't go, there was a fire there last night. Momma, it's a holiday today, no school, they told me.

But never a direct protest, never rebellion. I think of our others in their three-, four-year-oldness – the explosions, the tempers, the denunciations, the demands – and I feel suddenly ill. I put the iron down. What in me demanded that goodness in her? And what was the cost, the cost to her of such goodness?

The old man living in the back once said in his gentle way: 'You should smile at Emily more when you look at her.' What *was* in my face when I looked at her? I loved her. There were all the acts of love.

It was only with the others I remembered what he said, and it was the face of joy, and not of care or tightness or worry I turned to them – too late for Emily. She does not smile easily, let alone almost always as her brothers and sisters do. Her face is closed and sombre, but when she wants, how

44

fluid. You must have seen it in her pantomimes, you spoke of her rare gift for comedy on the stage that rouses a laughter out of the audience so dear they applaud and applaud and do not want to let her go.

Where does it come from, that comedy? There was none of it in her when she came back to me that second time, after I had had to send her away again. She had a new daddy now to learn to love, and I think perhaps it was a better time. Except when we left her alone nights, telling ourselves she was old enough.

'Can't you go some other time, Mommy, like tomorrow?' she would ask. 'Will it be just a little while you'll be gone? Do you promise?'

The time we came back, the front door open, the clock on the floor in the hall. She rigid awake. 'It wasn't just a little while. I didn't cry. Three times I called you, just three times, and then I ran downstairs to open the door so you could come faster. The clock talked loud. I threw it away, it scared me what it talked.'

She said the clock talked loud again that night I went to the hospital to have Susan. She was delirious with the fever that comes before red measles, but she was fully conscious all the week I was gone and the week after we were home when she could not come near the new baby or me.

She did not get well. She stayed skeleton thin, not wanting to eat, and night after night she had nightmares. She would call for me, and I would rouse from exhaustion to sleepily call back: 'You're all right, darling, go to sleep, it's just a dream,' and if she still called, in a sterner voice, 'now go to sleep, Emily, there's nothing to hurt you.' Twice, only twice, when I had to get up for Susan anyhow, I went in to sit with her.

Now when it is too late (as if she would let me hold and comfort her like I do the others) I get up and go to her at once at her moan or restless stirring. 'Are you awake, Emily?

45

Can I get you something, dear?' And the answer is always the same: 'No, I'm all right, go back to sleep, Mother.'

They persuaded me at the clinic to send her away to a convalescent home in the country where 'she can have the kind of food and care you can't manage for her, and you'll be free to concentrate on the new baby'. They still send children to that place. I see pictures on the society page of sleek young women planning affairs to raise money for it, or dancing at the affairs, or decorating Easter eggs or filling Christmas stockings for the children.

They never have a picture of the children so I do not know if the girls still wear those gigantic red bows and the ravaged looks on the every other Sunday when parents can come to visit 'unless otherwise notified' – as we were notified the first six weeks.

Oh it is a handsome place, green lawns and tall trees and fluted flower beds. High up on the balconies of each cottage the children stand, the girls in their red bows and white dresses, the boys in white suits and giant red ties. The parents stand below shrieking up to be heard and the children shriek down to be heard, and between them the invisible wall 'Not To Be Contaminated by Parental Germs or Physical Affection.'

There was a tiny girl who always stood hand in hand with Emily. Her parents never came. One visit she was gone. 'They moved her to Rose Cottage,' Emily shouted in explanation. 'They don't like you to love anybody here.'

She wrote once a week, the laboured writing of a seven-year-old. 'I am fine. How is the baby. If I write my leter nicly I will have a star. Love.' There never was a star. We wrote every other day, letters she could never hold or keep but only hear read – once. 'We simply do not have room for children to keep any personal possessions,' they patiently explained when we pieced one Sunday's shrieking together to plead how much it would mean to Emily, who loved so to keep things, to be allowed to keep her letters and cards.

Each visit she looked frailer. 'She isn't eating,' they told us.

46

(They had runny eggs for breakfast or mush with lumps, Emily said later, I'd hold it in my mouth and not swallow. Nothing ever tasted good, just when they had chicken.)

It took us eight months to get her released home, and only the fact that she gained back so little of her seven lost pounds convinced the social worker.

I used to try to hold and love her after she came back, but her body would stay stiff, and after a while she'd push away. She ate little. Food sickened her, and I think much of life too. Oh she had physical lightness and brightness, twinkling by on skates, bouncing like a ball up and down up and down over the jump rope, skimming over the hill; but these were momentary.

She fretted about her appearance, thin and dark and foreign-looking at a time when every little girl was supposed to look or thought she should look a chubby blonde replica of Shirley Temple. The doorbell sometimes rang for her, but no one seemed to come and play in the house or be a best friend. Maybe because we moved so much.

There was a boy she loved painfully through two school semesters. Months later she told me how she had taken pennies from my purse to buy him candy. 'Liquorice was his favourite and I brought him some every day, but he still liked Jennifer better'n me. Why, Mommy?' The kind of question for which there is no answer.

School was a worry to her. She was not glib or quick in a world where glibness and quickness were easily confused with ability to learn. To her overworked and exasperated teachers she was an overconscientious 'slow learner' who kept trying to catch up and was absent entirely too often.

I let her be absent, though sometimes the illness was imaginary. How different from my now-strictness about attendance with the others. I wasn't working. We had a new baby, I was home anyhow. Sometimes, after Susan grew old enough, I would keep her home from school, too, to have them all together.

47

Mostly Emily had asthma, and her breathing, harsh and laboured, would fill the house with a curiously tranquil sound. I would bring the two old dresser mirrors and her boxes of collections to her bed. She would select beads and single ear-rings, bottle tops and shells, dried flowers and pebbles, old postcards and scraps, all sorts of oddments; then she and Susan would play Kingdom, setting up landscapes and furniture, peopling them with action.

Those were the only times of peaceful companionship between her and Susan. I have edged away from it, that poisonous feeling between them, that terrible balancing of hurts and needs I had to do between the two, and did so badly, those earlier years.

Oh there are conflicts between the others too, each one human, needing, demanding, hurting, taking – but only between Emily and Susan, no, Emily toward Susan that corroding resentment. It seems so obvious on the surface, yet it is not obvious. Susan, the second child, Susan, golden- and curly-haired and chubby, quick and articulate and assured, everything in appearance and manner Emily was not; Susan, not able to resist Emily's precious things, losing or sometimes clumsily breaking them; Susan telling jokes and riddles to company for applause while Emily sat silent (to say to me later: that was *my* riddle, Mother, I told it to Susan); Susan, who· for all the five years' difference in age was just a year behind Emily in developing physically.

I am glad for that slow physical development that widened the difference between her and her contemporaries, though she suffered over it. She was too vulnerable for that terrible world of youthful competition, of preening and parading, of constant measuring of yourself against every other, of envy, 'If I had that copper hair,' or 'If I had that skin . . .' She tormented herself enough about not looking like the others, there was enough of the unsureness, the having to be conscious of words before you speak, the constant caring – what are they thinking of me? What kind of an impression am I making? – there was enough without having it all magnified by the merciless physical drives.

Ronnie is calling. He is wet and I change him. It is rare there is such a cry now. That time of motherhood is almost behind me when the ear is not one's own but must always be racked and listening for the child cry, the child call. We sit for a while and I hold him, looking out over the city spread in charcoal with its soft aisles of light. '*Shoogily*,' he breathes and curls closer. I carry him back to bed, asleep. *Shoogily*. A funny word, a family word, inherited from Emily, invented by her to say: *comfort*.

In this and other ways she leaves her seal, I say aloud. And startle at my saying it. What do I mean? What did I start to gather together, to try and make coherent? I was at the terrible, growing years. War years. I do not remember them well. I was working, there were four smaller ones now, there was not time for her. She had to help be a mother, and housekeeper, and shopper. She had to set her seal. Mornings of crisis and near hysteria trying to get lunches packed, hair combed, coats and shoes found, everyone to school or Child Care on time, the baby ready for transportation. And always the paper scribbled on by a smaller one, the book looked at by Susan then mislaid, the homework not done. Running out to that huge school where she was one, she was lost, she was a drop; suffering over her unpreparedness, stammering and unsure in her classes.

There was so little time left at night after the kids were bedded down. She would struggle over books, always eating (it was in those years she developed her enormous appetite that is legendary in our family) and I would be ironing, or preparing food for the next day, or writing V-mail to Bill, or tending the baby. Sometimes, to make me laugh, or out of her despair, she would imitate happenings or types at school.

I think I said once: 'Why don't you do something like this in the school amateur show?' One morning she phoned me at work, hardly understandable through the weeping: 'Mother,

I did it. I won, I won; they gave me first prize; they clapped and clapped and wouldn't let me go.'

Now suddenly she was Somebody, and as imprisoned in her difference as she had been in her anonymity.

She began to be asked to perform at other high schools, even in colleges, then at city and state-wide affairs. The first one we went to, I only recognized her that first moment when thin, shy, she almost drowned herself into the curtains. Then: Was this Emily? The control, the command, the convulsing and deadly clowning, the spell, then the roaring, stamping audience, unwilling to let this rare and precious laughter out of their lives.

Afterwards: You ought to do something about her with a gift like that – but without money or knowing how, what does one do? We have left it all to her, and the gift has as often eddied inside, clogged and clotted, as been used and growing.

She is coming. She runs up the stairs two at a time with her light graceful step, and I know she is happy tonight. Whatever it was that occasioned your call did not happen today.

'Aren't you ever going to finish the ironing, Mother? Whistler painted his mother in a rocker. I'd have to paint mine standing over an ironing-board.' This is one of her communicative nights and she tells me everything and nothing as she fixes herself a plate of food out of the icebox.

She is so lovely. Why did you want me to come in at all? Why were you concerned? She will find her way.

She starts up the stairs to bed. 'Don't get me up with the rest in the morning.' 'But I thought you were having mid-terms.' 'Oh, those,' she comes back in, kisses me, and says quite lightly, 'in a couple of years when we'll all be atom-dead they won't matter a bit.'

She has said it before. She *believes* it. But because I have been dredging the past, and all that compounds a human being is so heavy and meaningful in me, I cannot endure it tonight.

I will never total it all. I will never come in to say: She was a child seldom smiled at. Her father left me before she was a year old. I had to work her first six years when there was work, or I sent her home to his relatives. There were years she had care she hated. She was dark and thin and foreign-looking in a world where the prestige went to blondeness and curly hair and dimples, she was slow where glibness was prized. She was a child of anxious, not proud, love. We were poor and could not afford for her the soil of easy growth. I was a young mother, I was a distracted mother. There were the other children pushing up, demanding. Her younger sister seemed all that she was not. There were years she did not let me touch her. She kept too much in herself, her life was such that she had to keep too much in herself. My wisdom came too late. She has much to her and probably little will come of it. She is a child of her age, of depression, of war, of fear.

Let her be. So all that is in her will not bloom – but in how many does it? There is still enough left to live by. Only help her to know – help make it so there is cause for her to know that she is more than this dress on the ironing-board, helpless before the iron.

Elizabeth Taylor

Flesh

Phyl was always one of the first to come into the hotel bar in the evenings, for what she called her *aperitif*, and which, in reality, amounted to two hours' steady drinking. After that, she had little appetite for dinner, a meal to which she was not used.

On this evening, she had put on one of her beaded tops, of the kind she wore behind the bar on Saturday evenings in London, and patted back her tortoiseshell hair. She was massive and glittering and sunburnt – a wonderful sight, Stanley Archard thought, as she came across the bar towards him.

He had been sitting waiting for her. They had found their own level in one another on about the third day of the holiday. Both being heavy drinkers drew them together. Before that had happened, they had looked one another over warily as, in fact, they had all their fellow guests.

Travelling on their own, speculating, both had watched and wondered. Even at the airport, she had stood out from the others, he remembered, as she had paced up and down in her emerald green coat. Then their flight number had been called, and they had gathered with others at the same channel, with the same pink labels tied to their hand luggage, all going to the same place; a polite, but distant little band of people, no one knowing with whom friendships were to be made – as like would no doubt drift to like. In the days that followed, Stanley had wished he had taken more notice of Phyl from the beginning, so that at the end of the holiday he would have that much more to remember. Only the emerald green coat had stayed in his mind. She had not worn it since – it was too warm – and he dreaded the day when she would put it on again to make the return journey.

Arriving in the bar this evening, she hoisted herself up on a stool beside him. 'Well, here we are,' she said, glowing, taking one peanut; adding, as she nibbled, 'Evening, George,' to the barman. 'How's tricks?'

'My God, you've caught it today,' Stanley said, and he put his hands up near her plump red shoulders as if to warm them at a fire. 'Don't overdo it,' he warned her.

'Oh, I never peel,' she said airily.

He always put in a word against the sunbathing when he could. It separated them. She stayed all day by the hotel swimming-pool, basting herself with oil. He, bored with basking – which made him feel dizzy – had hired a car and spent his time driving about the island, and was full of alienating information about the locality, which the other guests – resenting the hired car, too – did their best to avoid. Only Phyl did not mind listening to him. For nearly every evening of her married life she had stood behind the bar and listened to other people's boring chat: she had a technique for dealing with it and a fund of vague phrases. 'Go on!' she said now, listening – hardly listening – to Stanley, and taking another nut. He had gone off by himself and found a place for lunch: *hors d'œuvre*, nice-sized slice of veal, two veg, *crème caramel*, half bottle of rosé, coffee – twenty-two shillings the lot. 'Well, I'm blowed,' said Phyl, and she took a pound note from her handbag and waved it at the barman. When she snapped up the clasp of the bag it had a heavy, expensive sound.

One or two other guests came in and sat at the bar. At this stage of the holiday they were forming into little groups, and this was the jokey set who had come first after Stanley and Phyl. According to them all sorts of funny things had happened during the day, and little screams of laughter ran round the bar.

'Shows how wrong you can be,' Phyl said in a low voice, 'I thought they were ever so starchy on the plane. I was wrong about you, too. At the start, I thought you were . . . you know . . . one of *those*. Going about with that young boy all the time.'

Stanley patted her knee. 'On the contrary,' he said, with a meaning glance at her. 'No, I was just at a bit of a loose end, and he seemed to cotton on. Never been abroad before, he hadn't, and didn't know the routine. I liked it for the first day or two. It was like taking a nice kiddie out on a treat. Then it seemed to me he was sponging. I'm not mean, I don't think; but I don't like that – sponging. It was quite a relief when he suddenly took up with the Lisper.'

By now, he and Phyl had nicknames for most of the other people in the hotel. They did not know that the same applied to them, and that to the jokey set he was known as Paws and she as the Shape. It would have put them out and perhaps ruined their holiday if they had known. He thought his little knee-pattings were of the utmost discretion, and she felt confidence from knowing her figure was expensively controlled under her beaded dresses when she became herself again in the evenings. During the day, while sun-bathing, she considered that anything went – that, as her mind was a blank, her body became one also.

The funny man of the party – the awaited climax – came into the bar, crabwise, face covered slyly with his hand, as if ashamed of some earlier misdemeanour. 'Oh, my God, don't look round. Here comes trouble!' someone said loudly, and George was called for from all sides. 'What's the poison, Harry? No, my shout, old boy. George, if you *please*.'

Phyl smiled indulgently. It was just like Saturday night with the regulars at home. She watched George with a professional eye, and nodded approvingly. He was good. They could have used him at The Nelson. A good quick boy.

'Heard from your old man?' Stanley asked her.

She cast him a tragic, calculating look. 'You must be joking. He can't *write*. No, honest, I've never had a letter from him in the whole of my life. Well, we always saw each other every day until I had my hysterectomy.'

Until now, in conversations with Stanley, she had always referred to 'a little operation'. But he had guessed what it was – well, it always was, wasn't it? – and knew that it was the reason for her being on holiday. Charlie, her husband, had sent her off to recuperate. She had sworn there was no need, that she had never felt so well in her life – was only a bit weepy sometimes late on a Saturday night. 'I'm not really the crying sort,' she had explained to Stanley. 'So he got worried, and sent me packing.' 'You clear off to the sun,' he had said, 'and see what that will do.'

What the sun had done for her was to burn her brick-red, and offer her this nice holiday friend. Stanley Archard, retired widower from Hove.

She enjoyed herself, as she usually did. The sun shone every day, and the drinks were so reasonable – they had many a long discussion about that. They also talked about his little flat in Hove; his strolls along the front; his few cronies at the club; his sad, orderly and lonely life.

This evening, he wished he had not brought up the subject of Charlie's writing to her, for it seemed to have fixed her thoughts on him and, as she went chatting on about him, Stanley felt an indefinable distaste, an aloofness.

She brought out from her note-case a much-creased cutting

from *The Morning Advertiser.* 'Phyl and Charlie Parsons
welcome old friends and new at The Nelson, Southwood. In
licensed hours only!' 'That was when we changed Houses,'
she explained. There was a photograph of them both standing
behind the bar. He was wearing a dark blazer with a large
badge on the pocket. Sequins gave off a smudged sparkle
from her breast, her hair was newly, elaborately done, and
her large, ringed hand rested on an ornamental beer-handle.
Charlie had *his* hands in the blazer pockets, as if he were
there to do the welcoming, and his wife to do the work: and
this, in fact, was how things were. Stanley guessed it, and felt
a twist of annoyance in his chest. He did not like the look of
Charlie, or anything he had heard about him – how, for
instance, he had seemed like a fish out of water visiting his
wife in hospital. 'He used to sit on the edge of the chair and
stare at the clock, like a boy in school,' Phyl had said,
laughing. Stanley could not bring himself to laugh, too. He
had leaned forward and taken her knee in his hand and
wobbled it sympathetically to and fro.

No, she wasn't the crying sort, he agreed. She had a
wonderful buoyancy and gallantry, and she seemed to knock
years off his age by just *being* with him, talking to him.

In spite of their growing friendship, they kept to their
original, separate tables in the hotel restaurant. It seemed too
suddenly decisive and public a move for him to join her now,
and he was too shy to carry it off at this stage of the holiday,
before such an alarming audience. But after dinner, they
would go for a walk along the sea-front, or out in the car for
a drink at another hotel.

Always, for the first minute or two in a bar, he seemed to
lose her. As if she had forgotten him, she would look about
her critically, judging the set-up, sternly drawing attention to
a sticky ring on the counter where she wanted to rest her
elbow, keeping a professional eye on the prices.

When they were what she called 'nicely grinned-up', they
liked to drive out to a small headland and park the car,

watching the swinging beam from a lighthouse. Then, after the usual knee-pattings and neck-strokings, they would heave and flop about in the confines of the Triumph Herald, trying to make love. Warmed by their drinks, and the still evening and the romantic sound of the sea idly turning over down below them, they became frustrated, both large, solid people, she much corseted and, anyhow, beginning to be painfully sunburnt across the shoulders, he with the confounded steering wheel to contend with.

He would grumble about the car and suggest getting out onto a patch of dry barley grass; but she imagined it full of insects; the chirping of the cicadas was almost deafening.

She also had a few scruples about Charlie, but they were not so insistent as the cicadas. After all, she thought, she had never had a holiday romance – not even a honeymoon with Charlie – and she felt that life owed her just one.

After a time, during the day, her sunburn forced her into the shade, or out in the car with Stanley. Across her shoulders she began to peel, and could not bear – though desiring his caress – him to touch her. Rather glumly, he waited for her flesh to heal, told her 'I told you so'; after all, they had not forever on this island, had started their second, their last week already.

'I'd like to have a look at the other island,' she said, watching the ferry leaving, as they sat drinking nearby.

'It's not worth just going there for the inside of a day,' he said meaningfully, although it was only a short distance.

Wasn't this, both suddenly wondered, the answer to the too small car, and the watchful eyes back at the hotel. She had refused to allow him into her room there. 'If anyone saw you going in or out. Why, they know where I live. What's to stop one of them coming into The Nelson any time, and chatting Charlie up?'

'Would you?' he now asked, watching the ferry starting off across the water. He hardly dared to hear her answer.

After a pause, she laughed. 'Why not?' she said, and took his hand. 'We wouldn't really be doing any harm to anyone.' (Meaning Charlie.) 'Because no one could find out, could they?'

'Not over there,' he said, nodding towards the island. 'We can start fresh over there. Different people.'

'They'll notice we're both not at dinner at the hotel.'

'That doesn't prove anything.'

She imagined the unknown island, the warm and starlit night and, somewhere, under some roof or other, a large bed in which they could pursue their daring, more than middle-aged adventure, unconfined in every way.

'As soon as my sunburn's better,' she promised. 'We've got five more days yet, and I'll keep in the shade till then.'

A chambermaid advised yoghourt, and she spread it over her back and shoulders as best she could, and felt its coolness absorbing the heat from her skin.

Damp and cheesy-smelling in the hot night, she lay awake, cross with herself. For the sake of a tan, she was wasting her holiday – just to be a five minutes' wonder in the bar on her return, the deepest brown any of them had had that year. The darker she was, the more *abroad* she would seem to have been, the more prestige she could command. All summer, pallid herself, she had had to admire others.

Childish, really, she decided, lying rigid under the sheet, afraid to move, burning and throbbing. The skin was taut behind her knees, so that she could not stretch her legs; her flesh was on fire.

Five more days, she kept thinking. Meanwhile, even this sheet upon her was unendurable.

On the next evening, to establish the fact that they would not always be in to dinner at the hotel, they complained in the bar about the dullness of the menu, and went elsewhere.

It was a drab little restaurant, but they scarcely noticed

their surroundings. They sat opposite one another at a corner table and ate shellfish briskly, busily – he, from his enjoyment of the food; she, with a wish to be rid of it. They rinsed their fingers, quickly dried them and leaned forward and twined them together – their large placid hands, with heavy rings, clasped on the tablecloth. Phyl, glancing aside for a moment, saw a young girl, at the next table with a boy, draw in her cheekbones to suppress laughter then, failing, turn her head to hide it.

'At *our* age,' Phyl said gently, drawing away her hands from his. 'In public, too.'

She could not be defiant; but Stanley said jauntily, 'I'm damned if I care.'

At that moment, their chicken was placed before them, and he sat back, looking at it, waiting for vegetables.

As well as the sunburn, the heat seemed to have affected Phyl's stomach. She felt queasy and nervy. It was now their last day but one before they went over to the other island. The yoghourt – or time – had taken the pain from her back and shoulders, though leaving her with a dappled, flaky look, which would hardly bring forth cries of admiration or advance her prestige in the bar when she returned. But, no doubt, she thought, by then England would be too cold for her to go sleeveless. Perhaps the trees would have changed colour. She imagined – already – dark Sunday afternoons, their three o'clock lunch done with, and she and Charlie sitting by the electric log fire in a lovely hot room smelling of oranges and the so-called hearth littered with peel. Charlie – bless him – always dropped off amongst a confusion of newspapers, worn out with banter and light ale, switched off, too, as he always was with her, knowing that he could relax – be nothing, rather – until seven o'clock, because it was Sunday. Again, for Phyl, imagining home, a little pang, soon swept aside or, rather, swept aside *from*.

She was in a way relieved that they would have only one

night on the little island. That would make it seem more like a chance escapade than an affair, something less serious and deliberate in her mind. Thinking about it during the daytime, she even felt a little apprehensive; but told herself sensibly that there was really nothing to worry about: knowing herself well, she could remind herself that an evening's drinking would blur all the nervous edges.

'I can't get over that less than a fortnight ago I never knew you existed,' she said, as they drove to the afternoon ferry. 'And after this week,' she added, 'I don't suppose I'll ever see you again.'

'I wish you wouldn't talk like that – spoiling things,' he said heavily, and he tried not to think of Hove, and the winter walks along the promenade, and going back to the flat, boiling himself a couple of eggs, perhaps; so desperately lost without Ethel.

He had told Phyl about his wife and their quiet happiness together for many years, and then her long, long illness, during which she seemed to be going away from him gradually; but it was dreadful all the same when she finally did.

'We could meet in London on your day off,' he suggested.

'Well, maybe.' She patted his hand, leaving that disappointment aside for him.

There were only a few people on the ferry. It was the end of summer, and the tourists were dwindling, as the English community was reassembling, after trips 'back home'.

The sea was intensely blue all the way across to the island. They stood by the rail looking down at it, marvelling, and feeling like two people in a film. They thought they saw a dolphin, which added to their delight.

'Ethel and I went to Jersey for our honeymoon,' Stanley said. 'It poured with rain nearly all the time, and Ethel had one of her migraines.'

'I never had a honeymoon,' Phyl said. 'Just the one night

at the Regent Palace. In our business, you can't both go away together. This is the first time I've ever been abroad.'

'The places I could take you to,' he said.

They drove the car off the ferry and began to cross the island. It was hot and dusty, hillsides terraced and tilled; green lemons hung on the trees.

'I wouldn't half like to actually *pick* a lemon,' she said.

'You shall,' he said, 'somehow or other.'

'And take it home with me,' she added. She would save it for a while, showing people, then cut it up for gin and tonic in the bar one evening, saying casually, 'I picked this lemon with my own fair hands.'

Stanley had booked their hotel from a restaurant, on the recommendation of a barman. When they found it, he was openly disappointed; but she managed to be gallant and optimistic. It was not by the sea, with a balcony where they might look out at the moonlit waters or rediscover brightness in the morning; but down a dull side street, and opposite a garage.

'We don't *have* to,' Stanley said doubtfully.

'Oh, come on! We might not get in anywhere else. It's only for sleeping in,' she said.

'It *isn't* only for sleeping in,' he reminded her.

An enormous man in white shirt and shorts came out to greet them. 'My name is Radam. Welcome,' he said, with confidence. 'I have a lovely room for you, Mr and Mrs Archard. You will be happy here, I can assure you. My wife will carry up your cases. Do not protest, Mr Archard. She is quite able to. Our staff has slackened off at the end of the season, and I have some trouble with the old ticker, as you say in England. I know England well. I am a Bachelor of Science of England University. Once had digs in Swindon.'

A pregnant woman shot out of the hotel porch and seized their suitcases, and there was a tussle as Stanley wrenched them from her hands. Still serenely boasting, Mr Radam led them upstairs, all of them panting but himself.

The bedroom was large and dusty and overlooked a garage.

'Oh, God, I'm sorry,' Stanley said, when they were left alone. 'It's still not too late, if you could stand a row.'

'No. I think it's rather sweet,' Phyl said, looking round the room. 'And, after all, don't blame yourself. You couldn't know any more than me.'

The furniture was extraordinarily fret-worked, as if to make more crevices for the dust to settle in; the bedside lamp base was an old gin bottle filled with gravel to weight it down, and when Phyl pulled off the bed cover to feel the bed she collapsed with laughter, for the pillow-cases were embroidered 'Hers' and 'Hers'.

Her laughter eased him, as it always did. For a moment, he thought disloyally of the dead – of how Ethel would have started to be depressed by it all, and he would have hard work jollying her out of her dark mood. At the same time, Phyl was wryly imagining Charlie's wrath, how he would have carried on – for only the best was good enough for him, as he never tired of saying.

'He's quite right – that awful fat man,' she said gaily. 'We shall be very happy here. I dread to think who he keeps 'His' and 'His' for, don't you?'

'I don't suppose the maid understands English,' he said, but warming only slightly. 'You don't expect to have to read off pillowcases.'

'I'm sure there *isn't* a maid.'

'The bed is very small,' he said.

'It'll be better than the car.'

He thought, she is such a woman as I have never met. She's like a marvellous Tommy in the trenches – keeping everyone's pecker up. He hated Charlie for his luck.

I shan't ever be able to tell anybody about 'Hers' and 'Hers', Phyl thought regretfully – for she dearly loved to amuse their regulars back home. Given other circumstances, she might have worked up quite a story about it.

A tap on the door, and in came Mr Radam with two cups of tea on a tray. 'I know you English,' he said, rolling his eyes roguishly. 'You can't be happy without your tea.'

As neither of them ever drank it, they emptied the cups down the hand basin when he had gone.

Phyl opened the window and the sour, damp smell of new cement came up to her. All round about, building was going on; there was also the whine of a saw-mill, and a lot of clanking from the garage opposite. She leaned farther out, and then came back smiling into the room, and shut the window on the dust and noise. 'He was quite right – that barman. You *can* see the sea from here. It's down the bottom of the street. Let's go and have a look as soon as we've unpacked.'

On their way out of the hotel, they came upon Mr Radam, who was sitting in a broken old wicker chair, fanning himself with a folded newspaper.

'I shall prepare your dinner myself,' he called after them. 'And shall go now to make soup. I am a specialist of soup.'

They strolled in the last of the sun by the glittering sea, looked at the painted boats, watched a man beating an octopus on a rock. Stanley bought her some lace-edged handkerchiefs, and even gave the lace-maker an extra five shillings, so that Phyl could pick a lemon off one of the trees in her garden. Each bought for the other a picture-postcard of the place, to keep.

'Well, it's been just about the best holiday I ever had,' he said. 'And there I was in half a mind not to come at all.' He had for many years dreaded the holiday season, and only went away because everyone he knew did so.

'I just can't remember when I last had one,' she said. There was not – never would be, he knew – the sound of self-pity in her voice.

This was only a small fishing village; but on one of the headlands enclosing it and the harbour was a big new hotel, with balconies overlooking the sea, Phyl noted. They picked their way across a rubbly car-park and went in. Here, too, was the damp smell of cement; but there was a brightly-lighted empty bar with a small dance floor, and music playing.

'We could easily have got in here,' Stanley said. 'I'd like to wring that bloody barman's neck.'

'He's probably some relation, trying to do his best.'

'I'll best him.'

They seemed to have spent a great deal of their time together hoisting themselves up on bar stools.

'Make them nice ones,' Stanley added, ordering their drinks. Perhaps he feels a bit shy and awkward, too, Phyl thought.

'Not very busy,' he remarked to the barman.

'In one week we close.'

'Looks as if you've hardly opened,' Stanley said, glancing round.

It's not *his* business to get huffy, Phyl thought indignantly, when the young man, not replying, shrugged and turned aside to polish some glasses. Customer's always right. He should know that. Politics, religion, colour-bar – however they argue together, they're all of them always right, and if you know your job you can joke them out of it and on to something safer. The times she had done that, making a fool of herself, no doubt, anything for peace and quiet. By the time the elections were over, she was usually worn out.

Stanley had hated her buying him a drink back in the hotel; but she had insisted. 'What all that crowd would think of me!' she had said; but here, although it went much against her nature, she put aside her principles, and let him pay; let him set the pace, too. They became elated, and she was sure it would be all right – even having to go back to the soup specialist's dinner. They might have avoided that; but too late now.

The barman, perhaps with a contemptuous underlining of

their age, shuffled through some records and now put on *Night and Day*. For them both, it filled the bar with nostalgia.

'Come *on!*' said Stanley. 'I've never danced with you. This always makes me feel . . . I don't know.'

'Oh, I'm a terrible dancer,' she protested. The Licensed Victuallers' Association annual dance was the only one she ever went to, and even there stayed in the bar most of the time. Laughing, however, she let herself be helped down off her stool.

He had once fancied himself a good dancer; but, in later years, got no practice, with Ethel being ill, and then dead. Phyl was surprised how light he was on his feet; he bounced her round, holding her firmly against his stomach, his hand pressed to her back, but gently, because of the sunburn. He had perfect rhythm and expertise, side-stepping reversing, taking masterly control of her.

'Well, I never!' she cried. 'You're making me quite breathless.'

He rested his cheek against her hair, and closed his eyes, in the old, old way, and seemed to waft her away into a different dimension. It was then that he felt the first twinge, in his left toe. It was doom to him. He kept up the pace, but fell silent. When the record ended, he hoped that she would not want to stay on longer. To return to the hotel and take his gout pills was all he could think about. Some intuition made her refuse another drink. 'We've got to go back to the soup specialist some time,' she said. 'He might even be a good cook.'

'Surprise, surprise!' Stanley managed to say, walking with pain towards the door.

Mr Radam was the most abominable cook. They had – in a large cold room with many tables – thin greasy chicken soup, and after that the chicken that had gone through the soup. Then peaches; he brought the tin and opened it before them, as if it were a precious wine, and no hanky-panky going on. He then stood over them, because he had much to say. 'I was offered a post in Basingstoke. Two thousand pounds a year, and a car and a house thrown in. But what use is that to a man like me? Besides, Basingstoke has a most detestable climate.'

Stanley sat, tight-lipped, trying not to lose his temper; but this man, and the pain, were driving him mad. He did not – dared not – drink any of the wine he had ordered.

'Yes, the Basingstoke employment I regarded as not *on*,' Mr Radam said slangily.

Phyl secretly put out a foot and touched one of Stan's – the wrong one – and then thought he was about to have a heart attack. He screwed up his eyes and tried to breathe steadily, a slice of peach slithering about in his spoon. It was then she realized what was wrong with him.

'Oh, sod the peaches,' she said cheerfully, when Mr Radam had gone off to make coffee, which would be the best they had ever tasted, he had promised. Phyl knew they would not complain about the horrible coffee that was coming. The more monstrous the egoist, she had observed from long practice, the more normal people hope to uphold the fabrication – either for ease, or from a terror of any kind of collapse. She did not know. She was sure, though, as she praised the stringy chicken, hoisting the unlovable man's self-infatuation a notch higher, that she did so, because she feared him falling to pieces. Perhaps it was only fair, she decided, that weakness should get preferential treatment. Whether it would continue to do so, with Stanley's present change of mood, she was uncertain.

She tried to explain her thoughts to him when, he leaving his coffee, she having gulped hers down, they went to their bedroom. He nodded. He sat on the side of the bed, and put his face into his hands.

'Don't let's go out again,' she said. 'We can have a drink in here. I love a bedroom gin, and I brought a bottle in my case.' She went busily to the wash-basin, and held up a dusty tooth-glass to the light.

'You have one,' he said.

He was determined to keep unruffled, but every step she took across the uneven floorboards broke momentarily the steady pain into burning splinters.

'I've got gout,' he said sullenly. 'Bloody hell, I've got my gout.'

'I thought so,' she said. She put down the glass very quietly and came to him. 'Where?'

He pointed down.

'Can you manage to get into bed by yourself?'

He nodded.

'Well, then!' she smiled. 'Once you're in, I know what to do.'

He looked up apprehensively, but she went almost on tiptoe out of the door and closed it softly.

He undressed, put on his pyjamas, and hauled himself onto the bed. When she came back, she was carrying two pillows. 'Don't laugh, but they're "His" and "His",' she said. 'Now, this is what I do for Charlie. I make a little pillow house for his foot, and it keeps the bedclothes off. Don't worry, I won't touch.'

'On this one night,' he said.

'You want to drink a lot of water.' She put a glass beside him. 'My husband's got a touch of gout,' I told them down there. And I really felt quite married to you when I said it.'

She turned her back to him as she undressed. Her body, set free at last, was creased with red marks, and across her shoulders the bright new skin from peeling had ragged, dirty edges of the old. She stretched her spine, put on a transparent night-gown and began to scratch her arms.

'Come here,' he said unmoving. 'I'll do that.'

So gently she pulled back the sheet and lay down beside him that he felt they had been happily married for years. The pang was that this was their only married night and his foot burned so that he thought that it would burst. And it will be a damn sight worse in the morning, he thought, knowing the pattern of his affliction. He began with one hand to stroke her itching arm.

Almost as soon as she had put the light off, an ominous sound zig-zagged about the room. Switching on again, she said, 'I'll get that devil, if it's the last thing I do. You lie still.'

She got out of bed again and ran round the room, slapping at the walls with her *Reader's Digest*, until at last she caught the mosquito, and Stanley's (as was apparent in the morning) blood squirted out.

After that, once more in the dark, they lay quietly. He endured his pain, and she without disturbing him rubbed her flaking skin.

'So this is our wicked adventure,' he said bitterly to the moonlit ceiling.

'Would you rather be on your own?'

'No, no!' He groped with his hand towards her.

'Well, then . . .'

'How can you forgive me?'

'Let's worry about you, eh? Not me. That sort of thing doesn't matter much to me nowadays. I only really do it to be matey. I don't know . . . by the time Charlie and I have locked up, washed up, done the till, had a bit of something to eat . . .'

Once, she had been as insatiable as a flame. She lay and remembered the days of her youth; but with interest, not wistfully.

Only once did she wake. It was the best night's sleep she'd had for a week. Moonlight now fell over the bed, and on one chalky whitewashed wall. The sheet draped over them rose in a peak above his feet, so that he looked like a figure on a tomb. If Charlie could see me now, she suddenly thought. She tried not to have a fit of giggles for fear of shaking the bed. Stanley shifted, groaned in his sleep, then went on snoring, just as Charlie did.

*

He woke often during that night. The sheets were as abrasive as sandpaper. I knew this damn bed was too small, he thought. He shifted warily onto his side to look at Phyl who, in her sleep, made funny little whimpering sounds like a puppy. One arm flung above her head looked, in the moonlight, quite black against the pillow. Like going to bed with a coloured woman, he thought. He dutifully took a sip or two of water and then settled back again to endure his wakefulness.

'Well, *I* was happy,' she said, wearing her emerald green coat again, sitting next to him in the plane, fastening her safety-belt.

His face looked worn and grey.

'Don't mind me asking,' she went on, 'but did he charge for that tea we didn't order.'

'Five shillings.'

'I *knew* it. I wish you'd let me pay my share of everything. After all, it was me as well wanted to go.'

He shook his head, smiling at her. In spite of his prediction, he felt better this departure afternoon, though tired and wary about himself.

'If only we were taking off on holiday now,' he said. 'Not coming back. Why can't we meet up in Torquay or somewhere? Something for me to look forward to,' he begged her, dabbing his mosquito-bitten forehead with his handkerchief.

'It was only my hysterectomy got me away this time,' she said.

They ate, they drank, they held hands under a newspaper, and presently crossed the twilit coast of England, where farther along grey Hove was waiting for him. The trees had not changed colour much and only some – she noticed, as she looked down on them, coming in to land – were yellower.

She knew that it was worse for him. He had to return to his empty flat; she, to a full bar, and on a Saturday, too. She wished there was something she could do to send him off cheerful.

'To me,' she said, having refastened her safety-belt, taking his hand again. 'To me, it was lovely. To me it was just as good as if we had.'

Willa Cather

The Sentimentality of William Tavener

It takes a strong woman to make any sort of success of living in the West, and Hester undoubtedly was that. When people spoke of William Tavener as the most prosperous farmer in McPherson County, they usually added that his wife was a 'good manager'. She was an executive woman, quick of tongue and something of an imperatrix. The only reason her husband did not consult her about his business was that she did not wait to be consulted.

It would have been quite impossible for one man, within the limited sphere of human action, to follow all Hester's advice, but in the end William usually acted upon some of her suggestions. When she incessantly denounced the 'shiftlessness' of letting a new threshing machine stand unprotected in the open, he eventually built a shed for it. When she sniffed contemptuously at his notion of fencing a hog corral with sod walls, he made a spiritless beginning on the structure – merely to 'show his temper,' as she put it – but in the end he went off quietly to town and bought enough barbed wire to complete the fence. When the first heavy rains came on, and the pigs rooted down the sod wall and made little paths all over it to facilitate their ascent, he heard his wife relate with relish the story of the little pig that built a mud house, to the minister at the dinner table, and William's gravity never relaxed for an instant. Silence, indeed, was William's refuge and his strength.

William set his boys a wholesome example to respect their mother. People who knew him very well suspected that he even admired her. He was a hard man towards his neighbors, and even towards his sons: grasping, determined and ambitious.

There was an occasional blue day about the house when William went over the store bills, but he never objected to items relating to his wife's gowns or bonnets. So it came about that many of the foolish, unnecessary little things that Hester bought for the boys, she had charged to her personal account.

One spring night Hester sat in a rocking chair by the sitting room window, darning socks. She rocked violently and sent her long needle vigorously back and forth over her gourd, and it took only a very casual glance to see that she was wrought up over something. William sat on the other side of the table reading his farm paper. If he had noticed his wife's agitation, his calm, clean-shaven face betrayed no sign of concern. His must have noticed the sarcastic turn of her remarks at the supper table, and he must have noticed the moody silence of the older boys as they ate. When supper was but half over little Billy, the youngest, had suddenly pushed back his plate and slipped away from the table, manfully trying to swallow a sob. But William Tavener never heeded ominous forecasts in the domestic horizon, and he never looked for a storm until it broke.

After supper the boys had gone to the pond under the willows in the big cattle corral, to get rid of the dust of plowing. Hester could hear an occasional splash and a laugh

ringing clear through the stillness of the night, as she sat by
the open window. She sat silent for almost an hour reviewing
in her mind many plans of attack. But she was too vigorous a
woman to be much of a strategist, and she usually came to
her point with directness. At last she cut her thread and
suddenly put her darning down, saying emphatically:

'William, I don't think it would hurt you to let the boys
go to that circus in town tomorrow.'

William continued to read his farm paper, but it was not
Hester's custom to wait for an answer. She usually divined
his arguments and assailed them one by one before he uttered
them.

'You've been short of hands all summer, and you've
worked the boys hard, and a man ought to use his own flesh
and blood as well as he does his hired hands. We're plenty
able to afford it, and it's little enough our boys ever spend. I
don't see how you can expect 'em to be steady and hard
workin', unless you encourage 'em a little. I never could see
much harm in circuses, and our boys have never been to one.
Oh, I know Jim Howley's boys get drunk an' carry on when
they go, but our boys ain't that sort, an' you know it,
William. The animals are real instructive, an' our boys don't
get to see much out here on the prairie. It was different where
we were raised, but the boys have got no advantages here, an'
if you don't take care, they'll grow up to be greenhorns.'

Hester paused a moment, and William folded up his paper,
but vouchsafed no remark. His sisters in Virginia had often
said that only a quiet man like William could ever have lived
with Hester Perkins. Secretly, William was rather proud of
his wife's 'gift of speech', and of the fact that she could talk
in prayer meetings as fluently as a man. He confined his own
efforts in that line to a brief prayer at Covenant meetings.

Hester shook out another sock and went on.

'Nobody was ever hurt by goin' to a circus. Why, law me!
I remember I went to one myself once, when I was little. I
had most forgot about it. It was over at Pewtown, an' I

remember how I had set my heart on going. I don't think I'd ever forgiven my father if he hadn't taken me, though that red clay road was in a frightful way after the rain. I mind they had an elephant and six poll parrots, an' a Rocky Mountain lion, an' a cage of monkeys, an' two camels. My! but they were a sight to me then!'

Hester dropped the black sock and shook her head and smiled at the recollection. She was not expecting anything from William yet, and she was fairly startled when he said gravely, in much the same tone in which he announced the hymns in prayer meeting:

'No, there was only one camel. The other was a dromedary.'

She peered around the lamp and looked at him keenly.

'Why, William, how come you to know?'

William folded his paper and answered with some hesitation, 'I was there, too.'

Hester's interest flashed up. 'Well, I never, William! To think of my finding it out after all these years! Why, you couldn't have been much bigger'n our Billy then. It seems queer I never saw you when you was little, to remember about you. But then you Back Creek folks never have anything to do with us Gap people. But how come you to go? Your father was stricter with you than you are with your boys.'

'I reckon I shouldn't a' gone,' he said slowly, 'but boys will do foolish things. I had done a good deal of fox hunting the winter before, and father let me keep the bounty money. I hired Tom Smith's Tap to weed the corn for me, an' I slipped off unbeknownst to father an' went to the show.'

Hester spoke up warmly: 'Nonsense, William! It didn't do you no harm, I guess. You was always worked hard enough. It must have been a big sight for a little fellow. That clown must have just tickled you to death.'

William crossed his knees and leaned back in his chair.

'I reckon I could tell all that fool's jokes now. Sometimes I can't help thinkin' about 'em in meetin' when the sermon's long. I mind I had on a pair of new boots that hurt me like the mischief, but I forgot all about 'em when that fellow rode the donkey. I recall I had to take them boots off as soon as I got out of sight o' town, and walked home in the mud barefoot.'

'O poor little fellow!' Hester ejaculated, drawing her chair nearer and leaning her elbows on the table. 'What cruel shoes they did use to make for children. I remember I went up to Back Creek to see the circus wagons go by. They came down from Romney, you know. The circus men stopped at the creek to water the animals, an' the elephant got stubborn an' broke a big limb off the yellow willow tree that grew there by the toll house porch, an' the Scribners were 'fraid as death he'd pull the house down. But this much I saw him do; he waded in the creek an' filled his trunk with water and squirted it in at the window and nearly ruined Ellen Scribner's pink lawn dress that she had just ironed an' laid out on the bed ready to wear to the circus.'

'I reckon that must have been a trial to Ellen,' chuckled William, 'for she was mighty prim in them days.'

Hester drew her chair still nearer William's. Since the children had begun growing up, her conversation with her husband had been almost wholly confined to questions of economy and expense. Their relationship had become purely a business one, like that between landlord and tenant. In her desire to indulge her boys she had unconsciously assumed a defensive and almost hostile attitude towards her husband. No debtor ever haggled with his usurer more doggedly than did Hester with her husband on behalf of her sons. The strategic contest had gone on so long that it had almost crowded out the memory of a closer relationship. This exchange of confidences tonight, when common recollections took them unawares and opened their hearts, had all the miracle of romance. They talked on and on; of old neighbors, of old familiar faces in the valley where they had grown up,

75

of long forgotten incidents of their youth – weddings, picnics, sleighing parties and baptizings. For years they had talked of nothing else but butter and eggs and the prices of things, and now they had as much to say to each other as people who meet after a long separation.

When the clock struck ten, William rose and went over to his walnut secretary and unlocked it. From his red leather wallet he took out a ten dollar bill and laid it on the table beside Hester.

'Tell the boys not to stay late an' not to drive the horses hard,' he said quietly, and went off to bed.

Hester blew out the lamp and sat still in the dark a long time. She left the bill lying on the table where William had placed it. She had a painful sense of having missed something, or lost something; she felt that somehow the years had cheated her.

The little locust trees that grew by the fence were white with blossoms. Their heavy odor floated in to her on the night wind and recalled a night long ago, when the first whippoorwill of the Spring was heard, and the rough, buxom girls of Hawkins Gap had held her laughing and struggling under the locust trees, and searched in her bosom for a lock of her sweetheart's hair, which is supposed to be on every girl's breast when the first whippoorwill sings. Two of those same girls had been her bridesmaids. Hester had been a very happy bride. She rose and went softly into the room where William lay. He was sleeping heavily, but occasionally moved his hand before his face to ward off the flies. Hester went into the parlor and took the piece of mosquito net from the basket of wax apples and pears that her sister had made before she died. One of the boys had brought it all the way from Virginia, packed in a tin pail, since Hester would not risk shipping so precious an ornament by freight. She went back to the bedroom and spread the net over William's head. Then she sat down by the bed and listened to his deep, regular breathing until she heard the boys returning. She went out to meet them and warn them not to waken their father.

'I'll be up early to get your breakfast, boys. Your father says you can go to the show.' As she handed the money to the eldest, she felt a sudden throb of allegiance to her husband and said sharply, 'And you be careful of that, an' don't waste it. Your father works hard for his money.'

The boys looked at each other in astonishment and felt that they had lost a powerful ally.

Rosamond Lehmann

A Dream of Winter

In the middle of the great frost she was in bed with
influenza; and that was the time the bee man came from
the next village to take the swarm that had been for years
buried in the wall of her country house; deep under the leads
roofing the flat platform of the balcony outside her bedroom
window.

She lay staring out upon a mineral landscape: iron, ice and
stone. Powdered with a wraith of spectral blue, the chalky
frost-fog stood, thickened in the upper air; and behind it a
glassy disc stared back, livid, drained of heat, like a gas lamp
turned down, forgotten, staring down uselessly, aghast, upon
the impersonal shrouded objects and dark relics in an abandoned house. The silence was so absolute that it reversed
itself and became in her ears continuous reverberation. Or
was it the bees, still driving their soft throbbing dynamo, as
mostly they did, day in, day out, all the year round? – all
winter a subdued companionship of sound, a buried murmur;
fiercer, louder, daily more insistent with the coming of the

warm days; materializing then into that snarling, struggling, multiple-headed organism pinned as if by centripetal force upon the outside of the wall, and seeming to strive in vain to explode away from its centre and disperse itself.

No. The bees were silent. As for the children, not one cry. They were in the garden somewhere: frost-struck perhaps like all the rest.

All at once, part of a ladder oscillated across the window space, became stationary. A pause; then a battered hat appeared, then a man's head and shoulders. Spying her among the pillows, his face creased in a wide grin. He called cheerfully: 'Good-morning!'

She had lost her voice, and waved and smiled, pointing to her throat.

'Feeling a bit rough? Ah, that's a shame. There's a lot of nasty colds and that about. Bed's the best place this weather, if you ask *me*.'

He stepped up on to the little balcony, and stood framed full-length in the long sash window – a short, broad figure in a roll-collared khaki pull-over, with a twinkling blue small peasant's eye in a thin lined face of elliptical structure, a comedian's face, blurred in its angles and hollows by a day's growth of beard.

'Come to take that there swarm. Wrong weather to take a swarm. I don't like the job on a day like this. Bad for 'em. Needs a mild spell. Still, it don't look like breaking and I hadn't nothink else on and you wanted the job done.'

His speech had a curious humming drawl, not altogether following the pattern of the local dialect: brisker, more positive. She saw that, separated by the frosty pane, they were to be day-long companions. The lady of the house, on her bed of sickness, presented him with no problems in etiquette. He experienced a simple pleasure in her society: someone to chat to on a long job.

'I'll fetch my mate up.'

He disappeared, and below in the garden he called:

'George!' Then an unintelligible burr of conversation, and up he came again, followed by a young workman with a bag of tools. George felt the embarrassment of the situation, and after one constricted glance through the window, addressed himself to his task and never looked towards her again. He was very young, and had one of those nobly modelled faces of working men; jaw, brows profoundly carved out, lips shutting clearly, salient cheekbone, sunk cheek, and in the deep cavities of the eye-sockets, eyes of extreme sadness. The sorrow is fixed, impersonal, expressing nothing but itself, like the eyes of animals or of portraits. This face was abstract, belonging equally to youth or age, turning up here and there, with an engine driver's cap on, or a soldier's; topping mechanics' overalls, lifting from the roadmender's gang to gaze at her passing car. Each time she saw it, so uncorrupted, she thought vaguely, romantically, it was enough to believe in. She had had a lot of leisure in her life to look at faces. She had friends with revolutionary ideas, and belonged to the Left Book Club.

'Be a long job this,' called the bee man. 'Looks like they've got down very deep.'

A sense of terror overcame her, as if some dreaded exploratory physical operation of doubtful issue, and which she would be forced to witness, was about to take place. This growth was deep down in the body of the house. The waves of fever started to beat up again.

The men disappeared. She waited for the children to appear upon the ladder; and soon, there they were. John had taken the precaution of tucking his sister's kilt into her bloomers. In his usual manner of rather disgusted patience, he indicated her footing for her. They pranced on the balcony, tapped on the pane, peered in with faces of lunatic triumph, presenting themselves as the shock of her life.

'A man's come to do the bees!'

'It's perfectly safe,' yelled John, in scorn, forestalling her. But voiceless, she could only nod, beam, roll her eyes.

'Shall we get Jock up?'

Frantically she shook her head.

'But he's whining to come up,' objected Jane, dismayed.

The hysterical clamour of a Cairn terrier phenomenally separated from his own rose up from below.

'We'd better go down to him,' said John wearily, acknowledging one more victory for silliness. 'Here come the workmen anyway. We'd only be in their way. Here – put your foot *here*, ass.'

They vanished. Insane noises of reunion uprose; then silence. She knew that Jane had made off, her purely subjective frivolous interest exhausted; but that John had taken up his post for the day, a scientific observer with ears of deepening carmine, waiting, under the influence of an inexpressible desire for co-operation, for a chance to steady the ladder, hand up a tool, or otherwise insinuate himself within the framework of the ritual.

Up came the bee man and his mate. They set to work to lift the leads. They communicated with each other in a low drone, bee-like, rising and sinking in a minor key, punctuated by an occasional deep-throated 'Ah!' Knocking, hammering, wrenching developed. Somebody should tell them she could not stand it. Nobody would. She rang for the curtains to be drawn, and when they were, she lay down flat and turned her face to the wall and sank into burning sleep.

She woke to the sound of John shouting through her door.

'They've gone to have their lunch. He's coming back this afternoon to take the swarm. Most of the roof's off. I've seen the bees. If only you'd drawn back your curtains you could have too. I called to you but you didn't seem to hear. The cat's brought in two more birds, a pigeon and a tit, but we saved them and we're thawing them behind the boiler.'

Down the passage he went, stumping and whistling.

*

Three o'clock. The petrified day had hardened from hour to hour. But as light began to fail, there came a moment when the blue spirit drew closer, explored the treetops, bloomed against the ghostly pane; like a blue tide returning, invading the white caves, the unfructifying salt stones of the sea.

The ladder shook. He was there again, carrying a kind of lamp with a funnel from which poured black smoke.

'Take a look,' he called cheerfully. 'It's worth it. Don't suppose you ever see nothink o' the kind before.'

She rose from her bed, put on dressing-gown and shawl and stumbled to the window. With a showman's flourish he flung off the black sacking – and what a sight was revealed! Atolls of pale honeycomb ridging the length and breadth of beam and lath, thrusting down in serrated blocks into the cavity; the vast amorphous murmuring black swarm suddenly exposed, stirring resentful, helpless, transfixed in the icy air. A few of the more vigorous insects crawled out from the conglomeration, spun up into the air, fell back stupefied.

'They're more lively than you'd think for,' said the bee man, thoughtful. She pointed to his face, upon which three or four bees were languidly creeping. He brushed them off with a chuckle. 'They don't hurt me. Been stung too often. Inoculated like.'

He broke off a piece of honeycomb and held it up. She wished so much to hold it in her hand that she forced herself to push down the window, receiving the air's shock like a blow on the face; and took it from him. Frail, blond, brittle, delicate as coral in construction, weightless as a piece of dried sponge or seaweed.

'Dry, see,' said the bee man. 'You won't get much honey out of here. It's all that wet last summer. If I'd 'a' taken this swarm a year ago, you'd a' got a whole heap. You won't get anythink to speak of out of here now.'

She saw now: the papery transparent aspect of these ethereal growths meant a world extinct. She shivered violently, her spirit overwhelmed by symbols of frustration. Her dream had been rich: of honey pouring bountifully out from beneath her roof tree, to be stored up in family jars, in pots and bowls, to spread on the bread and sweeten the puddings, and save herself a little longer from having to tell the children: No more sugar.

Too late! The sweet cheat gone.

'It's no weather to take a swarm,' repeated the bee man. Dejectedly he waved the lamp over the bubbling glistening clumps, giving them a casual smoke-over. 'Still, you wanted the job done.'

She wished to justify herself, to explain the necessity of dispossessing the bees, to say that she had been waiting for him since September; but she was dumb. She pushed up the window, put the honeycomb on her dressing-table, and tumbled heavily into bed again.

Her Enemy, so attentive since the outbreak of the war, whispered in her ear:

'Just as I thought. Another sentimental illusion. Schemes to produce food by magic strokes of fortune. Life doesn't arrange stories with happy endings any more, see? *Never again*. This source of energy whose living voice comforted you at dawn, at dusk, saying: We work for you. Our surplus is yours, there for the taking – vanished! You left it to accumulate, thinking: There's time; thinking: when I will. You left it too late. What you took for the hum of growth and plenty is nothing, you see, but the buzz of an outworn machine running down. The workers have eaten up their fruits, there's nothing left for you. It's no use this time, my girl! Supplies are getting scarce for people like you. An end, soon, of getting more than their fair share for dwellers in country houses. Ripe gifts unearned out of traditional walls, no more. All the while your roof was being sealed up patiently, cunningly, with spreading plasters and waxy shrouds.'

Through half-closed eyes she watched him bending, peering here and there. Suddenly he whipped out his knife, plunging his arm forward out of sight. A pause; then up came knife, hand again, lifting a clot of thick yellow sticky stuff. Honey.

'Honey!'

There it was, the richness, the substance. The knife carried a packed edge of crusted sugar, and as he held it up, the syrup began to drip down slow, gummy, amber-dark. Isled in the full attack of total winter there it hung, inviolable, a microcosm of summer, melting in sweet oils.

'Honey!' yelled John from below.

'*Now* we're all right,' called back the bee man in a happy voice, as if released all at once from his own weight of disappointment. 'Plenty here – right in the corner. Did you ever see anythink so artful? Near shave me not spotting it. Oh, we'll get you some! Run and beg us a dish off Cook, Sonny, and I'll dish you out a nice little lot for your tea.'

She heard the urgency of the start of her son's boots. It was as if he ran away with her, ran through her, bursting all obstacles to be back with the dish before he had gone, to offer it where it was required: his part in the serious task. This pure goodwill and disinterestedness of children, this concentration of spirit so entire that they seemed to fuse with and become the object, lifted her on a cool wave above her sickness, threw her up in a moment of absolute peace, as after love or childbirth, upon a white and abstract shore.

'That's a nice boy you've got,' said the bee man, cutting, scraping busily.'Sensible. I'm ever so glad to see this honey. There's one thing I do hate to see, and that's a swarm starved.'

The words shocked her. Crawling death by infinitesimal stages. Not a question of no surplus, but of the bare necessities of life. Not making enough to live on. A whole community entombed, like miners trapped.

A scuffle below. John's fluting voice came up:

'This do?'

'Fine. Bring it up, Sonny.'

The largest meat platter from the kitchen dresser hove in sight.

'Thanks, mate. Now we'll get you a bit o' somethink to sweeten you. Need it? What does your Mammy think, eh?' He shouted with laughter.

Unable to cope with repartee of so personal a character, John cast her a wry self-conscious grin, and rapidly vanished.

Light was rapidly failing, but the rising moon arrested the descent of darkness. In the opaque bleached twilight his silhouette persisted on the pane, bending, straightening. He hummed and whistled. Now and then he spoke softly to the bees. 'Run off, my girl, run off.' Once he held up his hands to show her the insects clustering upon them.

'They don't worry me, the jokers. Just a sore sort of a tingle, like as if I'd rapped myself over the fingers with a hammer.'

He brushed them off and they fell down like a string of beads breaking. They smiled at one another. She closed her eyes.

Roused by a rap on the pane, she lay in confused alarm. The lower window ran up with a swift screech, and, heaving towards her over the sill in the semi-darkness, she saw a phantasmagoric figure climb in and straighten itself up. A headless figure. Where the face should have been, nothing but swaying darkness. It's the fever. Wait, and it will go away.

She found courage to switch on the lamp and saw the bee man. He was wearing a round hat with a long circular veil of thick gauze that hung to his shoulders.

Fishing up a fragment of voice she croaked:

'Is that your hat for taking swarms?'

'Oh, him,' he said laughing, removing it. 'Forgot I had him on. Did I give you a scare?'

'Stylish,' she said.

'Thought you'd like to know the job's done. I've got 'em

down below there. Got you a nice bit of honey, too. I'm glad of that. I hate to see a swarm starved.'

He drew her curtains together. 'Better dror 'em or you'll get into trouble with the black-out, bother it.' Then he moved over to the fireplace. 'You fire's gorn right down. That's why I come in. Thought I'd make it up for you.' He knelt down, riddled the ashes, and with his bruised, swollen, wax-stuck fingers piled on more coal. 'That'll be more cheerful soon. Ain't you got nobody to see to you then?'

'Oh, yes,' she whispered. 'There'll be somebody coming soon. I forgot to ring.' She felt self-pity, and wanted to weep.

'You do seem poorly. You need giving your chest a good rub with camphorated. I believe in that.'

In another few moments he would be rubbing her chest.

But he remained by the fire, looking thoughtfully round the room. 'This is a nice old place. I knew it when I was a young lad, of course. The old Squire used to have us up for evening classes. Improve our minds. He was a great one for that.' He chuckled. 'Must be ten years since he died. I'm out o' touch. Went out to Canada when I was seventeen. Twenty years ago that was. Never got a wife, nor a fortune, nor nothink.' He chuckled again. 'I'm glad I got back before this war. Back where I started – that's where I am. Living with my married sister.'

She said:

'Won't you have a cup of tea?'

'No, I'll be off home, thanks all the same. I'd best get that swarm in. They're in a bad way.'

'Will they recover?'

'Ah, I couldn't say. It wasn't no weather to take a swarm. And then it demoralizes 'em like when you steals their honey. They sings a mournful song – ever so mournful.' He strode to the window. 'Still, we'll hope for the best. George'll be up in the morning to put them leads right. Well, I'll wish you goodnight. Hope you'll be more yourself tomorrow.' At the window he paused. 'Well, there's no call to go out that way, is there?' he remarked. 'Might as well go out like a Christian.'

He marched briskly across the room, opened her bedroom door, closed it quietly after him. She heard his light feet on the oak staircase, dying away.

She took her temperature and found it was lower: barely a hundred. He had done her good. Then she lay listening to the silence she had created. One performs acts of will, and in doing so one commits acts of negation and destruction. A portion of life is suppressed for ever. The image of the ruined balcony weighed upon her: torn out, exposed, violated, obscene as the photograph of a bombed house.

What an extraordinary day, what an odd meeting and parting. It seemed to her that her passive, dreaming, leisured life was nothing, in the last analysis, but a fluid element for receiving and preserving faint paradoxical images and symbols. They were all she ultimately remembered.

Somewhere in the garden a big branch snapped off and fell crackling down.

The children burst in, carrying plates of honey.

'Want some?'

'Not now, thanks. I can't really swallow anything, not even delicious honey.'

'It isn't delicious. It's beastly. It looks like seccotine and it tastes *much* too sweet. Ugh!'

It was certainly an unappetising colour – almost brown; the texture gluey. It had been there too long. She croaked:

'You oughtn't to be in this room. Where's Mary? Don't come near me.'

'Oh, we shan't catch your old 'flu,' said John, throwing himself negligently backwards over the arm of the sofa and writhing on the floor. 'Look here, Mum, what on earth did you want to get rid of the poor blighters for? They never did any harm.'

'Think what a maddening noise they made.'

'We like the noise. If you can't stand the hum of a wretched little bee, what'll you do in an air-raid?'

'You had a lovely day watching the bee man.'

'I dare say.'

But now all was loss, satiety, disappointment.

'Think how everybody got stung last summer. Poor Robert. And Mr Fanshawe.'

'Oh, your old visitors.'

What an entertainment the bees had been, a topic, a focusing point at weekends. But from now on, of course, there would be no more weekend parties. It was time for the bees to go.

'Remember Jane's eye, all bandaged up for days.'

'I remember that.' Jane flushed, went solemn. 'It didn't 'alf 'urt.'

'Your *English*!' cried John, revolted.

'I got not 'alf off Pippy Didcock,' said Jane, complacent. 'They all says that. It's Oxfordshire accident.'

She started to run up and down the room, kilt flying, hair bouncing, then stood still, her hand on her chest.'

'What's the most important thing about a person?' she said.

'Dopey,' said her brother. 'What's biting you?'

'Don't you know?' said Jane. 'Your heart. If it stops, you die. I can hear mine after that running.'

'It won't stop,' said her mother.

'It will some day,' said John. 'It might stop tonight. Reminds me – ' He fished in his pocket and drew out a dark object. 'I brought up this tit to give it a last chance by your fire. It was at the back of the boiler, but the cats would keep prowling about. They got the pigeon. It must have been stiff eating.' He examined the tit. 'It's alive!'

He rushed with it to the fire and crouched down, holding it in his palms before the now leaping flames. 'Its eyes opened. It's fluttering.'

Jane came and knelt beside him.

'Isn't it a *sweet* little tiny bird?'

Suddenly it flew straight up out of his hands, dashed against the mantelpiece, fell down again upon the hearthrug. They were all perfectly silent.

After a moment his hand went out to pick it up again. Then it flew straight into the fire, and started to roast, to whirr and cheep over the coals.

In a split second she was there, plunged in her hand, out again. Smell of burnt feathers, charred fragments flaking down. It was on the hearthstone. Everybody stared.

Suddenly it revived, it began to stagger about. The tenacity of life in its minute frame appalled her. Over the carpet it bounced, one wing burnt off, one leg shrivelled up under its breast, no tail; up and down, vigorously round and about.

'Is it going to be alive?' said Jane.

'Yes,' said John coldly, heavily. 'We can't do anything about it now.'

Djuna Barnes

The Jest of Jests

T he name of the heroine of this story is the Madeleonette. Why, never seemed to matter any more than
that the hero should have been called the Physician
when he had never so much as seen a case of measles in his
life.

The place of climax is Long Beach, but that you will not
understand until you reach the very end, though I might as
well warn you that it was there the Madeleonette and the
Physician fell into each other's arms, much to the consternation of the 'regulars' on the boardwalk.

However, there was a third party to this story, and his
name was Josiah Illock, a small, good-for-nothing type of
man, who looked as though he should have been laying drain
pipes in a small suburban town rather than making love to
the Madeleonette.

On the other hand the Physician was tall and dark and
even handsome. He wore a long, old-fashioned frock coat
and gray tweed trousers, and had an habitual expression of

forceful timidity. He kept his hands in his pockets much of the time, with that backward thrust that made him seem to be encouraging his receding backbone.

Now both of the gentlemen loved the Madeleonette, or they said so, and love and advertisements must be believed. For Josiah, she was the lily of existence; for the Physician, she was the rock on which faith or a home is founded.

For herself the Madeleonette was only a fast aging woman, who had managed somehow to keep a certain amount of looks and some of youth's fine hair in spite of the ravages of time. She was a widow who had been left in rather comfortable circumstances. Her husband, who had been an antique collector, had supplied her with arm chairs, sofas and cabinets enough to have started a small museum, but I would hesitate to say that this fact had anything to do with the affections of the two gentlemen just mentioned.

When upon occasion these men met in her green and white parlor, they glared, for they hated each other heartily. The Physician did not waste time intriguing to do away with Josiah, but when Josiah was alone with the Madeleonette, he could speak of little else until he defeated his own plans and set the Madeleonette's heart over in the direction of the Physician.

Sometimes Josiah would say to her: 'Some day you are going to wake up to the fact that the Physician is not as crazy about you as you think. All men begin by loving a woman for what she isn't and end by perceiving what she is. In the beginning they caress the skin with kisses, and in the end they puncture with the pistol.'

'Great God!' the Madeleonette would cry. 'Do you think so?'

And he would answer: 'Always it's an instinct. Men shoot what they do not understand. That is, they track the lion instead of the fox. They bring to the bitter dust the highest flying hawk and to the pitfalls they at last drag the antelope.'

'There are no pitfalls for the woman over forty,' the Madeleonette would answer. 'There's only one possibility for her, and that is she will end life on a sofa with hot bottles at head and feet.'

'Look here,' he said, leaning forward. 'You know what I mean. Shooting is simple. A woman can get over that – if – ' There was a long pause. 'If,' he finished, 'he keeps right on loving her – but he won't. They never do.'

'The Physician would die,' she answered simply.

'Want to prove it?' Josiah questioned.

She looked at him a long time as a woman does who is taking chances.

'All right,' she said at last. 'It's worth it.'

He talked on, sketching his plan, but she did not pay any attention until she heard him saying: 'I'll see to it that it's loaded with blanks, of course. All you have to do is to fall over and pretend dead. Stop breathing for a few seconds, but watch. If he really cares for you he will raise hell. If he doesn't, he'll merely leave the room with you and the revolver together to prove it suicide.'

She laughed, 'You're a fool, ain't you? As if any one, especially the Physician, were going to risk his neck, even if he does love me. What's he to shoot for?'

'A provocation.'

'What provocation?'

'Jealousy,' he answered, pretending to be absorbed in his cigar band.

'You're all crazy, you men,' she said, dropping off into an acceptable silence.

In the meantime the Physician, who looked back upon a life of thirty-nine years of timid shudderings, catapulted out upon the veranda of his home and stood there breathing hard.

He was more than a timid man. Like a carpenter's foot rule, he was long and powerful in sections, but too apt to double up and cease his calculations. He adored bravery because he had none of it. It was his reason for his affection for the Madeleonette. He knew her for a brave woman. He had a rock, while she had only a lover.

'Yet,' he reflected sanely, 'one should test the Madeleonette. A woman without courage would be my ruin. I lack that quality so myself.'

He watched a long dust gray line of children with a certain keen shrillness of breath that did more to eat up tobacco than forty mouths applied simultaneously.

Now while the Physician mused, the Madeleonette prepared for the death.

When a woman decides to lie down and play 'possum she always selects with fearful care her hosiery, her petticoats and her shoes.

The pumps that the Madeleonette picked out were chosen for the newness of soles, the petticoats for its lace and ribbons and the hosiery for its irreproachable unity.

In her daily life she had considered her hats, her gloves and her buckles. When she decided to lean back against destiny, she concentrated on her lingerie. She tied her laces tighter, powdered her neck lower, put her fingers into rings, her neck into the willing slavery of a halter of pearls, and upon her face she put that fixed smile which advertizes a perception of the angels.

There was a sharp ring of the far distant bell. She ran out into the kitchen to press the button – waited at the door for the ascending steps to turn into a man.

Josiah Illock came in, removed his hat and shuffled over to a chair. He sat there gasping.

'You like it?' she said, indicating her gown.

'It is beautiful,' he assented. 'What is it?'

'Chiffon. It falls nicely,' she confided with a slight blush. 'It falls nicely.'

He grinned. 'It's going to be the jest of jests, ain't it?' he remarked guardedly. But there was a nervous twitching of his mind that betrayed itself in the muscles of his neck.

'Yes,' she answered. 'I've been practicing the fall, Josiah. I'm black and blue, but I have made it not only a fall, but a disaster. It has become an art.'

'Um,' he answered. 'You love him pretty much, don't you?'

'Quite a bit,' she assented. 'But I love art more.' She tried to look natural.

'There must be some subtle, fine, masterful touch that will make him realize that not only has a candle been snuffed out, but that an arc light has given up its flame; not only that a soul has passed into the night, but that a professional has given her last performance on any stage; not only that a grave shall open for the Madeleonette, but that an abyss shall remain forever gaping.'

Josiah Illock did not understand.

'What will you do?' he questioned.

'I shall die smoking a cigarette,' she said and watched for the effect.

She knew that she was not going to die. Had not Josiah Illock assured her, and did not Josiah love her?

Once Juliet had done this thing.

'My God!' she said, and started toward the window. Sudden ideas always take us to the casement. The tears ran unmolested down her cheeks. 'What if the Physician, swayed with remorse and with despair, should take the paper cutter or the curling irons and thrust them into his startled soul? What if he should lurch over to the window and fling himself to the pavement? What if he should tie a noose of handkerchiefs about his throat and spoil the gas fixture for the next tenant? What – '

The tears ceased. 'What a fool I am,' she thought as she smiled. 'I should wake up directly.'

She went back to her wardrobe to hunt for a becoming

dress. She laid it out upon the bed and, taking the cologne bottle, doused a liberal quantity of its contents upon the chiffon exterior. Then she laid it to her nose to ascertain if it was scented within the bounds of delicacy.

Next she took her hair out of curl papers and combed it into a ravishing coiffure. Presently, with her feet in bronze slippers and her electric coffee pot beside her, she gave herself up to pleasant expectancy, while she set the social crackers straight.

His eyes narrowed. 'I don't see anything professional in that, though perhaps you are right,' he assented and took to making nervous movements. Then abruptly he caught her hand.

'Can't you transfer that affection to me? Really it would be safer – please, I love you.'

She drew her hand back. 'You're messing things up a good bit, Josiah. I can love no one but the Physician. It is more than a conviction; it is something that has been bitten into my heart as a rose bug bites a rose.'

Josiah winced. 'You wouldn't have to go through this business then,' he commented.

She turned upon him. 'Not go through this business? Why, this is dress rehearsal. I wouldn't stop if I were married to him. You're a fool, Josiah. I have left the pistol in the hall on the stand. You'd better put those blanks in,' she added as he arose.

When he returned, she failed to notice that perspiration stood out upon his upper lip. She set the teapot on. The doorbell rang. They both started. She opened the door.

The Physician entered, hat in hand, and bowed over his fingers. Then they both stood up.

'Give me your hat,' she said.

Then Josiah came in with his behavior calculated to enrage to the point of madness. First he put his arm about the waist of the Madeleonette and, second, he kissed her. Third he opened his mouth to say some cutting things, but a look in

95

the Physician's face stopped him with his tongue raised. The Physician was staring at the nodding pansies in their box at the window in a way that seemed to him little ease. Then with a long step he reached the door and, at the same instant, came the short contralto song of a revolver shot. The Madeleonette dropped over sideways, with her cigarette still in her fingers. As she hit the floor, an abrupt flare of smoke burst from between her lips and ascended slowly in a gravely widening ring.

There was silence which was in its turn broken by the shutting of a back door.

The Physician laughed. A short, sad and very disillusioned laugh, and tossed the weapon upon the couch. He did not lean over her to look into her face. He did not stoop to kiss her lips. He did not cross those still hands above her breast. Instead he reached for the handle of the door and was gone.

In an instant, like a cat the Madeleonette was on her feet. She whirled a chair against the jamb and, drawing her chin above the transom top, watched with blazing eyes the exit of the Physician.

She watched him pass down the carpeted stair and on the the lower landing. She caught a tune from 'Chin-Chin' as he went. She said sadly: 'Now I shall have that little fool Josiah running around calling me beloved.'

She dropped to the floor as a plumb to the sod.

'Josiah!' she called.

There was no answer. She groped her way into the kitchen. It was empty.

She did not understand.

But one thing she did. It was growing in a widening pain. The Physician had been tested and found wanting.

He had not only tried to kill her and had, so far as he knew, but he had gone out as a man leaves a lavatory after washing his hands. She represented the suds after an experiment.

So that was the man he was. Just on outside appearances he had grown blindly jealous and flared up. Well, anyway, she knew him before it was too late. What was the matter with Josiah, though? Why had he bolted? She got up and went back into the parlor, where she wrote a note.

She even smiled now and finished the cigarette.

How frightened he would be when he found out that she was not dead after all. What would he not suffer in the way of humiliation and perception of his great inefficiency. How deliciously miserable he would be when he discovered he had lost her forever.

She went on to tell him of her trick to test him and added a bitter little jab such as women fashion. 'I shall no longer darken the doors of this place, defiled as it is by its acquaintance with you. I am leaving – shall have left by the time this reaches you – for Long Beach. I shall need a little rest in which to recover from this wound.'

She sent the note by messenger boy that it might reach its destination before the blood of self-accusation should recede from his cheeks.

Some five minutes later a small messenger boy appeared at the door. 'No answer,' he said, and departed with that casualness indulged in by Western Union children in the face of death and reunion.

The note was from the Physician.

'When you read this,' it said, 'I shall already be gone. I tested you and found you wanting. At the sound of a pistol shot you fainted. Oh, woman, that pistol was loaded with blanks! Ah, how shall I ever recover! You whom I loved – a coward! I shall always love you, but where I place that love there must I also have faith.

'Forever I leave this sad, disillusioned home. I go to Long Beach, there to recover a little of my former gaiety.

'PS – By the way, as I went out I found a loaded revolver on the table. What is the meaning of this?'

The Madeleonette sat down sharply. 'I'm the antelope all right,' she said.

Thus it comes about that the second paragraph of this story is the last.

Antonia White

The House of Clouds

The night before, Helen had tried to drown herself. She did not know why, for she had been perfectly happy. The four of them, she and Robert and Dorothy and Louis, had been getting supper. Louis had been carrying on one of his interminable religious arguments, and she remembered trying to explain to him the difference between the Virgin Birth and the Immaculate Conception as she carried plates out of the kitchen. And then, suddenly, she had felt extraordinarily tired and had gone out into the little damp courtyard and out through the gate into the passage that led to the Thames. She wasn't very clear what happened next. She remembered that Robert had carried her back to Dorothy's room and had laid her on the bed and knelt beside her for a long time while neither of them spoke. And then they had gone back into the comfortable noise and warmth of Louis's studio next door, and the others had gone on getting supper exactly as if nothing had happened. Helen had sat by the fire, feeling a little sleepy and remote, but amazingly happy. She had not wanted any supper, only a little bread and salt. She was insistent about the salt, because salt keeps away evil spirits, and they had given it to her quietly without any fuss. They were gentle with her, almost reverent. She felt they understood that something wonderful was going to happen to her. She would let no one touch her, not Robert even. It was as if she were being charged with some force, fiery and beautiful, but so dangerous that a touch would explode it.

She did not remember how she got home. But today had been quite normal, till at dinner-time this strong impulse had come over her that she must go to Dorothy's, and here, after walking for miles in the fog, she was. She was lying in Dorothy's bed. There was a fire in the room, but it could not warm her. She kept getting up and wandering over to the door and looking out into the foggy courtyard. Over and over again, gently and patiently, as if she were a child, Dorothy had put her back to bed again. But she could not sleep. Sometimes she was in sharp pain; sometimes she was happy. She could hear herself singing over and over again, like an incantation:

> O Deus, ego amo te
> Nec amo te ut salves me
> Nec quia non amantes te
> Aeterno punis igne.

The priest who had married her appeared by her bed. She thought he was his own ghost come to give her the last sacraments and that he had died at that very moment in India. He twisted his rosary round her wrist. A doctor came too; the Irish doctor she hated. He tried to give her an injection, but she fought him wildly. She had promised someone (was it Robert?) that she would not let them give her drugs. Drugs would spoil the sharpness of this amazing experience that was just going to break into flower. But, in spite of her fighting, she felt the prick of the needle in her arm, and sobbing and struggling still, she felt the thick wave of the drug go over her. Was it morphia? Morphia, a word she loved to say, lengthening the first syllable that sounded like the note of a horn. 'Morphia, mo-orphia, put an "M" on my forehead,' she moaned in a man's voice.

Morning came. She felt sick and mortally tired. The doctor was there still; her father, in a brown habit, like a monk, sat talking to him. Her father came over to the bed to kiss her, but a real physical dislike of him choked her, and she pushed him away. She knew, without hearing, what he and the doctor had been talking about. They were going to take her away to use her as an experiment. Something about the war. She was willing to go; but when they lifted her out of bed she cried desperately, over and over again, for Robert.

She was in a cab, with her head on a nurse's shoulder. Her father and two other men were there. It seemed odd to be driving through South Kensington streets in broad daylight, dressed only in one of Dorothy's nightgowns and an old army overcoat of Robert's. They came to a tall house. Someone, Louis, perhaps, carried her up flights and flights of steps. Now she was in a perfectly ordinary bedroom. An old nurse with a face she liked sat by the fire; a young one, very pink and white and self-conscious, stood near her. Helen wandered over to the window and looked out. There went a red bus, normal and reassuring. Suddenly the young nurse was at her elbow, leading her away from the window.

'I shouldn't look out of the window if I were you, dear,' she said in a soft hateful voice. 'It's so ugly.' Helen let herself be led away. She was puzzled and frightened; she wanted to explain something; but she was tired and muddled; she could not speak. Presently she was in bed, alone but for the old nurse. The rosary was still on her wrist. She felt that her parents were downstairs, praying for her. Her throat was dry; a fearful weariness weighed her down. She was in her last agony. She must pray. As if the old nurse understood, she began the 'Our Father' and 'Hail Mary'. Helen answered. Decade after decade they recited in a mechanical rhythm. There were cold beads on Helen's forehead, and all her limbs felt bruised. Her strength was going out of her in holy words. She was fighting the overpowering sleepiness that she knew was death. 'Holy Mary, Mother of God,' she forced out in beat after beat of sheer will-power. She lapsed at last. She was dead, but unable to leave the flesh. She waited, light, happy, disembodied.

Now she was a small child again and the nurse was the old Nanny at the house in Worcestershire. She lay very peacefully watching the nurse at her knitting under the green lamp. Pleasant thoughts went through her head of the red walled kitchen garden, of the frost on the rosemary tufts, of the firelight dancing in the wintry panes before the curtains were drawn. Life would begin again here, a new life perfected day by day through a new childhood, safe and warm and orderly as this old house that smelt of pines and beeswax. But the nightmares soon began. She was alone in a crypt watching by the coffin of a dead girl, an idiot who had died at school and who lay in a glass-topped coffin in her First Communion dress, with a gilt paper crown on her head. Helen woke up and screamed.

Another nurse was sitting by the green lamp.

'You must be quiet, dear,' said the nurse.

There were whispers and footsteps outside.

'I hear she is wonderful,' said a woman's voice.

'Yes,' said another, 'but all the conditions must be right, or it will be dangerous for her.'

'How?'

'You must all dress as nurses,' said the second voice, 'then she thinks she is in a hospital. She lives through it again, or rather, they do.'

'Who . . . the sons?'

'Yes. The House of Clouds is full of them.'

One by one, women wearing nurses' veils and aprons

tiptoed in and sat beside her bed. She knew quite well that they were not nurses; she even recognized faces she had seen in picture papers. These were rich women whose sons had been killed, years ago, in the war. And each time a woman came in, Helen went through a new agony. She became the dead boy. She spoke with his voice. She felt the pain of amputated limbs, of blinded eyes. She coughed up blood from lungs torn to rags by shrapnel. Over and over again, in trenches, in field hospitals, in German camps, she died a lingering death. Between the bouts of torture, the mothers, in their nurses' veils, would kiss her hands and sob out their gratitude.

'She must never speak of the House of Clouds,' one said to another.

And the other answered:

'She will forget when she wakes up. She is going to marry a soldier.'

Months, perhaps years, later, she woke up in a small, bare cell. The walls were whitewashed and dirty and she was lying on a mattress on the floor, without sheets, with only rough, red striped blankets over her. She was wearing a linen gown, like an old-fashioned nightshirt, and she was bitterly cold. In front of her was the blank yellow face of a heavy door without a handle of any kind. Going over to the door, she tried frantically to push it open. It was locked. She began to call out in panic and to beat on the door till her hands were red and swollen. She had forgotten her name. She did not know whether she were very young or very old; a man or a woman. Had she died that night in Dorothy's studio? She could remember Dorothy and Robert, yet she knew that her memory of them was not quite right. Was this place a prison? If only, only her name would come back to her.

Suddenly the door opened. A young nurse was there, a nurse with a new face. As suddenly as the door had opened, Helen's own identity flashed up again. She called wildly, 'I know who I am. I'm Helen Ryder. You must ring up my

103

father and tell him I'm here. I must have lost my memory. The number is Western 2159.'

The nurse did not answer, but she began to laugh. Slowly, mockingly, inch by inch, though Helen tried with all her strength to keep it open, she closed the door.

The darkness and the nightmare came back. She lost herself again; this time completely. For years she was not even a human being; she was a horse. Ridden almost to death, beaten till she fell, she lay at last on the straw in her stable and waited for death. They buried her as she lay on her side, with outstretched head and legs. A child came and sowed turquoises round the outline of her body in the ground, and she rose up again as a horse of magic with a golden mane, and galloped across the sky. Again she woke on the mattress in her cell. She looked and saw that she had human hands and feet again, but she knew that she was still a horse. Nurses came and dragged her, one on each side, to an enormous room filled with baths. They dipped her into bath after bath of boiling water. Each bath was smaller than the last, with gold taps that came off in her hands when she tried to clutch them. There was something slightly wrong about everything in this strange bathroom. All the mugs were chipped. The chairs had only three legs. There were plates lying about with letters round the brim, but the letters never read the same twice running. The nurses looked like human beings, but Helen knew quite well that they were wax dolls stuffed with hay.

They could torture her for all that. After the hot baths, they ducked her, spluttering and choking, into an ice-cold one. A nurse took a bucket of cold water and splashed it over her, drenching her hair and half blinding her. She screamed, and nurses, dozens of them, crowded round the bath to laugh at her. 'Oh, Nelly, you naughty, naughty girl,' they giggled. They took her out and dried her and rubbed something on her eyes and nostrils that stung like fire. She had human limbs, but she was not human; she was a horse or a stag being prepared for the hunt. On the wall was a looking-glass, dim with steam.

'Look, Nelly, look who's there,' said the nurses.

She looked and saw a face in the glass, the face of a fairy horse or stag, sometimes with antlers, sometimes with a wild, golden mane, but always with the same dark, stony eyes and nostrils red as blood. She threw up her head and neighed and made a dash for the door. The nurses caught and dragged her along a passage. The passage was like a long room; it had a shiny wooden floor with double iron tracks in it like the tracks of a model railway. The nurses held her painfully by the armpits so that her feet only brushed the floor. The passage was like a musty old museum. There were wax flowers under cases and engravings of Queen Victoria and Balmoral. Suddenly the nurses opened a door in the wall, and there was her cell again. They threw her down on the mattress and went out, locking the door.

She went to sleep. She had a long nightmare about a girl who was lost in the dungeons under an old house on her wedding-day. Just as she was, in her white dress and wreath and veil, she fell into a trance and slept for thirty years. She woke up, thinking she had slept only a few hours, and found her way back to the house, and remembering her wedding, hurried to the chapel. There were lights and flowers and a young man standing at the altar. But as she walked up the aisle, people pushed her back, and she saw another bride going up before her. Up in her own room, she looked in the glass to see an old woman in a dirty satin dress with a dusty wreath on her head. And somehow, Helen herself was the girl who had slept thirty years, and they had shut her up here in the cell without a looking-glass so that she should not know how old she had grown.

And then again she was Robert, endlessly climbing up the steps of a dark tower by the sea, knowing that she herself was imprisoned at the top. She came out of this dream suddenly to find herself being tortured as a human being. She was lying on her back with two nurses holding her down. A young man with a signet ring on his finger was bending over her, holding a funnel with a long tube attached. He forced the tube down her nose and began to pour some liquid down her throat. There was a searing pain at the back of her nose: she choked and struggled, but they held her down ruthlessly. At last the man drew out the tube and dropped it coiling in a basin. The nurses released her, and all three went out and shut the door.

This horror came at intervals for days. She grew to dread the opening of the door, which was nearly always followed by the procession of nurses and the man with the basin and the funnel. Gradually she became a little more aware of her surroundings. She was no longer lying on the floor, but in a sort of wooden manger clamped to the ground in the middle of a cell. Now she had not even a blanket, only a kind of stiff canvas apron, like a piece of sailcloth, stretched over her. And she was wearing, not a shirt, but a curious enveloping garment, very stiff and rough, that encased her legs and feet and came down over her hands. It had a leather collar, like an animal's, and a belt with a metal ring. Between the visitations of the funnel she dozed and dreamt. Or she would lie quietly, quite happy to watch, hour after hour, the play of pearly colours on the piece of sailcloth. Her name had irrevocably gone, but whole pieces of her past life, people, episodes, poems, remained embedded in her mind. She could remember the whole of 'The Mistress of Vision' and say it over to herself as she lay there. But if a word had gone, she could not suggest another to fill the gap, unless it was one of those odd, meaningless words that she found herself making up now and then.

One night there was a thunderstorm. She was frightened. The manger had become a little raft; when she put out her hand she could feel waves lapping right up to the brim. She had always been afraid of water in the dark. Now she began to pray. The door opened and a nurse, with a red face and pale hair and lashes, peered round the door, and called to her:

'Rosa Mystica.'

Helen called back:

'Turris Davidica.'

'Turris Eburnea,' called the nurse.

'Domus Aurea,' cried Helen.

And so, turn by turn, they recited the whole of the Litany of Our Lady.

One day she discovered that, by standing up in the manger, she could see through a high window, covered with close wire-netting, out into a garden. This discovery gave her great pleasure. In the garden women and nurses were walking; they did not look like real people, but oddly thin and bright, like figures cut out of coloured paper. And she could see birds flying across the sky, not real birds, but bird shaped kites, lined with strips of white metal that flew on wires. Only the clouds had thickness and depth and looked as clouds had looked in the other world. The clouds spoke to her sometimes. They wrote messages in white smoke on the blue. They would take shape after shape to amuse her, shapes of swans, of feathers, of charming ladies with fluffy white muffs and toques, of soldiers in white busbies.

Once the door of her cell opened and there appeared, not a nurse, but a woman with short, frizzy hair, who wore a purple jumper, a tweed skirt, and a great many amber beads. Helen at once decided that this woman's name was Stella. She had a friendly, silly face, and an upper lip covered with dark down.

'I've brought you a pencil,' she announced suddenly. 'I think you're so sweet. I've seen you from the garden, often. Shall we be friends?'

But before Helen could answer, the woman threw up her head, giggled, shot Helen an odd, sly look, and disappeared. With a sudden, sharp, quite normal horror, Helen thought, 'She's mad.'

She thought of the faces she had seen in the garden, with that same sly, shallow look. There must be other people in the place, then. For the first time, she was grateful for the locked door. She had a horror of mad people, of madness. Her own private horror had always been that she would go mad.

She was feeling quiet and reasonable that day. Her name had not come back to her, but she could piece together some shreds of herself. She recognized her hands; they were thinner and the nails were broken, but they were the hands she had had in the life with Dorothy and Robert and the others. She recognized a birthmark on her arm. She felt light and tired, as if she had recovered from a long illness, but sufficiently interested to ask the nurse who came in:

'What is this place?'

The nurse, who was young and pretty, with coppery hair and green eyes, looked at Helen with pity and contempt. She was kindly, with the ineffable stupid kindliness of nurses.

'I'm not supposed to tell you anything, you know.'

'I won't give you away,' promised Helen. 'What is it?'

'Well! it's a hospital, if you must know.'

'But what *kind* of a hospital?'

'Ah, that'd be telling.'

'What *kind* of a hospital?' persisted Helen.

'A hospital for girls who ask too many questions and have to give their brains a rest. Now go to sleep.'

She shook a playful finger and retreated.

It was difficult to know when the episode of the rubber room took place. Time and place were very uncertain, apt to remain stationary for months, and then to dissolve and fly in the most bewildering way. Sometimes it would take her a whole day to lift a spoon to her mouth; at other times she would live at such a pace that she could see the leaves of the ivy on the garden wall positively opening and growing before her eyes. The only thing she was sure of was that the rubber room came after she had been changed into a salmon and shut up in a little dry, waterless room behind a waterfall. She lay wriggling and gasping, scraping her scales on the stone floor, maddened by the water pouring just beyond the bars that she could not get through. Perhaps she died as a salmon as she had died as a horse, for the next thing she remembered was waking in a small, six-sided room whose walls were all thick bulging panels of grey rubber. The door was rubber-padded too, with a small red window, shaped like an eye, deeply embedded in it. She was lying on the floor, and through the red, a face, stained red too, was watching her and laughing.

She knew without being told, that the rubber room was a compartment in a sinking ship, near the boiler room, which would burst at any minute and scald her to death. Somehow she must get out. She flung herself wildly against the rubber walls as if she could beat her way out by sheer force. The air was getting hotter. The rubber walls were already warm to touch. She was choking, suffocating: in a second her lungs would burst. At last the door opened. They were coming to rescue her. But it was only the procession of nurses and the funnel once more.

The fantasies were not always horrible. Once she was in a cell that was dusty and friendly, like an attic. There were spider webs and an old ship's lamp on the ceiling. In the lamp was a face like a fox's mask, grinning down at her. She was sitting on a heap of straw, a child of eleven or so, with hair the colour of straw, and an old blue pinafore. Her name was Veronica. With crossed legs and folded arms she sat there patiently making a spell to bring her brother Nicholas safe home. He was flying back to her in a white aeroplane with a green propeller. She could see his face quite clearly as he sat between the wings. He wore a fur cap like a cossack's and a square green ring on his little finger. Enemies had put Veronica in prison, but Nicholas would come to rescue her as he had always come before. She and Nicholas loved each other with a love far deeper and more subtle than any love between husband and wife. She knew at once if he were in pain or danger, even if he were a thousand miles away.

Nicholas came to her window and carried her away. They flew to Russia, and landed on a plain covered with snow. Then they drove for miles in a sledge until they came to a dark pine forest. They walked through the forest, hand in hand, Veronica held close in Nicholas's great fur cape. But at last she was tired, dazed by the silence and the endless trees, all exactly alike. She wanted to sit down in the snow, to sleep.

Nicholas shook her: 'Never go to sleep in the snow, Ronnie, or you will die.'

But she was too tired to listen, and she lay down in the snow that was soft and strangely warm, and fell into an exquisite dreamy torpor. And perhaps she did die in the snow as Nicholas had said, for the next thing she knew was that she was up in the clouds, following a beautiful Indian woman who sailed before her, and sifting snow down on the world through the holes in her pinafore.

Whenever things became too intolerable, the Indian woman would come with her three dark, beautiful sons, and comfort her. She would draw her sweet smelling yellow veil over Helen and sing her songs that were like lullabies. Helen could never remember the songs, but she could often feel the Indian woman near, when she could not see her, and smell her sweet, musky scent.

She had a strange fantasy that she was Lord of the World. Whatever she ordered came about at once. The walls of the garden outside turned to blue ice that did not melt in the sun. All the doors of the house flew open and the passages were filled with children dressed in white and as lovely as dreams. She called up storms; she drove ships out of their courses; she held the whole world in a spell. Only herself she could not command. When the day came to an end she was tired out, but she could not sleep. She had forgotten the charm, or never known it, and there was no one powerful enough to say to her, 'Sleep.'

She raved, she prayed, but no sleep came. At last three women appeared.

'You cannot sleep unless you die,' they said.

She assented gladly. They took her to a beach and fettered her down on some stones, just under the bows of a huge ship that was about to be launched. One of the three gave a signal. Nothing could stop it now. On it came, grinding the pebbles to dust, deafening her with noise. It passed, slowly, right over her body. She felt every bone crack; felt the intolerable weight on her shoulders, felt her skull split like a shell. But she could sleep now. She was free from the intolerable burden of having to will.

After this she was born and re-born with incredible swiftness as a woman, as an imp, as a dog, and finally as a flower. She was some nameless, tiny bell, growing in a stream, with a stalk as fine as hair and a human voice. The water flowing through her flower throat made her sing all day a little monotonous song, 'Kulallah, Kulallah.' This happy flower life did not last long. Soon there came a day when the place was filled with nurses who called her 'Helen'. She did not recognize the name as her own, but she began to answer it mechanically as a dog answers a familiar sound.

She began to put on ordinary clothes, clumsily and with difficulty, as if she had only just learned how, and to be taken for walks in a dreary yard; an asphalt paved square with one sooty plane tree and a broken bench in the middle. Wearily she would trail round and round between two nurses who polished their nails incessantly as they walked and talked about the dances they had been to. She began to recognize some of her companions in the yard. There was the woman with the beads, the Vitriol woman, and the terrible Caliban girl. The Caliban girl was called Micky. She was tall and rather handsome, but Helen never thought of her except as an animal or a monster, and was horrified when Micky tried to utter human words. Her face was half-beautiful, half-unspeakable, with Medusa curls and great eyes that looked as if they were carved out of green stone. Two long, yellow teeth, like tiger's fangs, grew right down over her lip. She had a queer passion for Helen, who hated and feared her. Whenever she could, Micky would break away from her nurses and try to fondle Helen. She would stroke her hair, muttering, 'Pretty, pretty,' with her deformed mouth. Micky's breath on her cheek was hot and sour like an animal's, her black hair was rough as wire. The reality of Micky was worse than any nightmare; she was shameful, obscene.

The Vitriol woman was far more horrible to look at, but far less repulsive. Helen had heard the nurses whispering how the woman's husband had thrown acid at her. Her face was one raw, red, shining burn, without lid or brow, almost without lips. She always wore a neat black hat and a neat, common blue coat with a fur collar. Everyone she met she addressed with the same agonized question: 'Have you seen Fred? Where's Fred? Take me to Fred!'

On one of the dirty walls someone had chalked up:
'Baby.'
'Blood.'
'Murder.'
And no one had bothered to wipe it out.

The yard was a horror that seemed to have no place in the world, yet from beyond the walls would come pleasant ordinary noises of motors passing, and people walking and bells ringing. Above the walls, Helen could see a rather beautiful, slender dome, pearl coloured against the sky, and tipped with a gilt spear. It reminded her of some building she knew very well but whose name, like her own, she had forgotten.

One day, she was left almost alone in the yard. Sitting on the broken bench by the plane tree was a young girl, weeping. Helen went up to her. She had a gentle, bewildered face; with loose, soft plaits falling round it. Helen went and sat by her and drew the girl's head on to her own shoulder. It seemed years since she had touched another person with affection.

The girl nestled against her. Her neck was greenish white, like privet; when Helen touched it curiously, its warmth and softness were so lovely that tears came into her eyes. The girl was so gentle and defenceless, like some small, confiding animal, that Helen felt a sudden love for her run through all her veins. There was a faint country smell about her hair, like clover.

'I love you,' murmured Helen, hardly knowing what she said.

But suddenly a flock of giggling nurses were upon them with a chatter of:

'Look at this, will you?' and,

'Break away there.'

She never saw the country girl again.

And so day after day went past, punctuated by dreary meals and drearier walks. She lived through each one because she knew that sooner or later Robert must come to fetch her away, and this hope carried her through each night. There were messages from him sometimes, half-glimpsed in the flight of birds, in the sound of a horn beyond the walls, in the fine lines ruled on a blade of grass. But he himself never came, and at last there came a day when she ceased to look for him. She gave up. She accepted everything. She was no longer Helen or Veronica, no longer even a fairy horse. She had become an Inmate.

Nell Dunn

Out with the Girls

We stand, the three of us, me, Sylvie and Rube, pressed up against the saloon door, brown ales clutched in our hands. Rube, neck stiff so as not to shake her beehive, stares sultrily round the packed pub. Sylvie eyes the boy hunched over the mike and shifts her gaze down to her breasts snug in her new pink jumper. 'Kiss! Kiss! Kiss!' he screams. Three blokes beckon us over to their table.

'Fancy 'em?'

Rube doubles up with laughter. 'Come on, then. They can buy us some beer.'

'Hey, look out, yer steppin' on me winkle!'

Dignified, the three of us squeeze between tables and sit ourselves, knees tight together, daintily on the chairs.

'Three browns, please,' says Sylvie before we've been asked.

'I've seen you in here before, ain't I?' A boy leans luxuriously against the leather jacket slung over the back of his chair.

'Might 'ave done.'

'You come from Battersea, don't yer?'

'Yeah, me and Sylvie do. She don't though. She's an heiress from Chelsea.'

'Really? You really an heiress?' Jimmy Dean moves his chair closer to mine, sliding his arm along the back.

'Are yer married?'

'Course she is. What do yer think that is? Scotch mist?' Rube points to my wedding ring.

Sylvie says, 'Bet they're all married, dirty ginks!'

'Like to dance?'

Rube moves onto the floor. She hunches up her shoulders round her ears, sticks out her lower lip and swings in time to the shattering music.

'What's it like havin' a ton of money?'

'You can't buy love.'

'No, but you can buy a bit of the other.' Sylvie chokes, spewing out brown ale.

'I'd get a milk-white electric guitar.'

'Yeah and a milk-white Cadillac convertible – walk in the shop and peel off the notes. Bang 'em down on the counter and drive out – that's what yer dad does, I bet . . .'

We were crushed in the toilets. All round girls smeared on pan-stick.

'I can't go with him, he's too short.'

'All the grey glitter I put on me hair come off on his cheek and I hadn't the heart to tell him.'

'I wouldn't mind goin' with a married man 'cept I couldn't abear him goin' home and gettin' into bed with his wife.'

'Me hair all right?'

'Yeah, lend us yer lacquer.'

'Now don't get pissin' off and leavin' me.' Rube pulled at her mauve skirt so it clung to her haunches and stopped short of her round knees.

Outside revving bikes were splitting the night.

'Where we going?'

'Let's go swimmin' up the Common.'

'We ain't got no swim-suits with us.'

'We'll swim down one end and you down the other. It's dark, ain't it?'

'Who do yer think's going to see yer? The man in the moon?'

'Yeah and what's to stop yer hands wandering?'

'We'll tie 'em behind our backs.'

'Here, I'll never git on there, I can't get me knees apart.'

'Hitch yer skirt up under yer coat.'

'Help, me grandmother'll catch cold!'

The three of us climb onto the bikes, each behind a boy. We burn up Tooting Broadway and streak round a corner.

'I did this bend at eighty once,' he shouts over my shoulder.

'Ninety-two people bin decapitated on them iron girders, taking it too fast.' We race across the Common, then shudder to a halt under some trees. He wears jeans, black boots with double gold buckles and a fine lawn shirt beneath his unzipped jacket.

'There are two things I'd like to be – a racing driver or a pilot. But you've gotta have money for that.'

We clambered over the high wall, pulled and pushed by the boys, went giggling through the coke pile to where the gleaming pool lay. Huddled beneath the cabin eaves, we watched the naked boys plunge into the thick water.

'I wouldn't trust Ronnie, you can tell by his eyes.'

'I'm bloody well going to keep me drawers on.'

A train howls by across the Common, a flickering light in the crowded trees, and then darkness except for an orange glow from distant street lamps.

I swim off towards the dark end. He puts an arm around my neck and I see tattooed on his greenish-white skin I AM ELVIS. Suddenly we are lit up. Searchlights. The law.

'Quick, me clobber!' Rube is running towards me, bulging

out of her bra, a pink jelly, her black hair wet down her back. Jimmy grabs my wrist and we run into the trees. He rubs his blond hair dry on his shirt.

'Sometimes we go camping. Take tents and something to cover you over and go down to the seaside. The girls tell their mums they're going camping four or five together and then they come with us – fabulous sleeping out with a bird to keep yer warm.

'All I want is a bike and ten pounds a week in me pocket – there's one thing I can't stand and that's being skint.

'Comin' home with me? There's a place I know, matter of fact it's right in the buildings. I'm the only one what knows it. I nick me mum's key to the washhouse, she's got an old mattress tied up in there – I just untie it.'

Sylvie's laugh rips the night. 'Hey, you two, we're going!'

'I bet she's well away!'

'Know what happened in work today? I was sittin' on the steps outside McCrindle's eatin' me dinner when this Fred, Indian gink, says, "Look out, love, I can see yer drawers." So I says, "What colour are they then?" "Pink," he says. "No, they're not," I says, "because I ain't got none on."'

'You work up McCrindle's?'

'Yeah, I've had a scrub, so don't go saying you can smell the butter on me.'

Sylvie whispers, 'He undid me brassieres, so I told him to do them up again. "You certainly know where the hook is," I says.'

''E believes in grabbin' hold of yer and bitin' yer ear-'ole.

'I like it rough. You get more feelin' out of it that way.

'I was tuckin' in his shirt for him and he says, "Don't put yer hand down there or you'll get a shock!"'

The boys pushed the bikes out of the trees and once again we shot off into the night.

'I've never bin beaten except once in a burn-up on the Sidcup mile. Then I found the other bloke dead at the end. He hit an island – peaceful he looked, no blood nor nothing.'

We were standing in the concrete stairwell of some LCC flats.

A ball of paper blew about. A girl in stilettos clattered down the stairs. 'Cor, we used to belt along that road, round the bends, and the girls would be lollin' on the banks wavin' and callin' out, "Give us a ride" . . .'

'Yeah, let's face it, it's dicin' with death, it's gettin' just that inch in front . . .'

'You must think I'm slow. I don't know what to say to a decent girl. If you was an old slag, I'd just say, "Come 'ere . . ."'

'All me mates are gettin' married, it's the rage . . .

'I went steady once, but she broke it off after me accident. I remember openin' me eyes and seein' me mate carryin' me shoe across the road. "That's it," I thought, "I've lost me bloody foot!" And I passed out for twenty-four hours. When I come to it was still there . . .

'Yeah, when me mates get to twenty or twenty-one, they see the girls they mucked around with getting married and they think, "If I don't hurry up all the best ones will be gone." So they get married and then they're bloody miserable . . .'

'Is it ever wrong to do what you want to?'

He leant back against the concrete wall, scrawled over with chalk drawings and girls' names, the silver chain taut against his narrow throat. Then he says, 'Do me a favour.'

'What is it?'

'Seduce me.'

Edith Wharton

Souls Belated

I

Their railway carriage had been full when the train left Bologna; but at the first station beyond Milan their only remaining companion – a courtly person who ate garlic out of a carpet-bag – had left his crumb-strewn seat with a bow.

Lydia's eye regretfully followed the shiny broadcloth of his retreating back till it lost itself in the cloud of touts and cab drivers hanging about the station; then she glanced across at Gannett and caught the same regret in his look. They were both sorry to be alone.

'*Par-ten-za!*' shouted the guard. The train vibrated to a sudden slamming of doors; a waiter ran along the platform with a tray of fossilized sandwiches; a belated porter flung a bundle of shawls and band-boxes into a third-class carriage; the guard snapped out a brief *Partenza!* which indicated the purely ornamental nature of his first shout; and the train swung out of the station.

The direction of the road had changed, and a shaft of

EDIT WHARTON

sunlight struck across the dusty red velvet seats into Lydia's
corner. Gannett did not notice it. He had returned to his
Revue de Paris, and she had to rise and lower the shade of
the farther window. Against the vast horizon of their leisure
such incidents stood out sharply.

Having lowered the shade, Lydia sat down, leaving the
length of the carriage between herself and Gannett. At length
he missed her and looked up.

'I moved out of the sun,' she hastily explained.

He looked at her curiously: the sun was beating on her
through the shade.

'Very well,' he said pleasantly; adding, 'You don't mind?'
as he drew a cigarette-case from his pocket.

It was a refreshing touch, relieving the tension of her spirit
with the suggestion that, after all, if he could *smoke* – ! The
relief was only momentary. Her experience of smokers was
limited (her husband had disapproved of the use of tobacco)
but she knew from hearsay that men sometimes smoked to
get away from things; that a cigar might be the masculine
equivalent of darkened windows and a headache. Gannett,
after a puff or two, returned to his review.

It was just as she had foreseen; he feared to speak as much
as she did. It was one of the misfortunes of their situation
that they were never busy enough to necessitate, or even to
justify, the postponement of unpleasant discussions. If they
avoided a question it was obviously, unconcealably because
the question was disagreeable. They had unlimited leisure and
an accumulation of mental energy to devote to any subject
that presented itself; new topics were in fact at a premium.
Lydia sometimes had premonitions of a famine-stricken
period when there would be nothing left to talk about, and
she had already caught herself doling out piecemeal what, in
the first prodigality of their confidences, she would have
flung to him in a breath. Their silence therefore might simply
mean that they had nothing to say; but it was another
disadvantage of their position that it allowed infinite oppor-

tunity for the classification of minute differences. Lydia had learned to distinguish between real and factitious silences; and under Gannett's she now detected a hum of speech to which her own thoughts made breathless answer.

How could it be otherwise, with that thing between them? She glanced up at the rack overhead. The *thing* was there, in her dressing-bag, symbolically suspended over her head and his. He was thinking of it now, just as she was; they had been thinking of it in unison ever since they had entered the train. While the carriage had held other travellers they had screened her from his thoughts; but now that he and she were alone she knew exactly what was passing through his mind; she could almost hear him asking himself what he should say to her . . .

The thing had come that morning, brought up to her in an innocent-looking envelope with the rest of their letters, as they were leaving the hotel at Bologna. As she tore it open, she and Gannett were laughing over some ineptitude of the local guidebook – they had been driven, of late, to make the most of such incidental humors of travel. Even when she had unfolded the document she took it for some unimportant business paper sent abroad for her signature, and her eye travelled inattentively over the curly *Whereases* of the preamble until a word arrested her: – Divorce. There it stood, an impassable barrier, between her husband's name and hers.

She had been prepared for it, of course, as healthy people are said to be prepared for death, in the sense of knowing it must come without in the least expecting that it will. She had known from the first that Tillotson meant to divorce her – but what did it matter? Nothing mattered, in those first days of supreme deliverance, but the fact that she was free; and not so much (she had begun to be aware) that freedom had released her from Tillotson as that it had given her to Gannett. This discovery had not been agreeable to her self-esteem. She had preferred to think that Tillotson had himself embodied all her reasons for leaving him; and those he represented had seemed cogent enough to stand in no need of reinforcement. Yet she had not left him till she met Gannett. It was her love for Gannett that had made life with Tillotson so poor and incomplete a business. If she had never, from the first, regarded her marriage as a full cancelling of her claims upon life, she had at least, for a number of years, accepted it as a provisional compensation – she had made it 'do'. Existence in the commodious Tillotson mansion in Fifth Avenue – with Mrs Tillotson senior commanding the approaches from the second-story front windows – had been reduced to a series of purely automatic acts. The moral atmosphere of the Tillotson interior was as carefully screened and curtained as the house itself: Mrs Tillotson senior dreaded ideas as much as a draught on her back. Prudent people liked an even temperature; and to do anything unexpected was as foolish as going out in the rain. One of the chief advantages of being rich was that one need not be exposed to unforeseen contingencies: by the use of ordinary firmness and common sense one could make sure of doing exactly the same thing every day at the same hour. These doctrines, reverentially imbibed with his mother's milk, Tillotson (a model son who had never given his parents an hour's anxiety) complacently expounded to his wife, testifying to his sense of their importance by the regularity with which he wore goloshes on damp days, his punctuality at meals, and his elaborate precautions against burglars and contagious diseases. Lydia, coming from a smaller town, and entering New York life through the portals of the Tillotson mansion, had mechanically accepted this point of view as inseparable from having a front pew in church and a parterre box at the opera. All the people who came to the house revolved in the same small circle of prejudices. It was the kind of society in which, after dinner, the ladies compared the exorbitant charges of their children's teachers, and agreed that, even with the new duties on French clothes, it was cheaper in the end to get everything from Worth; while the husbands, over their cigars, lamented municipal corruption, and decided that the men to start a reform were those who had no private interests at stake.

To Lydia this view of life had become a matter of course, just as lumbering about in her mother-in-law's landau had come to seem the only possible means of locomotion, and listening every Sunday to a fashionable Presbyterian divine the inevitable atonement for having thought oneself bored on the other six days of the week. Before she met Gannett her life had seemed merely dull: his coming made it appear like one of those dismal Cruikshank prints in which the people are all ugly and all engaged in occupations that are either vulgar or stupid.

It was natural that Tillotson should be the chief sufferer from this readjustment of focus. Gannett's nearness had made her husband ridiculous, and a part of the ridicule had been reflected on herself. Her tolerance laid her open to a suspicion of obtuseness from which she must, at all costs, clear herself in Gannett's eyes.

She did not understand this until afterwards. At the time she fancied that she had merely reached the limits of endurance. In so large a charter of liberties as the mere act of leaving Tillotson seemed to confer, the small question of divorce or no divorce did not count. It was when she saw that she had left her husband only to be with Gannett that she perceived the significance of anything affecting their relations. Her husband, in casting her off, had virtually flung her at Gannett: it was thus that the world viewed it. The measure of alacrity with which Gannett would receive her would be the subject of curious speculation over afternoon-tea tables and in club corners. She knew what would be said – she had heard it so often of others! The recollection bathed her in misery. The men would probably back Gannett to 'do the decent thing'; but the ladies' eyebrows would emphasize the worthlessness of such enforced fidelity; and after all, they would be right. She had put herself in a position where

Gannett 'owed' her something; where, as a gentleman, he was bound to 'stand the damage'. The idea of accepting such compensation had never crossed her mind; the so-called rehabilitation of such a marriage had always seemed to her the only real disgrace. What she dreaded was the necessity of having to explain herself; of having to combat his arguments; of calculating, in spite of herself, the exact measure of insistence with which he pressed them. She knew not whether she most shrank from his insisting too much or too little. In such a case the nicest sense of proportion might be at fault; and how easy to fall into the error of taking her resistance for a test of his sincerity! Whichever way she turned, an ironical implication confronted her: she had the exasperated sense of having walked into the trap of some stupid practical joke.

Beneath all these preoccupations lurked the dread of what he was thinking. Sooner or later, of course, he would have to speak; but that, in the meantime, he should think, even for a moment, that there was any use in speaking, seemed to her simply unendurable. Her sensitiveness on this point was aggravated by another fear, as yet barely on the level of consciousness; the fear of unwillingly involving Gannett in the trammels of her dependence. To look upon him as the instrument of her liberation; to resist in herself the least tendency to a wifely taking possession of his future; had seemed to Lydia the one way of maintaining the dignity of their relation. Her view had not changed, but she was aware of a growing inability to keep her thoughts fixed on the essential point – the point of parting with Gannett. It was easy to face as long as she kept it sufficiently far off: but what was this act of mental postponement but a gradual encroachment on his future? What was needful was the courage to recognize the moment when, by some word or look, their voluntary fellowship should be transformed into a bondage the more wearing that it was based on none of those common obligations which make the most imperfect marriage in some sort a centre of gravity.

When the porter, at the next station, threw the door open, Lydia drew back, making way for the hoped-for intruder, but none came, and the train took up its leisurely progress through the spring wheat fields and budding copses. She now began to hope that Gannett would speak before the next station. She watched him furtively, half-disposed to return to the seat opposite his, but there was an artificiality about his absorption that restrained her. She had never before seen him read with so conspicuous an air of warding off interruption. What could he be thinking of? Why should he be afraid to speak? Or was it her answer that he dreaded?

The train paused for the passing of an express, and he put down his book and leaned out of the window. Presently he turned to her with a smile.

'There's a jolly old villa out here,' he said.

His easy tone relieved her, and she smiled back at him as she crossed over to his corner.

Beyond the embankment, through the opening in a mossy wall, she caught sight of the villa, with its broken balustrades, its stagnant fountains, and the stone satyr closing the perspective of a dusky grass-walk.

'How should you like to live there?' he asked as the train moved on.

'There?'

'In some such place, I mean. One might do worse, don't you think so? There must be at least two centuries of solitude under those yew trees. Shouldn't you like it?'

'I – I don't know,' she faltered. She knew now that he meant to speak.

He lit another cigarette. 'We shall have to live somewhere, you know,' he said as he bent above the match.

Lydia tried to speak car lessly. '*Je n'en vois pas la nécessité!* Why not live everywhere, as we have been doing?'

'But we can't travel forever, can we?'

'Oh, forever's a long word,' she objected, picking up the review he had thrown aside.

'For the rest of our lives then,' he said, moving nearer.

She made a slight gesture which caused his hand to slip from hers.

'Why should we make plans? I thought you agreed with me that it's pleasanter to drift.'

He looked at her hesitantly. 'It's been pleasant, certainly; but I suppose I shall have to get at my work again some day. You know I haven't written a line since – all this time,' he hastily emended.

She flamed with sympathy and self-reproach. 'Oh, if you mean *that* – if you want to write – of course we must settle down. How stupid of me not to have thought of it sooner! Where shall we go? Where do you think you could work best? We oughtn't to lose any more time.'

He hesitated again. 'I had thought of a villa in these parts. It's quiet; we shouldn't be bothered. Should you like it?'

'Of course I should like it.' She paused and looked away. 'But I thought – I remember your telling me once that your best work had been done in a crowd – in big cities. Why should you shut yourself up in a desert?'

Gannett, for a moment, made no reply. At length he said, avoiding her eye as carefully as she avoided his: 'It might be different now; I can't tell, of course, till I try. A writer ought not to be dependent on his *milieu*; it's a mistake to humor oneself in that way; and I thought that just at first you might prefer to be – '

She faced him. 'To be what?'

'Well – quiet. I mean – '

'What do you mean by "at first"?' she interrupted.

He paused again. 'I mean after we are married.'

She thrust up her chin and turned toward the window. 'Thank you!' she tossed back at him.

'Lydia!' he exclaimed blankly; and she felt in every fibre of her averted person that he had made the inconceivable, the unpardonable mistake of anticipating her acquiescence.

The train rattled on and he groped for a third cigarette. Lydia remained silent.

'I haven't offended you?' he ventured at length, in the tone of a man who feels his way.

She shook her head with a sigh. 'I thought you understood,' she moaned. Their eyes met and she moved back to his side.

'Do you want to know how not to offend me? By taking it for granted, once for all, that you've said your say on this odious question and that I've said mine, and that we stand just where we did this morning before that – that hateful paper came to spoil everything between us!'

'To spoil everything between us? What on earth do you mean? Aren't you glad to be free?'

'I was free before.'

'Not to marry me,' he suggested.

'But I don't *want* to marry you!' she cried.

She saw that he turned pale. 'I'm obtuse, I suppose,' he said slowly. 'I confess I don't see what you're driving at. Are you tired of the whole business? Or was I simply a – an excuse for getting away? Perhaps you didn't care to travel alone? Was that it? And now you want to chuck me?' His voice had grown harsh. 'You owe me a straight answer, you know; don't be tenderhearted!'

Her eyes swam as she leaned to him. 'Don't you see it's because I care – because I care so much? Oh, Ralph! Can't you see how it would humiliate me? Try to feel it as a woman would! Don't you see the misery of being made your wife in this way? If I'd known you as a girl – that would have been a real marriage! But now – this vulgar fraud upon society – and upon a society we despised and laughed at – this sneaking back into a position that we've voluntarily forfeited: don't you see what a cheap compromise it is? We neither of us believe in the abstract "sacredness" of marriage; we both know that no ceremony is needed to consecrate our love for each other; what object can we have in marrying, except the secret

127

fear of each that the other may escape, or the secret longing to work our way back gradually – oh, very gradually – into the esteem of the people whose conventional morality we have always ridiculed and hated? And the very fact that, after a decent interval, these same people would come and dine with us – the women who talk about the indissolubility of marriage, and who would let me die in a gutter today because I am "leading a life of sin" – doesn't that disgust you more than their turning their backs on us now? I can stand being cut by them, but I couldn't stand their coming to call and asking what I meant to do about visiting that unfortunate Mrs So-and-so!'

She paused, and Gannett maintained a perplexed silence.

'You judge things too theoretically,' he said at length, slowly. 'Life is made up of compromises.'

'The life we ran away from – yes! If we had been willing to accept them' – she flushed – 'we might have gone on meeting each other at Mrs Tillotson's dinners.'

He smiled slightly. 'I didn't know that we ran away to found a new system of ethics. I supposed it was because we loved each other.'

'Life is complex, of course; isn't it the very recognition of that fact that separates us from the people who see it *tout d'une pièce*? If *they* are right – if marriage is sacred in itself and the individual must always be sacrificed to the family – then there can be no real marriage between us, since our – our being together is a protest against the sacrifice of the individual to the family.' She interrupted herself with a laugh. 'You'll say now that I'm giving you a lecture on sociology! Of course one acts as one can – as one must, perhaps – pulled by all sorts of invisible threads; but at least one needn't pretend, for social advantages, to subscribe to a creed that ignores the complexity of human motives – that classifies people by arbitrary signs, and puts it in everybody's reach to be on Mrs Tillotson's visiting list. It may be necessary that the world should be ruled by conventions – but if we believed in them, why did we break through them? And if we don't believe in them, is it honest to take advantage of the protection they afford?'

Gannett hesitated. 'One may believe in them or not; but as long as they do rule the world it is only by taking advantage of their protection that one can find a *modus vivendi*.'

'Do outlaws need a *modus vivendi*?'

He looked at her hopelessly. Nothing is more perplexing to man than the mental process of a woman who reasons her emotions.

She thought she had scored a point and followed it up passionately. 'You do understand, don't you? You see how the very thought of the thing humiliates me! We are together today because we choose to be – don't let us look any farther than that!' She caught his hands. '*Promise* me you'll never speak of it again; promise me you'll never *think* of it even,' she implored, with a tearful prodigality of italics.

Through what followed – his protests, his arguments, his final unconvinced submission to her wishes – she had a sense of his but half-discerning all that, for her, had made the moment so tumultuous. They had reached that memorable point in every heart-history when, for the first time, the man seems obtuse and the woman irrational. It was the abundance of his intentions that consoled her, on reflection, for what they lacked in quality. After all, it would have been worse, incalculably worse, to have detected any overreadiness to understand her.

II

When the train at nightfall brought them to their journey's end at the edge of one of the lakes, Lydia was glad that they were not, as usual, to pass from one solitude to another. Their wanderings during the year had indeed been like the flight of outlaws: through Sicily, Dalmatia, Transylvania and Southern

Italy they had persisted in their tacit avoidance of their kind. Isolation, at first, had deepened the flavor of their happiness, as night intensifies the scent of certain flowers; but in the new phase on which they were entering, Lydia's chief wish was that they should be less abnormally exposed to the action of each other's thoughts.

She shrank, nevertheless, as the brightly looming bulk of the fashionable Anglo-American hotel on the water's brink began to radiate toward their advancing boat its vivid suggestion of social order, visitors' lists, Church services, and the bland inquisition of the *table-d'hôte*. The mere fact that in a moment or two she must take her place on the hotel register as Mrs Gannett seemed to weaken the springs of her resistance.

They had meant to stay for a night only, on their way to a lofty village among the glaciers of Monte Rosa; but after the first plunge into publicity, when they entered the dining-room, Lydia felt the relief of being lost in a crowd, of ceasing for a moment to be the centre of Gannett's scrutiny; and in his face she caught the reflection of her feeling. After dinner, when she went upstairs, he strolled into the smoking-room, and an hour or two later, sitting in the darkness of her window, she heard his voice below and saw him walking up and down the terrace with a companion cigar at his side. When he came up he told her he had been talking to the hotel chaplain – a very good sort of fellow.

'Queer little microcosms, these hotels! Most of these people live here all summer and then migrate to Italy or the Riviera. The English are the only people who can lead that kind of life with dignity – those soft-voiced old ladies in Shetland shawls somehow carry the British Empire under their caps. *Civis Romanus sum*. It's a curious study – there might be some good things to work up here.'

He stood before her with the vivid preoccupied stare of the novelist on the trail of a 'subject'. With a relief that was

half painful she noticed that, for the first time since they had
been together, he was hardly aware of her presence.

'Do you think you could write here?'

'Here? I don't know.' His stare dropped. 'After being out
of things so long one's first impressions are bound to be
tremendously vivid, you know. I see a dozen threads already
that one might follow – '

He broke off with a touch of embarrassment.

'Then follow them. We'll stay,' she said with sudden
decision.

'Stay here?' He glanced at her in surprise, and then,
walking to the window, looked out upon the dusky slumber
of the garden.

'Why not?' she said at length, in a tone of veiled irritation.

'The place is full of old cats in caps who gossip with the
chaplain. Shall you like – I mean, it would be different if – '

She flamed up.

'Do you suppose I care? It's none of their business.'

'Of course not; but you won't get them to think so.'

'They may think what they please.'

He looked at her doubtfully.

'It's for you to decide.'

'We'll stay,' she repeated.

Gannett, before they met, had made himself known as a
successful writer of short stories and of a novel which had
achieved the distinction of being widely discussed. The
reviewers called him 'promising', and Lydia now accused
herself of having too long interfered with the fulfilment of his
promise. There was a special irony in the fact, since his
passionate assurances that only the stimulus of her companionship could bring out his latent faculty had almost given
the dignity of a 'vocation' to her course: there had been
moments when she had felt unable to assume, before poster-
ity, the responsibility of thwarting his career. And, after all,
he had not written a line since they had been together: his
first desire to write had come from renewed contact with the

131

world! Was it all a mistake then? Must the most intelligent choice work more disastrously than the blundering combinations of chance? Or was there a still more humiliating answer to her perplexities? His sudden impulse of activity so exactly coincided with her own wish to withdraw, for a time, from the range of his observation, that she wondered if he too were not seeking sanctuary from intolerable problems.

'You must begin tomorrow!' she cried, hiding a tremor under the laugh with which she added, 'I wonder if there's any ink in the inkstand?'

Whatever else they had at the Hotel Bellosguardo, they had, as Miss Pinsent said, 'a certain tone'. It was to Lady Susan Condit that they owed this inestimable benefit; an advantage ranking in Miss Pinsent's opinion above even the lawn tennis courts and the resident chaplain. It was the fact of Lady Susan's annual visit that made the hotel what it was. Miss Pinsent was certainly the last to underrate such a privilege: – 'It's so important, my dear, forming as we do a little family, that there should be someone to give *the tone*; and no one could do it better than Lady Susan – an earl's daughter and a person of such determination. Dear Mrs Ainger now – who really *ought*, you know, when Lady Susan's away – absolutely refuses to assert herself.' Miss Pinsent sniffed derisively. 'A bishop's niece! – my dear, I saw her once actually give in to some South Americans – and before us all. She gave up her seat at table to oblige them – such a lack of dignity! Lady Susan spoke to her very plainly about it afterwards.'

Miss Pinsent glanced across the lake and adjusted her auburn front.

'But of course I don't deny that the stand Lady Susan takes is not always easy to live up to – for the rest of us, I mean. Monsieur Grossart, our good proprietor, finds it trying at times, I know – he has said as much, privately, to Mrs Ainger and me. After all, the poor man is not to blame for wanting to fill his hotel, is he? And Lady Susan is so difficult – so very difficult – about new people. One might almost say that she disapproves of them beforehand, on principle. And yet she's had warnings – she very nearly made a dreadful mistake once with the Duchess of Levens, who dyed her hair and – well, swore and smoked. One would have thought that might have been a lesson to Lady Susan.' Miss Pinsent resumed her knitting with a sigh. 'There are exceptions, of course. She took at once to you and Mr Gannett – it was quite remarkable, really. Oh, I don't mean that either – of course not! It was perfectly natural – we *all* thought you so charming and interesting from the first day – we knew at once that Mr Gannett was intellectual, by the magazines you took in; but you know what I mean. Lady Susan is so very – well, I won't say prejudiced, as Mrs Ainger does – but so prepared *not* to like new people, that her taking to you in that way was a surprise to us all, I confess.'

Miss Pinsent sent a significant glance down the long laurustinus alley from the other end of which two people – a lady and gentleman – were strolling toward them through the smiling neglect of the garden.

'In this case, of course, it's very different; that I'm willing to admit. Their looks are against them; but, as Mrs Ainger says, one can't exactly tell them so.'

'She's very handsome,' Lydia ventured, with her eyes on the lady, who showed, under the dome of a vivid sunshade, the hour-glass figure and superlative coloring of a Christmas chromo.

'That's the worst of it. She's too handsome.'

'Well, after all, she can't help that.'

'Other people manage to,' said Miss Pinsent sceptically.

'But isn't it rather unfair of Lady Susan – considering that nothing is known about them?'

'But, my dear, that's the very thing that's against them. It's infinitely worse than any actual knowledge.'

Lydia mentally agreed that, in the case of Mrs Linton, it possibly might be.

'I wonder why they came here?' she mused.

'That's against them too. It's always a bad sign when loud people come to a quiet place. And they've brought van-loads of boxes – her maid told Mrs Ainger's that they meant to stop indefinitely.'

'And Lady Susan actually turned her back on her in the *salon*?'

'My dear, she said it was for our sakes; that makes it so unanswerable! But poor Grossart *is* in a way! The Lintons have taken his most expensive *suite*, you know – the yellow damask drawing-room above the portico – and they have champagne with every meal!'

They were silent as Mr and Mrs Linton sauntered by; the lady with tempestuous brows and challenging chin; the gentleman, a blond stripling, trailing after her, head downward, like a reluctant child dragged by his nurse.

'What does your husband think of them, my dear?' Miss Pinsent whispered as they passed out of earshot.

Lydia stooped to pick a violet in the border.

'He hasn't told me.'

'Of your speaking to them, I mean. Would he approve of that? I know how very particular nice Americans are. I think your action might make a difference; it would certainly carry weight with Lady Susan.'

'Dear Miss Pinsent, you flatter me!'

Lydia rose and gathered up her book and sunshade.

'Well, if you're asked for an opinion – if Lady Susan asks you for one – I think you ought to be prepared,' Miss Pinsent admonished her as she moved away.

III

Lady Susan held her own. She ignored the Lintons, and her little family, as Miss Pinsent phrased it, followed suit. Even Mrs Ainger agreed that it was obligatory. If Lady Susan owed it to the others not to speak to the Lintons, the others clearly owed it to Lady Susan to back her up. It was generally found expedient, at the Hotel Bellosguardo, to adopt this form of reasoning.

Whatever effect this combined action may have had upon the Lintons, it did not at least have that of driving them away. Monsieur Grossart, after a few days of suspense, had the satisfaction of seeing them settle down in his yellow damask *premier* with what looked like a permanent installation of palm trees and silk sofa cushions, and a gratifying continuance in the consumption of champagne. Mrs Linton trailed her Doucet draperies up and down the garden with the same challenging air, while her husband, smoking innumerable cigarettes, dragged himself dejectedly in her wake; but neither of them, after the first encounter with Lady Susan, made any attempt to extend their acquaintance. They simply ignored their ignorers. As Miss Pinsent resentfully observed, they behaved exactly as though the hotel were empty.

It was therefore a matter of surprise, as well as of displeasure, to Lydia, to find, on glancing up one day from her seat in the garden, that the shadow which had fallen across her book was that of the enigmatic Mrs Linton.

'I want to speak to you,' that lady said, in a rich hard voice that seemed the audible expression of her gown and her complexion.

Lydia started. She certainly did not want to speak to Mrs Linton.

'Shall I sit down here?' the latter continued, fixing her intensely shaded eyes on Lydia's face, 'or are you afraid of being seen with me?'

'Afraid?' Lydia colored. 'Sit down, please. What is it that you wish to say?'

Mrs Linton, with a smile, drew up a garden chair and crossed one open-work ankle above the other.

'I want you to tell me what my husband said to your husband last night.'

Lydia turned pale.

'My husband – to yours?' she faltered, staring at the other.

'Didn't you know they were closeted together for hours in the smoking-room after you went upstairs? My man didn't get to bed until nearly two o'clock and when he did I couldn't get a word out of him. When he wants to be aggravating I'll back him against anybody living!' Her teeth and eyes flashed persuasively upon Lydia. 'But you'll tell me what they were talking about, won't you? I know I can trust you – you look so awfully kind. And it's for his own good. He's such a precious donkey and I'm so afraid he's got into some beastly scrape or other. If he'd only trust his own old woman! But they're always writing to him and setting him against me. And I've got nobody to turn to.' She laid her hand on Lydia's with a rattle of bracelets. 'You'll help me, won't you?'

Lydia drew back from the smiling fierceness of her brows.

'I'm sorry – but I don't think I understand. My husband has said nothing to me of – of yours.'

The great black crescents above Mrs Linton's eyes met angrily.

'I say – is that true?' she demanded.

Lydia rose from her seat.

'Oh, look here, I didn't mean that, you know – you mustn't take one up so! Can't you see how rattled I am?'

Lydia saw that, in fact, her beautiful mouth was quivering beneath softened eyes.

'I'm beside myself!' the splendid creature wailed, dropping into her seat.

'I'm so sorry,' Lydia repeated, forcing herself to speak kindly; 'but how can I help you?'

Mrs Linton raised her head sharply.

'By finding out – there's a darling!'

'Finding what out?'

'What Trevenna told him.'

'Trevenna – ?' Lydia echoed in bewilderment.

Mrs Linton clapped her hand to her mouth.

'Oh, Lord – there, it's out! What a fool I am! But I supposed of course you knew; I supposed everybody knew.' She dried her eyes and bridled. 'Didn't you know that he's Lord Trevenna? I'm Mrs Cope.'

Lydia recognized the names. They had figured in a flamboyant elopement which had thrilled fashionable London some six months earlier.

'Now you see how it is – you understand, don't you?' Mrs Cope continued on a note of appeal. 'I knew you would – that's the reason I came to you. I suppose *he* felt the same thing about your husband; he's not spoken to another soul in the place.' Her face grew anxious again. 'He's awfully sensitive, generally – he feels our position, he says – as if it wasn't *my* place to feel that! But when he does get talking there's no knowing what he'll say. I know he's been brooding over something lately, and I *must* find out what it is – it's to his interest that I should. I always tell him that I think only of his interest; if he'd only trust me! But he's been so odd lately – I can't think what he's plotting. You will help me, dear?'

Lydia, who had remained standing, looked away uncomfortably.

'If you mean by finding out what Lord Trevenna has told my husband, I'm afraid it's impossible.'

'Why impossible?'

'Because I infer that it was told in confidence.'

Mrs Cope stared incredulously.

'Well, what of that? Your husband looks such a dear – any one can see he's awfully gone on you. What's to prevent your getting it out of him?'

Lydia flushed.

'I'm not a spy!' she exclaimed.

'A spy – a spy? How dare you?' Mrs Cope flamed out. 'Oh, I don't mean that either! Don't be angry with me – I'm so miserable.' She essayed a softer note. 'Do you call that spying – for one woman to help out another? I do need help so dreadfully! I'm at my wits' end with Trevenna, I am indeed. He's such a boy – a mere baby, you know; he's only two-and-twenty.' She dropped her orbed lids. 'He's younger than me – only fancy! A few months younger. I tell him he ought to listen to me as if I was his mother; oughtn't he now? But he won't, he won't! All his people are at him, you see – oh, I know *their* little game! Trying to get him away from me before I can get my divorce – that's what they're up to. At first he wouldn't listen to them; he used to toss their letters over to me to read; but now he reads them himself, and answers 'em too, I fancy; he's always shut up in his room, writing. If I only knew what his plan is I could stop him fast enough – he's such a simpleton. But he's dreadfully deep too – at times I can't make him out. But I know he's told your husband everything – I knew that last night the minute I laid eyes on him. And I *must* find out – you must help me – I've got no one else to turn to!'

She caught Lydia's fingers in a stormy pressure.

'Say you'll help me – you and your husband.'

Lydia tried to free herself.

'What you ask is impossible; you must see that it is. No one could interfere in – in the way you ask.'

Mrs Cope's clutch tightened.

'You won't then? You won't?'

'Certainly not. Let me go, please.'

Mrs Cope released her with a laugh.

'Oh, go by all means – pray don't let me detain you! Shall you go and tell Lady Susan Condit that there's a pair of us – or shall I save you the trouble of enlightening her?'

Lydia stood still in the middle of the path, seeing her antagonist through a mist of terror. Mrs Cope was still laughing.

'Oh, I'm not spiteful by nature, my dear; but you're a little more than flesh and blood can stand! It's impossible, is it? Let you go, indeed! You're too good to be mixed up in my affairs, are you? Why, you little fool, the first day I laid eyes

on you I saw that you and I were both in the same box –
that's the reason I spoke to you.'

She stepped nearer, her smile dilating on Lydia like a lamp
through a fog.

'You can take your choice, you know; I always play fair.
If you'll tell I'll promise not to. Now then, which is it to be?'

Lydia, involuntarily, had begun to move away from the
pelting storm of words; but at this she turned and sat down
again.

'You may go,' she said simply. 'I shall stay here.'

IV

She stayed there for a long time, in the hypnotized contem-
plation, not of Mrs Cope's present, but of her own past.
Gannett, early that morning, had gone off on a long walk –
he had fallen into the habit of taking these mountain-tramps
with various fellow-lodgers; but even had he been within
reach she could not have gone to him just then. She had to
deal with herself first. She was surprised to find how, in the
last months, she had lost the habit of introspection. Since
their coming to the Hotel Bellosguardo she and Gannett had
tacitly avoided themselves and each other.

She was aroused by the whistle of the three o'clock
steamboat as it neared the landing just beyond the hotel gates.
Three o'clock! Then Gannett would soon be back – he had
told her to expect him before four. She rose hurriedly, her
face averted from the inquisitorial façade of the hotel. She
could not see him just yet; she could not go indoors. She
slipped through one of the overgrown garden alleys and
climbed a steep path to the hills.

It was dark when she opened their sitting-room door.
Gannett was sitting on the window-ledge smoking a cigarette.
Cigarettes were now his chief resource: he had not written a
line during the two months they had spent at the Hotel

Bellosguardo. In that respect, it had turned out not to be the right *milieu* after all.

He started up at Lydia's entrance.

'Where have you been? I was getting anxious.'

She sat down in a chair near the door.

'Up the mountain?' she said wearily.

'Alone?'

'Yes.'

Gannett threw away his cigarette: the sound of her voice made him want to see her face.

'Shall we have a little light?' he suggested.

She made no answer and he lifted the globe from the lamp and put a match to the wick. Then he looked at her.

'Anything wrong? You look done up.'

She sat glancing vaguely about the little sitting-room, dimly lit by the pallid globed lamp, which left in twilight the outlines of the furniture, of his writing-table heaped with books and papers, of the tea-roses and jasmine drooping on the mantelpiece. How like home it had all grown – how like home!

'Lydia, what is wrong?' he repeated.

She moved away from him, feeling for her hatpins and turning to lay her hat and sunshade on the table.

Suddenly she said: 'That woman has been talking to me.'

Gannett stared.

'That woman? What woman?'

'Mrs Linton – Mrs Cope.'

He gave a start of annoyance, still, as she perceived, not grasping the full import of her words.

'The deuce! She told you – ?'

'She told me everything.'

Gannett looked at her anxiously.

'What impudence! I'm so sorry that you should have been exposed to this, dear.'

'Exposed!' Lydia laughed.

Gannett's brow clouded and they looked away from each other.

'Do you know *why* she told me? She had the best of reasons. The first time she laid eyes on me she saw that we were both in the same box.'

'Lydia!'

'So it was natural, of course, that she should turn to me in a difficulty.'

'What difficulty?'

'It seems she has reason to think that Lord Trevenna's people are trying to get him away from her before she gets her divorce – '

'Well?'

'And she fancied he had been consulting with you last night as to – as to the best way of escaping from her.'

Gannett stood up with an angry forehead.

'Well – what concern of yours was all this dirty business? Why should she go to you?'

'Don't you see? It's so simple. I was to wheedle his secret out of you.'

'To oblige that woman?'

'Yes; or, if I was unwilling to oblige her, then to protect myself.'

'To protect yourself? Against whom?'

'Against her telling everyone in the hotel that she and I are in the same box.'

'She threatened that?'

'She left me the choice of telling it myself or of doing it for me.'

'The beast!'

There was a long silence. Lydia had seated herself on the sofa, beyond the radius of the lamp, and he leaned against the window. His next question surprised her.

'When did this happen? At what time, I mean?'

She looked at him vaguely.

'I don't know – after luncheon, I think. Yes, I remember; it must have been at about three o'clock.'

He stepped into the middle of the room and as he approached the light she saw that his brow had cleared.

'Why do you ask?' she said.

'Because when I came in, at about half-past three, the mail was just being distributed, and Mrs Cope was waiting as usual to pounce on her letters; you know she was always watching for the postman. She was standing so close to me that I couldn't help seeing a big official-looking envelope that was handed to her. She tore it open, gave one look at the inside, and rushed off upstairs like a whirlwind, with the director shouting after her that she had left all her other letters behind. I don't believe she ever thought of you again after that paper was put into her hand.'

'Why?'

'Because she was too busy. I was sitting in the window, watching for you, when the five o'clock boat left, and who should go on board, bag and baggage, valet and maid, dressing-bags and poodle, but Mrs Cope and Trevenna. Just an hour and a half to pack up in! And you should have seen her when they started. She was radiant – shaking hands with everybody – waving her handkerchief from the deck – distributing bows and smiles like an empress. If ever a woman got what she wanted just in the nick of time that woman did. She'll be Lady Trevenna within a week, I'll wager.'

'You think she has her divorce?'

'I'm sure of it. And she must have got it just after her talk with you.'

Lydia was silent.

At length she said, with a kind of reluctance, 'She was horribly angry when she left me. It wouldn't have taken long to tell Lady Susan Condit.'

'Lady Susan Condit has not been told.'

'How do you know?'

'Because when I went downstairs half an hour ago I met Lady Susan on the way – '

He stopped, half smiling.

'Well?'

'And she stopped to ask if I thought you would act as patroness to a charity concert she is getting up.'

In spite of themselves they both broke into a laugh. Lydia's ended in sobs and she sank down with her face hidden. Gannett bent over her, seeking her hands.

'That vile woman – I ought to have warned you to keep away from her; I can't forgive myself! But he spoke to me in confidence; and I never dreamed – well, it's all over now.'

Lydia lifted her head.

'Not for me. It's only just beginning.'

'What do you mean?'

She put him gently aside and moved in her turn to the window. Then she went on, with her face turned toward the shimmering blackness of the lake, 'You see of course that it might happen again at any moment.'

'What?'

'This – this risk of being found out. And we could hardly count again on such a lucky combination of chances, could we?'

He sat down with a groan.

Still keeping her face toward the darkness, she said, 'I want you to go and tell Lady Susan – and the others.'

Gannett, who had moved towards her, paused a few feet off.

'Why do you wish me to do this?' he said at length, with less surprise in his voice than she had been prepared for.

'Because I've behaved basely, abominably, since we came here: letting these people believe we were married – lying with every breath I drew – '

'Yes, I've felt that too,' Gannett exclaimed with sudden energy.

143

The words shook her like a tempest: all her thoughts seemed to fall about her in ruins.

'You – you've felt so?'

'Of course I have.' He spoke with low-voiced vehemence. 'Do you suppose I like playing the sneak any better than you do? It's damnable.'

He had dropped on the arm of a chair, and they stared at each other like blind people who suddenly see.

'But you have liked it here,' she faltered.

'Oh, I've liked it – I've liked it.' He moved impatiently. 'Haven't you?'

'Yes,' she burst out; 'that's the worst of it – that's what I can't bear. I fancied it was for your sake that I insisted on staying – because you thought you could write here; and perhaps just at first that really was the reason. But afterwards I wanted to stay myself – I loved it.' She broke into a laugh. 'Oh, do you see the full derision of it? These people – the very prototypes of the bores you took me away from, with the same fenced-in view of life, the same keep-off-the-grass morality, the same little cautious virtues and the same little frightened vices – well, I've clung to them, I've delighted in them, I've done my best to please them. I've toadied Lady Susan, I've gossiped with Miss Pinsent, I've pretended to be shocked with Mrs Ainger. Respectability! It was the one thing in life that I was sure I didn't care about, and it's grown so precious to me that I've stolen it because I couldn't get it in any other way.'

She moved across the room and returned to his side with another laugh.

'I who used to fancy myself unconventional! I must have been born with a card-case in my hand. You should have seen me with that poor woman in the garden. She came to me for help, poor creature, because she fancied that, having 'sinned', as they call it, I might feel some pity for others who had been tempted in the same way. Not I! She didn't know me. Lady Susan would have been kinder, because Lady Susan wouldn't have been afraid. I hated the woman – my one thought was not to be seen with her – I could have killed her for guessing my secret. The one thing that mattered to me at that moment was my standing with Lady Susan!'

Gannett did not speak.

'And you – you've felt it too!' she broke out accusingly. 'You've enjoyed being with these people as much as I have; you've let the chaplain talk to you by the hour about "The Reign of Law" and Professor Drummond. When they asked you to hand the plate in church I was watching you – *you wanted to accept.*'

She stepped close, laying her hand on his arm.

'Do you know, I begin to see what marriage is for. It's to keep people away from each other. Sometimes I think that two people who love each other can be saved from madness only by the things that come between them – children, duties, visits, bores, relations – the things that protect married people from each other. We've been too close together – that has been our sin. We've seen the nakedness of each other's souls.'

She sank again on the sofa, hiding her face in her hands.

Gannett stood above her perplexedly: he felt as though she were being swept away by some implacable current while he stood helpless on its bank.

At length he said, 'Lydia, don't think me a brute – but don't you see yourself that it won't do?'

'Yes, I see it won't do,' she said without raising her head.

His face cleared.

'Then we'll go tomorrow.'

'Go – where?'

'To Paris; to be married.'

For a long time she made no answer; then she asked slowly, 'Would they have us here if we were married?'

'Have us here?'

'I mean Lady Susan – and the others.'

'Have us here? Of course they would.'

145

'Not if they knew – at least, not unless they could pretend not to know.'

He made an impatient gesture.

'We shouldn't come back here, of course; and other people needn't know – no one need know.'

She sighed. 'Then it's only another form of deception and a meaner one. Don't you see that?'

'I see that we're not accountable to any Lady Susans on earth!'

'Then why are you ashamed of what we are doing here?'

'Because I'm sick of pretending that you're my wife when you're not – when you won't be.'

She looked at him sadly.

'If I were your wife you'd have to go on pretending. You'd have to pretend that I'd never been – anything else. And our friends would have to pretend that they believed what you pretended.'

Gannett pulled off the sofa-tassel and flung it away.

'You're impossible,' he groaned.

'It's not I – it's our being together that's impossible. I only want you to see that marriage won't help it.'

'What will help it then?'

She raised her head.

'My leaving you.'

'Your leaving me?' He sat motionless, staring at the tassel which lay at the other end of the room. At length some impulse of retaliation for the pain she was inflicting made him say deliberately:

'And where would you go if you left me?'

'Oh!' she cried, wincing.

He was at her side in an instant.

'Lydia – Lydia – you know I didn't mean it; I couldn't mean it! But you've driven me out of my senses; I don't know what I'm saying. Can't you get out of this labyrinth of self-torture? It's destroying us both.'

'That's why I must leave you.'

'How easily you say it!' He drew her hands down and made her face him. 'You're very scrupulous about yourself – and others. But have you thought of me? You have no right to leave me unless you've ceased to care – '

'It's because I care – '

'Then I have a right to be heard. If you love me you can't leave me.'

Her eyes defied him.

'Why not?'

He dropped her hands and rose from her side.

'Can you?' he said sadly.

The hour was late and the lamp flickered and sank. She stood up with a shiver and turned toward the door of her room.

V

At daylight a sound in Lydia's room woke Gannett from a troubled sleep. He sat up and listened. She was moving about softly, as though fearful of disturbing him. He heard her push back one of the creaking shutters; then there was a moment's silence, which seemed to indicate that she was waiting to see if the noise had roused him.

Presently she began to move again. She had spent a sleepless night, probably, and was dressing to go down to the garden for a breath of air. Gannett rose also; but some undefinable instinct made his movements as cautious as hers. He stole to his window and looked out through the slats of the shutter.

It had rained in the night and the dawn was gray and lifeless. The cloud muffled hills across the lake were reflected in its surface as in a tarnished mirror. In the garden, the birds were beginning to shake the drops from the motionless laurustinus boughs.

An immense pity for Lydia filled Gannett's soul. Her

seeming intellectual independence had blinded him for a time to the feminine cast of her mind. He had never thought of her as a woman who wept and clung: there was a lucidity in her intuitions that made them appear to be the result of reasoning. Now he saw the cruelty he had committed in detaching her from the normal conditions of life; he felt, too, the insight with which she had hit upon the real cause of their suffering. Their life was 'impossible,' as she had said – and its worst penalty was that it had made any other life impossible for them. Even had his love lessened, he was bound to her now by a hundred ties of pity and self-reproach; and she, poor child! must turn back to him as Latude returned to his cell . . .

A new sound startled him: it was the stealthy closing of Lydia's door. He crept to his own and heard her footsteps passing down the corridor. Then he went back to the window and looked out.

A minute or two later he saw her go down the steps of the porch and enter the garden. From his post of observation her face was invisible, but something about her appearance struck him. She wore a long travelling cloak and under its folds he detected the outline of a bag or bundle. He drew a deep breath and stood watching her.

She walked quickly down the laurustinus alley toward the gate; there she paused a moment, glancing about the little shady square. The stone benches under the trees were empty, and she seemed to gather resolution from the solitude about her, for she crossed the square to the steamboat landing, and he saw her pause before the ticket office at the head of the wharf. Now she was buying her ticket. Gannett turned his head a moment to look at the clock: the boat was due in five minutes. He had time to jump into his clothes and overtake her –

He made no attempt to move; an obscure reluctance restrained him. If any thought emerged from the tumult of his sensations, it was that he must let her go if she wished it. He had spoken last night of his rights: what were they? At

148

the last issue, he and she were two separate beings, not made one by the miracle of common forbearance, duties, abnegations, but bound together in a *noyade* of passion that left them resisting yet clinging as they went down.

After buying her ticket, Lydia had stood for a moment looking out across the lake; then he saw her seat herself on one of the benches near the landing. He and she, at that moment, were both listening for the same sound: the whistle of the boat as it rounded the nearest promontory. Gannett turned again to glance at the clock: the boat was due now.

Where would she go? What would her life be when she had left him? She had no near relations and few friends. There was money enough ... but she asked so much of life, in ways so complex and immaterial. He thought of her as walking barefooted through a stony waste. No one would understand her – no one would pity her – and he, who did both, was powerless to come to her aid ...

He saw that she had risen from the bench and walked toward the edge of the lake. She stood looking in the direction from which the steamboat was to come; then she turned to the ticket-office, doubtless to ask the cause of the delay. After that she went back to the bench and sat down with bent head. What was she thinking of?

The whistle sounded; she started up, and Gannett involuntarily made a movement toward the door. But he turned back and continued to watch her. She stood motionless, her eyes on the trail of smoke that preceded the appearance of the boat. Then the little craft rounded the point, a dead-white object on the leaden water: a minute later it was puffing and backing at the wharf.

The few passengers who were waiting – two or three peasants and a snuffy priest – were clustered near the ticket-office. Lydia stood apart under the trees.

The boat lay alongside now; the gangplank was run out and the peasants went on board with their baskets of vegetables, followed by the priest. Still Lydia did not move. A bell began to ring querulously; there was a shriek of steam, and someone must have called to her that she would be late, for she started forward, as though in answer to a summons. She moved waveringly, and at the edge of the wharf she paused. Gannett saw a sailor beckon to her; the bell rang again and she stepped upon the gangplank.

Halfway down the short incline to the deck she stopped again; then she turned and ran back to the land. The gangplank was drawn in, the bell ceased to ring, and the boat backed out into the lake. Lydia, with slow steps, was walking toward the garden . . .

As she approached the hotel she looked up furtively and Gannett drew back into the room. He sat down beside a table; a Bradshaw lay at his elbow, and mechanically, without knowing what he did, he began looking out the trains to Paris . . .

Jessie Kesson

Until Such Times

'They're coming the day.' Grandmother bustled into the kitchen, waving a letter aloft. 'Postie's just brought a line. Now! If,' she said, pausing to consider the matter, '*If* they were to catch the through train, they should manage to win here in time for a bite of dinner.'

'I'd be the better of a clean shawl, then,' the Invalid Aunt suggested, 'if they're coming the day.'

– A suggestion that stripped Grandmother clean of the good humour that had been over her. 'My hands are never out of the wash tub!' she snapped. 'The shawl that's on you is clean enough! It's barely been on your back a week! And, as for *you*! . . .' Grandmother's face bent down till it was level with your own. '*You* can just sup up your porridge! There's a lot of work to be got through. If they're coming the day. Your Aunt Millie and Cousin Alice.'

'A lot of help she'll be to you. That one!' the Invalid Aunt said. 'Her Cousin Alice is a different kettle of fish. Another bairn altogether. Well brought up. And biddable.'

'Alice is neither better nor worse than any other bairn!' Grandmother snorted, before turning in attack on you again. 'And there's no call for you to start banging the teapot on the table!'

'The din that one makes,' the Invalid Aunt grumbled, 'is enough to bring on one of my heads!'

'For pity's sake, Edith! She's only a bairn.'

Times like these, you loved Grandmother. Knowing she was on your side. Times like these, you hated the Invalid Aunt. Sat huddled in her shawl on the bed-chair by the window. The smell of disinfectant always around her. And that other smell of commode. The medicine bottles along the window-sill for when 'the head came on her' or 'the heart took her'. Even the Invalid Aunt's medicine bottles had taken on malevolence, getting you off to a bad start with Grandmother, at the very beginning of your stay.

'You *understand*! You understand, bairn. I'm telling you NOW! And I don't want to have to tell you again! You must never touch your Aunt Edith's medicine bottles. Never! Ever!'

'But she said the heart took her!'

'Not even when the heart takes her,' Grandmother had insisted. 'Mind you on that! You must never touch Aunt Edith's medicine bottles. Not as long as you are here!'

But you weren't here to stay forever! Your Aunt Ailsa had promised you that. You was only here to stay . . . 'Until Such Times', Aunt Ailsa had said on the day she took you to Grandmother's house . . . 'Until Such Times as I can find a proper place for you and me to bide. For you should be at school. But the authorities would just go clean mad if they found out they had a scholar who lived in a Corporation lodging house. And spent most of her time in the Corporation stables. Sat between the two dust cart horses! SO. You are going to school. And biding with Grandmother . . . Until Such Times . . .' You could never tell when Until Such Times had passed. But you began to recognize its passing. With Grandmother bringing each week to an end, always on the scold, on Sunday mornings.

'Learning your catechism on the *Sabbath*! Five minutes before you set off for the Sunday School! I told you to learn it last night!'

But you had learned it 'last night'. You knew it 'last night'. 'It's just . . .' you tried to explain to Grandmother, 'it's just the words. They might all change in the night. I'm looking up to make *sure*!'

'It's just . . .' Grandmother always maintained, 'it's just that you didn't put your mind to it, last night! So! Let's hear it now, then! What is the Chief End of Man?'

'Man's Chief End is to glorify God and enjoy Him forever – '

It was the coming of the dark night that told you summer was at an end. 'A *candle*!!! A candle up to her *bed*!' The Invalid Aunt had protested, prophesying that 'They would all be burned alive in their sleep!' And so paving the way for Grandmother's instant rejection of your request for a candle. 'It was only,' Grandmother had pointed out, 'the shadows of the fir trees that you've seen, moving against your window, and you should be used to that by this time! There was nothing,' she tried to assure, 'nothing to be feared of in the wood. It's a blithe place for a bairn. Wait you!' she had exhorted. 'Just wait you till summer comes round again!' – an exhortation that had dismayed you, that had extended time beyond all comprehension of its passing self.

'I'm *saying*!' Grandmother grabbed the teapot from your hands. 'I'm saying there's a lot of work to be got through. with your Aunt Millie and Cousin Alice already on their road!'

'If it had been *Ailsa* that was coming,' the Invalid Aunt said, 'she would have jumped to it! My word! She would that!'

153

But it *wasn't* your Aunt Ailsa that was coming. She never 'dropped a line'. She just arrived. Unexpected. Unannounced.

How you wished that she could have arrived unseen. That the wood, which hid everything else, could have hidden Aunt Ailsa, too. But the kitchen window looked out on the road, and on all who passed along it, and the Invalid Aunt's voice was always the first to rise up in forewarning. 'God help us! *She*'s on her way! Ailsa! Her ladyship! Taking up the whole of the road. Looks like she went into the Broadstraik Inn. And didn't come out till closing time!'

How you wanted to leap up off your stool, and hurtle yourself down the road to warn Aunt Ailsa. 'Walk straight, my Aunt Ailsa. Walk as straight as you can! They've seen you coming. They're all watching behind the curtains.'

'Thank God it's not Ailsa that's coming,' the Invalid Aunt concluded. 'We can do fine without her company.'

For once, you found yourself in agreement with the Invalid Aunt. Albeit with a sense of betrayal, and a pain for which you had not found the source, hidden somewhere, within the memory of your Aunt Ailsa's last – and first – 'official' visit.

You had recognized the man and his pony and trap, waiting at the small wayside railway station, but had not realized that he, too, was awaiting the arrival of your Aunt Ailsa. Not until he came towards you, in greeting . . . 'You mind on me? Surely you mind on me!' he had insisted, flummoxed by your silence. 'You'll mind on the pony then! I'll warrant you've forgotten the pony's name.'

'He's Donaldie,' you said, willing enough to claim acquaintance with the pony. 'He's Donaldie. His name's Donaldie.'

The cat, Aunt Ailsa grumbled, as the man elbowed her towards the trap, must have got her tongue, for this was a poor welcome, considering Aunt Ailsa had come all this way.

It was the man! you protested. HIM. Donaldie's dad. 'He belongs to his pony! Not to US. Not to you and me!'

*

It was only when they reached the wood that the old intimacy warmed up between them. Whoaing Donaldie to a halt, Aunt Ailsa spoke in the tone of time remembered, when the world was small enough to hold what she used to describe as . . . you and me. Ourselves two. And the both of us . . .

'You know,' Aunt Ailsa had confided, 'how Grandmother hates me smoking my pipe. So we're just going to take a turn up the wood for a smoke. I want you to do a small thing for me. To bide here, and keep an eye on Donaldie. We'll not be long. About five minutes just,' she emphasized, presenting you with another aspect of time.

'Five minutes *must* be up now, Donaldie,' you confided to the pony, munching away on the grass verge. His calm acceptance of passing time beginning to distress you, since animals differed from yourself in appearance only, never in understanding. 'It must be up, Donaldie. I've counted up to hundreds.'

'I know something about you, Donaldie,' you boasted, beginning to be irritated by the pony's indifference. 'Something about all horses. Something my Aunt Ailsa once told me. All horsemen have a secret word of command. "The horseman's *knacking* word," she called it. But no horseman will ever tell the secret word. He would lose his power, that way of it. I don't know the secret word,' she admitted to the pony. 'But you might know it, Donaldie. If I could just find it.'

Time poised upon, and passing within, all the words you could remember. Tried out and tested, with no reaction from the pony.

'Maybe,' you suggested at last, 'maybe the secret word's in Gaelic . . . Ay Roh. Ay Roh

'El Alooran
El Alooran

Ay Roh Ay Roh
Ay Roh'

JESSIE KESSON

'Stop wheebering away to yourself, there!' Aunt Ailsa commanded, as they turned up the track to Grandmother's house. 'And pay attention to what I am telling you! Not a word out of your head to Grandmother. Not one word about Donaldie's dad! We never saw him the day. We never set *eyes* on him. Just you mind on that.'

'Mind now,' Grandmother was saying, 'When your Cousin Alice comes the day, just you play quiet in the clearing. You know how her mother hates Alice getting her clothes all sossed up in the wood.'

'That one wouldn't worry,' the Invalid Aunt assured Grandmother. 'She would rive in the bushes till she hadn't a stitch to her back. It's high time she took herself through to the scullery and made a start on the dishes!'

'You cannot expect her to be stood out in the cold scullery all morning!' Grandmother snapped.

'But I'm needing the commode!' the Invalid Aunt protested. 'I'm needing to pay a big visit. And I can't do a thing! Not with that one. Stood there. All eyes!'

'She's taking no notice, Edith! She's got better things to look at, than you sat stuck there on the commode. Come on, bairn!' Grandmother said, elbowing you out of the kitchen. 'It's time you and me took a turn up the wood for a burthen of kindlers. And a breath of fresh air!'

'I'm needing the commode.' The Invalid Aunt's whine followed them to the porch door. 'I'm leaking! You know fine I can't contain!'

> I can contain
> I've never wet myself
> Nor ever will again

'*That*!' Grandmother said, when she caught up with you at the clearing, 'is a bad thing to say. And a worse thing to *think*!'

'I beg pardon.' Your apology was instant. And genuine. Moments shared alone with Grandmother were too rare, too precious, to be wasted in acrimony.

'I grant you grace,' Grandmother acknowledged, spreading herself down and across the log. 'But, if that's what they're learning you at the school . . .'

School, like Grandmother herself, was a separate thing, and shared only at times like these, beyond influence of the house and the Invalid Aunt.

'If,' you said, squeezing yourself down on the log beside her, 'if we were sitting out in the porch, on a fine summer evening, and a weary, thirsty traveller came by and begged us for a drink of milk. And he had wings instead of ears. And wings instead of feet. Do you know what that man's name would be?'

'Wings instead of ears, did you say!'

'And wings instead of feet!' you reminded Grandmother.

'No,' she admitted. 'You've gotten me fair beat there! I've never heard tell of that man before!'

'His name would be Mercury. He's in my school reader. He can fly all round the world in a minute!'

'I can well believe that!' she conceded. 'With all that wings he's gotten.'

In moments like that, with the mood of acceptance over Grandmother, a positive admission of time, and its passing, seemed feasible.

'I wouldn't need a candle at night, now,' you boasted. 'I'm not feared of the wood, now.'

'Of course you're not feared,' Grandmother agreed. 'The nights are stretching out, now.'

'I still wouldn't need a candle!' you insisted. 'But that's *one* thing! I won't be here when the dark nights come again. That's *one* thing!' you claimed, jumping down off the log. 'I won't be here when the dark nights come again. Do *you* think I'll still be here when the dark nights come again?'

'That's hard to say,' Grandmother pulled herself up off the log, and stood, considering. 'Hard to tell. But *no!*' she decided at last. 'No. I should hardly think you'd still be here, when the dark nights come again.'

Until Such Times
As we go home
A Hundred Hundred miles
And all the People
They bow down
And everybody smiles . . .

'I know,' Cousin Alice claimed, when they reached the clearing, 'I know why Grandfather says we mustn't go down through the woods where the men are working.'

'So do I though,' you assured her. 'It's because they *swear*! Something cruel! Grandmother says it's because they come from the south. And I know the swear the men say! It's a terrible swear. It begins with F! But mind!' you urged Cousin Alice. 'Don't you say it. *Ever*! They would just murder *me*! For telling!'

She hadn't heard that word before, Cousin Alice admitted. But you had heard it. Hundreds of times. In the Corporation lodging house. It didn't sound terrible then. Just like all the other words. It didn't sound terrible, until one day in the wood, when one of the wood men shouted it out.

'You should have seen the look on Grandfather's face!' you said to Cousin Alice. 'I wanted to cry out to him . . . it wasn't me that swore, Grandfather! It wasn't *me*! Just to make Grandfather speak to me. For once. And to let him know that I don't swear. And I wanted to stand as quiet as anything, so that the twigs wouldn't crackle, and Grandfather wouldn't see me at all. Sometimes,' you confessed to Cousin Alice, 'sometimes I'm never sure what to do . . .'

'Ankle strap shoes, like what Alice has got! Whatever would you be wanting next!' the Invalid Aunt wondered. 'Alice's Mother and Father worked hard for Alice's shoes!' she informed you. 'And Alice took good care of them when she got them!'

'Sorrow be on shoes!' Grandmother snapped. 'The lark needs no shoes to climb to heaven. Forbye!' she assured you. 'Thin shoes like yon wouldn't last you a week in this wood!'

'They wouldn't last you a day!' the Invalid Aunt said. 'But then, there's just no comparison.'

She would like you to be jealous of Alice, the Invalid Aunt. And that was the strange thing, although you envied Alice's shoes, you was never jealous of Alice herself. But glad for her. Proud of her. Willing to claim acquaintanceship. The glory that was Alice, somehow reflecting on yourself . . . Look everybody! Just look! This is Alice. She's *my* cousin! My cousin Alice. Did you ever see anybody so beautiful. So dainty. In all your life! With long golden hair. And blue ribbons. She's my cousin! *My* cousin . . . Alice. *Look*! Everybody just *L O O K*! That's *my* grandather's horses coming up the road. They're his horses . . . my grandfather.'

'My conscience, bairn!' Grandmother edged you out of her road, and away from the window. 'You should know every tree from this scullery window by heart! For I never did see anybody who could stand so long. Just looking!'

That was about all you was good for, the Invalid Aunt confided to Grandmother. It was high time, she insisted, that Ailsa found a place for herself and that bairn! But, being man-mad, a bairn on her hands would fair clip Ailsa's wings.

'Be quiet Edith!!' Grandmother admonished. 'It's your sister you're speaking about.'

'Sister or no sister,' the Invalid Aunt said, 'Ailsa died to me a long time ago.'

> My Aunt Ailsa died to me
> – Words of lament forming themselves in your mind –
> A long long time ago

A dirge for a death, beyond your comprehension, singing in your head.

'The *world*!' Grandmother announced, 'must surely be

coming to an end!' For, she informed you, this was only the second time your Aunt Ailsa had bothered to write!

'If she's bothered to write,' the Invalid Aunt said, 'she must be on the cadge for something or other. Either that, or she's lost her job again. It's my opinion . . .'

'There's a time and a place for opinions,' Grandmother declared, taking you by the hand into the scullery . . . 'Your Aunt Ailsa is coming to see you the day,' she confided. 'She might have some good news for you. So! Would it not be a good idea for you to take a turn up the wood for some dry kindlers for the fire.'

Until Such Times had maybe arrived at last. The very thought of it fixed your feet to the cement of the scullery floor. With the voices from the kitchen rising and falling to the rise and fall of your own heart beats . . .

It was to be hoped, the Invalid Aunt was saying, that this chield would marry Ailsa this time. Though any man that did that had all the Invalid Aunt's sympathy! Either that or he must be a poor, simple creature that was of him!

Neither poor nor simple, Grandmother pointed out. A decent enough chield. A disabled war soldier.

That would fit the bill! the Invalid Aunt maintained. Knowing *Ailsa*, she would have her eye on his bit pension! And lucky to get that! Better women than Ailsa had never even got the *chance* of a man! It was the Invalid Aunt's opinion that Ailsa had never 'let on' about the bairn.

O but she did! Grandmother confirmed. She said in her letter that she was bringing him to see the bairn.

And that, the Invalid Aunt concluded would be enough to put any man clean off! Unless of course, it was somebody they didn't know.

'We know of him,' Grandmother admitted. 'Summers. Dod Summers. His father's got that croft down by the railway.'

'I'm with you now!' The Invalid Aunt's voice shrilled out

in triumph. 'Peg Leg Summers. So that's who she's gotten. Old Peg Leg Summers. And he's got no pension. He shouldn't have been in the war in the first place. Well, well! Even I can mind on him! He used to go clop, clop, cloppin round the mart on a Friday!'

'Listen now,' Grandmother urged you. 'When your Aunt Ailsa comes the day, she'll maybe be bringing somebody with her . . .'

'She wouldn't!' you protested. 'I know she wouldn't. My Aunt Ailsa never *would*!'

'Good grief, bairn! What ails you?'

'What on earth are you on about?' Grandmother insisted, puzzled by your distress.

'My Aunt Ailsa. She wouldn't. She'd *never* marry a man with a wooden leg!'

'*Listening* again!' The Invalid Aunt snorted. 'Lugs cocking at the key hole!'

'Look a here. Just you look a here, now,' Grandmother said, easing you down on your stool by the door. 'A wooden leg's nothing. Nothing at all just. Many a brave man has a wooden leg. You like biding with your Aunt Ailsa,' she reminded you. 'Who has been making sore lament to get back to her Aunt Ailsa? Well then! You'll be happier with your Aunt Ailsa than you've been here. And fine you know that . . .'

'I wish to God she'd stop blubbering,' the Invalid Aunt complained. 'She should be thankful that somebody's willing to give her a home!'

'Now, listen, bairn, just you go and wash your face,' Grandmother suggested. 'And put on a clean pinny. You want to look your best to meet your Aunt Ailsa. But, first things first. I'll away to the well for some fresh water. You can follow on with the little pail.'

'Are you still blubbering there?' The Invalid Aunt's voice, battening itself against your hearing, was powerless to reach the horror of your imagination. 'You heard your Grand-mother! You could at least obey her. But no faith you! Obedience would be some much to expect! *My*! But you're stubborn! Just like Ailsa. The living spit of the mother of you ...'

'She's my Aunt Ailsa,' you said, protective of a relationship that was acceptable. 'She's my Aunt Ailsa ... She's not my *mother*!' The implication of the Invalid Aunt's words had penetrated at last, sending you hurtling towards her bed-chair. 'She's my Aunt Ailsa!' Grasping the aunt by the shoulders, you tried to shake her into understanding. My *mother* is ladies I cut out from pictures in books. Ladies I pick out passing in the street! You know fine she's not my mother! You're just saying that because ... because you're ugly! And you smell terrible! You're just a *fucker*!

... It wasn't *me* that swore, Grandfather. It wasn't me ...

'My Aunt Ailsa's coming!' you shouted to Grandmother, bent over the well at the edge of the wood. 'She's all by herself. She wouldn't. I knew she wouldn't. Marry a man with a wooden leg!'

'I doubt you're right,' Grandmother agreed, as you stood together watching Aunt Ailsa coming up the track. 'Ah well!' she sighed, 'maybe it's all for the best. Who knows! Who can tell! You'd better run on and meet her, then. You haven't even washed your face!' Grandmother admonished. 'Nor changed your pinny! Whatever keepit you so long?'

'It was Edith,' you told Grandmother. 'I think the heart took her. She was making that funny noise.'

'Heavens above! O good grief.' The water from the pail that Grandmother dropped swirling round your feet.

'I didn't touch her medicine bottles!' you reassured her retreating figure. 'I didn't *touch* them!'

Leonora Carrington

As They Rode Along the Edge

A s they rode along the edge, the brambles drew back their thorns like cats retracting their claws.

This was something to see: fifty black cats and as many yellow ones, and then her, and one couldn't really be altogether sure that she was a human being. Her smell alone threw doubt on it – a mixture of spices and game, the stables, fur and grasses.

Riding a wheel, she took the worst roads, between precipices, across trees. Someone who's never travelled on a wheel would think it difficult, but she was used to it.

Her name was Virginia Fur, she had a mane of hair yards long and enormous hands with dirty nails; yet the citizens of the mountain respected her and she too always showed a deference for their customs. True, the people up there were plants, animals, birds; otherwise things wouldn't have been the same. Of course, she had to put up with being insulted by the cats at times, but she insulted them back just as loudly and in the same language. She, Virginia Fur, lived in a village long abandoned by human beings. Her house had holes all over, holes she'd pierced for the fig tree that grew in the kitchen.

Apart from the garage for the wheel, all the rooms were occupied by cats; there were fourteen in all.

Every night she went out on her wheel to hunt; whatever their respect, the mountain beasts didn't let themselves be killed as easily as all that, so several days per week she was forced to live on lost sheepdog, and occasionally mutton or child, though this last was rare since no one ever came there.

It was one night in autumn when she found to her surprise that she was being followed by footsteps heavier than those of an animal; the footsteps came rapidly.

The sickening smell of a human entered her nostrils; she pushed her wheel as hard as she could, to no avail. She stopped when her pursuer was beside her.

'I am Saint Alexander,' he said. 'Get down, Virginia Fur, I want to talk to you.'

Who could this individual be who dared address her so familiarly? An individual, furthermore, of a rare filthiness, there in his monk's habit. The cats kept a contemptuous distance.

'I want to ask you to enter the Church,' he went on. 'I hope to win your soul.'

'My soul?' replied Virginia. 'I sold it a long time ago for a kilo of truffles. Go ask Igname the Boar for it.'

He considered this across the whole length of his greenish face. Finally he said with a cunning smile, 'I have a pretty little church not far from here. It's a marvel of location, and what comfort! My friend! Every night there are apparitions, and you really have to see the graveyard, really, it's a dream! There's a view of the surrounding mountains for a hundred miles and more. Come with me, Virginia.' He continued in a tender voice. 'I promise you, on the head of little baby Jesus, that you'll have a beautiful spot in my graveyard, right next to the statue of the Holy Virgin. (And believe me that's the very best place.) I'll conduct your funeral rites myself. Imagine, funeral rites celebrated by the great Saint Alexander!'

The cats growled impatiently, but Virginia was thinking it over. She'd heard there was good dinnerware in churches, some of it made of gold, and the rest would always have its uses. She alerted the cats in their language, and told the saint, 'Sir, what you're telling me interests me to a certain degree, but it is against my principles to interrupt the hunt. If I come with you, I shall have to dine with you, and so shall the hundred cats of course.'

He looked at the cats with a certain amount of apprehension, then nodded his head in agreement.

'To bring you to the path of True Light,' he murmured, 'I shall arrange a miracle. But understand that I am poor, very, very poor. I eat only once a week, and this solitary meal is sheep's droppings.'

The cats set off without enthusiasm.

About a hundred yards from the Church of Saint Alexander there was what he called 'my garden of the little Flowers of Mortification'. This consisted of a number of lugubrious instruments half buried in the earth: chairs made of wire ('I sit in them when they're white-hot and stay there until they cool off'); enormous, smiling mouths with pointed, poisonous teeth; underwear of reinforced concrete full of scorpions and adders; cushions made of millions of black mice biting one another – when the blessed buttocks were elsewhere.

Saint Alexander showed off his garden one object at a time, with a certain pride. 'Little Theresa never thought of underwear of reinforced concrete,' he said. 'In fact I can't at the moment think of anybody who had the idea. But then, we can't all be geniuses.'

The entrance of the church was lined with statues of Saint Alexander at various periods of his life. There were some of Jesus Christ too, but much smaller. The interior of the church was very comfortable: velvet cushions in ash pink, bibles of real silver, and *My Unblemished Life, or The Rosaries of the Soul of Saint Alexander* by himself, this in a binding of peacock blue jewels. Amber bas-reliefs on the walls gave intimate details of the life of the saint in childhood.

'Gather yourselves,' said Saint Alexander, and the hundred cats sat down on a hundred ash pink cushions.

Virginia remained standing and examined the church with interest. She sniffed the altar, which exuded a vaguely familiar smell, though she couldn't remember where she had smelled it.

Saint Alexander mounted the pulpit and explained that he was going to perform a miracle: everyone hoped he was talking about food.

He took a bottle of water and sprinkled drops everywhere.

> *Snow of purity*

he began in a very low voice,

> *Pillar of virtue*
> *Sun of beauty*
> *Perfume ...*

He continued in this vein until a cloud flowed from the altar, a cloud like sour milk. Soon the cloud took the shape of a fat lamb with baneful eyes. Immediately Saint Alexander cried out, more and more loudly, and the lamb floated up to the ceiling.

'Lamb of God, dearly beloved Jesus, pray for the poor sinners,' cried the saint. But his voice had reached its maximum strength and broke. The lamb, which had become enormous, burst and fell to the ground in four pieces. At this moment the cats, who had watched the miracle without moving, threw themselves on the lamb in one great bound. It was their first meal of the day.

They soon finished off the lamb. Saint Alexander was lost in a cloud of dust, all that was left of the odour of sanctity. A weak, remote voice hissed, 'Jesus has spilled his blood, Jesus is dead, Saint Alexander will avenge himself.'

Virginia took this opportunity to fill her bag with holy plates, and left the church with the hundred cats behind her.

The wheel crossed the woods at a hissing speed. Bats and moths were imprisoned in Virginia's hair; she gestured to the beasts with her strange hands that the hunt was over; she opened her mouth and a blind nightingale flew in: she swallowed it and sang in the nightingale's voice: 'Little Jesus is dead, and we've had a fine dinner.'

A wild boar lived near Virginia's house. This boar had a single eye in the middle of his forehead, surrounded by black curls. His hindquarters were covered with a thick russet fur, and his back with very tough bristles. Virginia was acquainted with this animal and did not kill it, since it knew where the truffles were hiding.

The boar was called Igname, and he was very pleased with his beauty. He enjoyed decorating himself with fruits, leaves, plants. He made himself necklaces of little animals and insects, which he killed solely to make himself look elegant, since he ate nothing but truffles.

Every evening when the moon was shining, he went to the lake to admire himself in the water. It was here, one evening, while bathing in the moonlight, that Igname decided to take Virginia as his mistress. He admired most her fruity smell and her long hair, always full of nocturnal animals. He decided she was very beautiful and probably a virgin. Igname rolled in the mud luxuriously, thinking of Virginia's charms.

'She has every reason for taking me. Am I not the finest animal in all the forest?'

When he had finished his moon- and mudbath, he got up to find the most sumptuous outfit in which to ask Virginia for her love.

No animal or bird ever looked so splendid as did Igname in his attire of love. Attached to his curly head was a young nightjar. This bird with its hairy beak and surprised eyes beat its wings and looked constantly for prey among the creatures that come out only at the full moon. A wig of squirrels' tails and fruit hung around Igname's ears, pierced for the occasion by two little pikes he had found dead on the lakeshore. His hoofs were dyed red by the blood of a rabbit he had crushed while galloping, and his active body was enveloped by a purple cape which had mysteriously emerged out of the forest. (He hid his russet buttocks, as he did not want to show all his beauty at one go.)

He walked slowly and with great dignity. The grass-hoppers fell silent with admiration. As he was passing under an oak tree, Igname saw a rosary hanging down among the leaves. He knew there must be a body attached to this rosary, and he heard a shrill and mocking laugh from above.

Any other time, thought Igname, and he'd be laughing on the other side of his face, and he continued on his way without turning his head.

Igname arrived at Virginia's house. She was sitting on her heels in front of a stewpot which trembled on the fire, making little musical noises. The cats were sitting motionless in every corner of the kitchen, staring at the stewpot.

When Virginia said Igname she jumped on the table.

'You look impressive coming out of the forest,' she breathed, dazzled by his beauty.

Igname's eye became pale and brilliant; the nightjar sent up its thin cry, almost too high to be heard by the ear. Igname advanced and sat down beside the fire on his russet backside.

'Do you recognize my garments of love?' said Igname gravely. 'Do you know, Virginia, that I am wearing them for you? Do you realize that the nightjar's claws are thrust deep into my skull? It's for you, I love you. I double up with laughter when I see the night, for my body is exploding with love. Answer me, Virginia, will this night belong to us?'

He faltered, since he had prepared his speech only to this point. Virginia, trembling, spat hard into the fire, a curse on the words of love. She was afraid of Igname's beauty. Then she spat into the stewpot and put her lips into the boiling liquid and swallowed a big mouthful. With a savage cry she brought her head back out of the pot; she jumped around Igname, tearing her hair out by the roots; Igname stood up, and together they danced a dance of ecstasy. The cats caterwauled and stuck their claws into one another's necks, then threw themselves in a mass onto Igname and Virginia, who disappeared under a mountain of cats. Where they made love.

Hunters came seldom to the mountains, but one morning Virginia Fur saw two humans with guns. She hid herself in a bramble bush, and the human beings passed near without noticing her smell. She was terrified by their ugliness and clumsy movements. Abusing them under her breath, she returned home to warn Igname. He wasn't there.

She went out again on her wheel, accompanied by the hundred cats.

In the forest Virginia learned that there had been several deaths. Flocks of birds and groups of wild beasts were having funeral feasts. Full of anguish, they filled their stomachs and cursed the hunters.

Virginia went looking for her lover, but found neither track nor scent of him.

Towards dawn she heard from a badger that Igname was dead: he had been murdered along with a thousand birds, forty hares, and as many deer.

The badger, sitting on a tree trunk, told the story:

'The hunters, who you noticed, passed close to the Church of Saint Alexander. The saint was sitting in his concrete underwear. He saw them coming, he was praying aloud. The hunters asked him news of game.

"I am the Protector of the Little Animals of God," he

169

answered. "But inside my church is a box of alms for the poor. If you put something in it, it's just possible the good Lord will show you the lake where every evening a big wild boar can be found."

After having a good look to see how much the hunters had put into the box, Saint Alexander led them to the lake.

Igname was looking deeply at himself in the water. The hunters fired, and the dogs finished him off. They put Igname into a big sack and said, "This one will do for the bistro in Glane, we'll get at least a hundred francs." '

Virginia returned home, followed by the cats. There, in the kitchen, she gave birth to seven little boars. Out of sentiment she kept the one most like Igname, and boiled the others for herself and the cats, as a funeral feast.

The wheel, the cats, and Virginia merged with the trees and the wind. Their shadows, black and disquieting, passed with extraordinary speed across the slope of the mountains. They were shouting something; the nightbirds replied: 'Wheeeeeeech? Saint Francis? That bore again! Let's kill him! Isn't he dead yet? Enough of his damned stupidities. It isn't him? Who then? Ah, Saint Alexander, ayyyyy! Kill him too, he's a saint.' And they flew along with the shadows, crying, 'Killll himmmm! Killll himmmm!'

Soon the earth moved with all the beasts out of their holes crying, 'Killll himmmm!'

Ninety thousand horses bounded and broke from their stables to gallop along, beating the earth with their hoofs and neighing, 'Killll himmmm, death to foul Alexander!'

Two ladies dressed in black were walking in the snow. One of them talked a lot, the other appeared to have had enough of walking, but wore the icy look of a dutiful lady. The other one, with her pinched, dry face, talked in a crystal clear voice, one of those voices that are so tiresome when one wants to go to sleep in a railway compartment.

'My husband,' she was saying, 'loves me very much, you know. My husband is so well-known. He's such a child, my husband. My husband has his flings, but I leave him totally free, my dear little husband. And yet I am very ill, I shall die soon, in a month I shall be dead.'

'No, no,' the other said, her attention elsewhere. 'Aren't the mountains ravishing in the snow?'

The talkative lady gave a laugh. 'Yes, aren't they? But all I see are the poor people who suffer in these isolated little villages. I feel my heart fill to bursting with love and pity.' She struck her flat chest, and the dutiful lady thought, 'There isn't room for a heart, her bust's too tight.'

The path climbed suddenly, and at the end of a long lane they saw a convent.

'What a beautiful place to die. I feel so pure with the Sisters of Jesus's Little Smile of Anguish. I know that there, with my prayers, I shall get back the soul of my darling little husband.'

Two men came down the path. They were carrying the corpse of a beautiful boar.

'I shall buy the boar and give it to the good sisters,' the lady said. 'I am very generous, you know. My little husband often scolded me, said I throw money out the window. But won't they be happy, the good sisters?' She gave the hunters some money and they said they'd take the boar to the convent. 'I myself eat very little, you know, I am too ill. I am very near to death, very near.'

'We're approaching the convent,' said the other, with a sigh.

'Kiss me, my dear little Engadine,' said the talkative one. 'You know I'm nothing but a capricious girl.' She offered her companion a shrivelled face. 'My little husband always said I was such a child!'

Engadine pretended not to hear, and walked faster. Her

companion had a certain nauseating smell of the sick about her that repelled her. She walked faster. The sun was hidden by heavy black clouds. A flock of goats and a billy goat passed close, the buck threatening them with a devil's look.

'They frighten me, these goats, they smell so bad. What a brutish smell!' The buck continued to stare at her.

The road became harder. The mountains darkened into rude animal shapes; in the distance they seemed to hear galloping horses.

They rang the bell at the great portal of the convent; it was opened by a creature that might have come from a lemon, she was so shrivelled and acid. 'The Abbot is in the middle of his prayers,' she wheezed. 'Mother Superior is on her knees. Come, come in the chapel.'

They followed her through the corridors, and finally arrived at the chapel. The Abbot had just finished his prayers. The Mother Superior of Jesus's Little Smile of Anguish got up from her knees with difficulty, weighted down by her greyish flesh.

'Poor little girl,' whispered the nun. 'Come along to the drawing room.'

Once there, the enormous woman enveloped the other in a fat, sturdy embrace. Then they talked:

'I've come to die in your convent and win the soul of my dear husband . . .'

'Board and lodging five hundred francs a month . . .'

'I'm very ill, very ill . . .'

'Plenary indulgences are supplementary, a thousand francs.'

'My darling little husband will come see me often . . .'

'Another thousand francs for food, of course.'

'I pray morning till night for my little husband.'

'A community like ours is very expensive.'

They talked like this for several hours.

At half past six an enormous bell rang for the dead and the evening meal, a meal to be taken in rigorous silence. On feast days, Sister Ignatius, headmistress, read aloud. She rang a little bell, and when everybody had something to eat, announced, 'This evening is among the greatest of occasions for our community; the Great Saint Alexander himself is coming to speak to us in the chapel at seven-thirty. Afterwards we shall have a meal in the great hall to celebrate the occasion.'

The eyes of a hundred nuns shone with joy.

'Now,' continued Sister Ignatius, 'we continue with chapter one thousand nine hundred and thirteen of the twentieth volume of the life of Christ as told to children.' The light disappeared in a hundred pairs of eyes.

When the chapel was full of nuns, the organ played a grand, sombre hymn for the saint's imperial entrance. In gold and purple and followed by five little boys, he got down on his knees before the altar.

A voice in the choir began to sing. Perhaps it was a hymn, but it went so fast that most of the nuns were two or three lines behind. The effect was odd; the Mother Superior appeared ill at ease; when the saint mounted the pulpit, followed by six fat cats, she was in a sweat.

'Dear sisters, I have come from far to gladden you with the word of God.'

It seemed as if the altar was filling with cats, gold cats and black cats.

'The harshness of life, the temptations of the flesh, the goodness of the good . . .'

A strong wild smell drifted through the church; raising their eyes, the sisters were horrified to see a large badger climbing tranquilly onto Saint Alexander's head. He continued, but every now and again made a movement with his hand as if trying to chase something away.

'Beware of sinful thoughts . . .'

The voice in the choir was still singing, but it scarcely resembled a hymn; Saint Alexander was obliged to shout to make himself heard.

'The good Lord sees your most secret thoughts . . .' The

ceiling was hidden by a million birds of the night crying: 'Death to foul Alexander . . .'

He descended the pulpit with as much dignity as he could muster, and went out, followed by the nuns, the cats, the badger, and a million birds of the night.

In the refectory a huge table groaned with platters of game, cakes, and great flagons of wine. The saint sat down in the place of honour at the top of the table and asked the good Lord for permission to eat. The good Lord made no reply, and everybody sat down and attacked with good appetite.

The Mother Superior, sitting on the saint's right, whispered, 'Holy Father, you weren't disturbed in your magnificent discourse?'

'Disturbed?' he asked in a surprised voice, though his face was covered in scratches. 'Disturbed, how?'

'Oh, nothing,' the mother replied, blushing. 'There are some flies in the church.'

'I notice nothing when I talk to the good Lord,' said the lady who'd taken up residence at the convent. 'Not even flies.'

The two ladies exchanged sour looks.

'That, dear madam, is a noble thought,' answered the saint. 'Are you familiar with a little poem I wrote in my youth:

> *In Paris the Pope*
> *In Aix Lord of the House,*
> *But before the good Lord*
> *I'm but a poor mouse.*

'It's fresh, and yet so strong at the same time,' the lady exclaimed ecstatically. How I love real poetry.'

'There's more where that came from,' said the saint. 'I find the lack of true poets forces me to write.'

Out of the corner of her eye, the Mother Superior saw seven large cats enter the room silently. They sat down beside the saint, curling their tails around themselves. She grew pale. 'Your husband, dear child, must be very busy to leave you alone so often?'

'My husband,' the lady replied in a sharp voice, 'is very tired. He's having a rest.'

'Well then,' replied the Mother Superior, 'no doubt he's having it on the Riviera? Remember the temptations of the flesh. If my husband were not Our Lord, if I had instead chosen among the poor sinners of this world, I would hardly feel easy with him on the Riviera, especially if I weren't in the first spring of youth anymore, let's be frank.'

The lady trembled with rage, and clenched her fingers. 'My darling little husband adores me. He does silly things, but we're made for each other.'

The moment had come for the roast to be carried in, and everyone looked with anticipation at the door that led to the kitchen. Sister Ignatius stood up and blew a long, melancholic note on a small leather trumpet: 'The boar!'

The door crashed open and all the beasts of the forest entered crying, 'Kill him, kill him.' In the turmoil that followed one could barely make out a human form sitting on a wheel that turned with incredible speed, who shouted with the others: 'Kill him!'

Translated from the French by Kathrine Talbot

Attia Hosain

Time is Unredeemable

When the second cable arrived, confirming the date he was to sail, Bano allowed herself to believe her husband was really coming back.

She was sitting in the thatched verandah sewing when her father-in-law came in. He held his spectacles in one hand, the cable in the other, and it trembled as if an unseen current caught it in the still air.

The women who observed purdah from him twittered like disturbed birds and hurried into the inner room.

'Read it to me,' said her mother-in-law. 'Tell me quickly what it says.' In her agitation the red betel juice sprayed from her mouth.

Bano kept her head lowered as she tried to thread the needle. Her father-in-law put on his spectacles, pulled at his beard, pushed back his woollen cap, and held the cable close to his eyes.

'How long you take . . .' grumbled her mother-in-law. Bano could hear her own heart's echoes sound like a drum within her ears, and at the back of her head.

Her father-in-law cleared his throat, translated the words of the cable and added, 'So, God willing, he will be home with us at the end of next month.'

'The end of the month,' sobbed her mother-in-law in her extremity of joy. 'God be praised!'

Bano felt sharp points of tears press against her eyelids, but her habit strengthened sense of propriety set a guard on her rebellious feelings, and her face was drained of emotion. Her mind, by its simplicity, reduced the complications of her thoughts, and her anxiety concentrated safely on external things as she wondered what her husband would look like after all these years, what he would think of her, what she would say to him, what she should wear when he first saw her. At the same time she responded to the sounds of the old couple's voices, picking key words to make them intelligible without breaking her own web of thought. Her mother-in-law made plans for immediate celebrations, her father-in-law for his son's future.

'What,' sighed the old man, 'will the boy do when others are already established? Ah, these years, these years destroyed!'

The sigh echoed mournfully in Bano's mind, and the chill of wasted years fell upon the formless future.

Her mother-in-law said, 'Whatever is in his Kismet and hers must happen. Their life is beginning, and, for all I care, mine can end. I have lived nine years for this day.'

Bano's father-in-law cleared his throat, blinked his eyes rapidly, and said, 'I must be going. My game of chess is unfinished . . .'

When he had gone the women crowded back, with so many questions to ask and opinions to express that one could not wait for another to begin a sentence or finish it, and their words formed a many-layered patchwork of sound obscuring Bano's silence.

Bano was sixteen when she was married to a reluctant Arshad a month before he sailed for England. In that brief, busy month she accepted the young stranger, barely two years older than herself, as the very focus of her being. To her mother and his the hurriedly arranged marriage was a moral insurance.

'To a mother of many girls both safety and wisdom counsel an early marriage,' said her mother.

'If you push a boy into a sea of temptation will a hair of his head remain dry? Now he will not bring home a foreign woman,' said Arshad's mother.

For two years after her marriage Bano's life was pleasant enough because there was no questioning of its circumscribed character. She was isolated from the outside world not only by physical seclusion but by mental oblivion. Arshad's letters came literally from a different world, yet both she and his mother were conscious only of the physical separation of distance. He wrote regularly to his father about his studies, to his mother of his health. To Bano he wrote short, formal letters, but she was content, not expecting more. Sometimes he sent her postcards from countries he visited, and she showed them to her friends with a sense of vicarious pleasure as if she were worldly-wise by their possession.

Her father-in-law, who considered himself a man of liberal ideas, was pleased when Bano decided to learn English from his old friend Hari Ram's English wife. Of Mrs Ram's shortcomings as a teacher, her dropped aitches, her ungrammatical colloquialisms, Bano was unaware; she was conscious only of the fact that Mrs Ram could help her prove to Arshad that she was not like the other girls in the family, ignorant and old-fashioned.

Mrs Ram lived in the small house next door, on the edge of penury. Her bleached, untidy, sagging appearance reflected her husband's failure as a lawyer, as a politician. They had settled in this small town after years of weary struggle to keep up appearances; and Mrs Ram, who had always been familiar with poverty, welcomed its gentler nature. She was touched by Bano's affection, and grateful.

Bano lived her dutiful uneventful life, and was not unhappy.

Then the war broke out.

To Bano and her mother-in-law war meant nothing except in terms of Arshad's safety, and the despairing knowledge that he would not return until it ended.

In the winter of 1940 Mrs Ram went away with her husband when he was given a good post in a new Government department. Bano put away her English books.

Without his friend Mr Ram her father-in-law's loneliness increased his morbid anxieties about Arshad and the fate of his shaken world. He retired with his family to his ancestral village home.

Bano drew further away in time and space from Arshad; her only consciousness of it was that his infrequent letters took longer to arrive.

Endless years of waiting, of living the life of neither a wife nor a widow, pitied by her relatives, wept over by her mother and mother-in-law, hag-ridden by her misgivings that Arshad might die or marry again, wrung the spirit out of her.

The war ended.

The sharp sting of anticipation revived Bano; in her happiness there was a mysterious suggestiveness of an expectant bride, a radiance that lent her beauty and gentleness. She took out her English books again, and tried painfully to remember all she had forgotten, daring even to ask her father-in-law's help.

When Arshad wrote it was difficult to get a passage and he would be indefinitely delayed, she was cast into a gloom which was as deep as the heights to which her joy had carried her. She was haunted by the suspicion that he did not wish to return, that he had found a woman. Then the habit of acceptance closed around her, obliterating all peaks of feeling, and she waited once again for the news that would clear the mist.

ATTIA HOSAIN

It came with the first cable, and was made real by the second.

Every breath and movement and thought now became a preparation of herself for the first moment of meeting Arshad. Above all else she wished to make him realize that she was not an ignorant girl of whom he, with his foreign education, need be ashamed.

Gradually a plan took shape in her mind: she would not even look like the other girls in the village, she would not wear the customary clothes no matter how much her mother-in-law insisted, she would wear a sari, new and modern. And a coat, not a shawl.

She confided in a favourite cousin who conveyed her wishes to her mother-in-law, as modesty forbade a direct approach in a matter which concerned her husband, however indirectly. The old lady, in her present mood of happiness, willingly gave her consent that Bano should go to the city to do her shopping.

Bano could think of no one more suitable than Mrs Ram to advise her, especially about the coat, which had to be of the latest English fashion, and asked her father-in-law to write and request Mrs Ram to help her, not trusting her own unpractised English.

A visit to the city was a rare and exciting event, usually on the occasion of a wedding or celebration, sometimes because of a serious illness or death in the family, seldom for very special shopping. It called for a great deal of bustle and preparation.

Bano's father-in-law insisted on making all the arrangements himself, and said he would go with her because he wished to take this opportunity to meet his friends and discuss Arshad's future.

The day she was to leave the young girls in the house joked with Bano as if she were on her way to her wedding; they shared her excitement.

The tonga which was to drive them to the small country

180

station for the first, bumping, dusty halfhour of the two-hour journey was drawn up near the door of the zenana. The bells on its harness rang gaily as the nondescript grey horse shook its head and flicked its tail to shake off the irritating flies. A sheet was tied round the back of the tonga and another to screen Bano from the driver, beside whom sat her father-in-law. Bano carried with her the shrouding 'burqa' she would wear to cross the platform.

When everything was ready for her to leave, the elder women embraced her, the young girls came with her to the door, and everyone called out, 'God protect you. God be with you.'

When she arrived at their house in the city Bano did not tell her relatives much beyond this, that she had some shopping to do for her mother-in-law. Their expected banter about her husband's return she welcomed with simulated shyness.

After her father-in-law had rested, he told her he was going to see Mr Ram, who lived some distance away in the Civil Lines. She asked him with a courage born of excited anxiety to tell Mrs Ram to come for her as early as possible the next day as there was so little time and so much to do.

Next morning she was up early, and ready long before she expected Mrs Ram to arrive. It seemed to her half the day was gone before she did come, though it was only ten o'clock.

Mrs Ram looked no older, was stouter, and a gleam of prosperity glanced lightly over her faded face. After the first moments of affectionate greeting and questioning that closed the gap of separating years, she asked Bano what she wished to buy. Bano was embarrassed and hesitant in the presence of her relatives.

'A few clothes,' she stammered.

'Ah,' smiled Mrs Ram with heavy coyness. 'In preparation for Arshad's return! Well, well, girls will be girls. But we must hurry, dear, as I'm ever so busy these days with parties and meetings.'

When Bano brought her 'burqa' from her room, Mrs Ram's pale eyes widened: 'Surely, dear, you will not wear that?'

Bano looked at her relatives diffidently. 'My father-in-law . . .' she began.

Mrs Ram shrugged her shoulders, and looked with distaste at the shapeless garment.

In the car she said, 'You must take it off when we get to the shop. It will attract ever so much attention, because no one that I know of wears it any more. And tell me, dear, exactly what you want to buy so that I can tell the driver where to go.'

Bano said softly, 'A sari, and a coat.'

'I know just the right shop. All the best people go there; they know me well and it makes all the difference when things are hard to get.'

Bano let herself drift on the stream of Mrs Ram's will. As they drove through the narrow streets towards the wide avenues of the Civil Lines she removed the offending 'burqa' but was glad the closed car hid her from passers-by. She tried to explain as well as her restrictive shyness would permit her about the kind of coat she wanted, but what it meant to her was impossible to convey because it was a small part of all she had carried within herself for years.

'Do you want it for the evening or the day?' That puzzled Bano, who did not know the difference.

'For all the time,' she said.

'I see, a nice practical warm coat. How much do you wish to spend?'

She had not thought of details. 'I have three hundred rupees altogether.'

'That is not much really, seeing as prices are so high.'

Bano looked with pained amazement at Mrs Ram. Not since she was a bride when special clothes and jewels were necessary had she spent more on herself at one time; surely it was more than Mr Ram had earned once. Mrs Ram, enjoying this new experience of being depended upon, felt generously eager to please.

'Oh well, don't worry, dear, we'll manage.'

In the shop Bano felt uncomfortably exposed to the glances of the strange men who served them. She nervously clutched the edge of her sari, with which she had covered her head and arms. Her self-consciousness made her unable to concentrate on the choice she had to make from the cloth that was unrolled in untidy heaps before her, and the saris that were piled around. She was glad to submit to Mrs Ram's choice.

The sari that was chosen was of deep red Benares net with large gold flowers scattered over it and formalized in two rows along the edge as a border.

'Red for a bride,' whispered Mrs Ram with a meaning smile. For the blouse Mrs Ram chose a piece of red satin, not exactly the same shade as the sari, but she considered it would not be noticed in the right light.

The coat presented a number of problems. There were none ready of the right size, the choice of materials was limited, and it would take three weeks to get it sewn.

'Not three weeks,' said Mrs Ram, 'not when I order it. You'll get it ready in ten days.'

'We do our best to please you, madam, but we can't promise. As for the cloth, as you know, madam, if you can't get it here you will not find it in any other shop.'

Mrs Ram nodded agreement. Among all those confident people Bano felt she knew nothing, and within her was a growing panic. She wanted to get away quickly. Suppose her father-in-law walked down the street and saw her without her 'burqa'?

She agreed happily when Mrs Ram said, 'Leave it to me. I'll choose the cloth.'

'What about fittings?' said the solicitous salesman.

'What about the fittings?' mused Mrs Ram. Bano looked lost in her puzzled ignorance.

Mrs Ram felt expansively helpful: 'Well, well, dear, leave

it all to me. I'll buy the cloth, have it made up, and send it to you with one of my husband's orderlies. Send for your tailor,' she ordered the salesman. 'He can take the measurements, and I know he is good enough not to need a fitting. He does all my work, mine and Mr Ram's, and the girls.'

Mrs Ram rode high on the waves of authority, and Bano was overwhelmed. She did not like being measured by a strange man, but by now she was prepared for anything.

As they were leaving the shop a young woman in a sari walked in, unaware of Bano's curious glance. But in Bano's mind the impression of her face remained after it was out of sight. She blushed and said to Mrs Ram, 'Could you please buy me some powder, and colour for my lips? And please don't mention it to anyone.'

'Lipstick and powder?' said Mrs Ram, and she leant back, the folds of her face and chin shaking with affectionate amusement. 'How our young Bano is changing!'

For some days after she returned to the village Bano carried within and around her the magic of the two-day visit to the city, then it merged into the growing excitement of Arshad's approaching arrival.

Mrs Ram kept her promise and two weeks later the coat arrived. Bano felt a vague disappointment when she unpacked it, because in her imagination it was something wonderful; but she thought it must be right because Mrs Ram had chosen it.

It was of heavy rough-surfaced material, maroon with faint flicks of grey, plain and belted. The sleeves pulled because it was somewhat narrow across the chest, and when buttoned was tight across the hips.

Her mother-in-law and other elders did not like it, preferring richer materials and more ornamentation, but they joked, 'Perhaps this is what is worn now by memsahibs, and now that her husband is coming back a sahib she must wear it.'

A week before Arshad was to return, welcoming relatives started arriving and soon the house was full. There were beds down the length of the thatched verandahs and in the rooms, and on them the women sat by day and slept at night.

Three extra women came as usual from the barber's family to help with the cooking; and the village songstresses, who sang in the zenanas, sang marriage songs every evening. The fat one, who was their leader and beat the rhythm on the long drum, started singing even the special suggestive songs, but Bano's mother-in-law stopped her.

The religious recital was to be on the day after Arshad was home, but for three days before, preparations were in full swing, and over a hundred guests were expected. Sweets were being prepared by the 'halwai' in a specially constructed shed in the outer courtyard, and in the zenana the women cut betel nuts and prepared 'pan', piling the small green cones in baskets covered with damp cloths. Bano's mother-in-law made a list of all the kinsfolk, those who would come to the 'Milād' and those who could not, and to all of whom the sweets must be distributed, each person getting an equal portion. In a corner of the courtyard were collected the shallow pottery saucers to hold the sweets.

Bano had no special importance in the general pattern. She did whatever her mother-in-law asked her to do.

A room that was easily accessible from the men's part of the house was prepared for Bano and Arshad, and she moved into it a day before his return. The silver-covered ornamental legs of her marriage bed were taken out of storage, and a frame fitted on them. In the plain whitewashed room the bed with its red satin counterpane gleamed when the sun shone through the window, and at night it was warm by lamplight.

Bano had hung muslin curtains on the windows and doors, dyed a pale pink and tied with ribbon bows; and on the table by the armchair she had put her favourite vase, a woman's hand holding up an ornamented cone coloured pink and blue. She had embroidered the tablecloth herself, and crocheted the head-rests on the chair.

In the evenings her cousins hung garlands of flowers in the

ATTIA HOSAIN

room, and they were strewn over the bed and the room was
sweet with their heavy fragrance.

Bano did not leave the room the day of Arshad's return.
She felt weak and unable to face the women who crowded
the rooms and courtyards. At the thought of food her
stomach turned sour. She locked the door of her room, and
would not open it until her mother-in-law made her do so in
the afternoon, and forced her to drink some tea.

As she lay alone, with the sounds of the shouting chattering
women shrilly penetrating the walls and locked door, she felt
the intense longing for the moment of Arshad's arrival turn
into a hysterical panic that exhausted her until she was drawn
further and further away from herself and her surroundings
and was in a void.

She woke to the sound of her name being called as
impatient fists beat the door. It was dark in the room, and as
she opened the door the light from the lamps outside made
her draw back with hurt, dilated pupils.

She did not need to hear her cousin's words, or see her
face; she did not need to feel the excitement that sent the
women crowding towards the outer door. He had come
home.

She shut the door, and held her hand to her heart to press
back the pain. Then, because she knew he would come to her
last of all, after being released from everyone's curiosity, and
the clinging hungry love of the mother and the father, she
tried to fill the great space between each moment with
commonplace action.

She opened the door to bring in the lit gas lamp that had
been put outside the room by her cousin, and by its light put
fresh coals on the brazier in the corner, saw that the small
night lamp had oil in it, and put it with a box of matches on
the table by the vase.

The noise of excited voices made her restless. She walked
to the door and back, sat on the chair, then picked up a

186

mirror from the shelf in the wall, where she had arranged the things she needed for her toilet.

She looked at herself critically, then impatiently put the mirror down, and went to wash her face.

She dressed slowly, oiled and combed her hair, and carefully plaited it. All the women admired her thick and long plait.

Once again she picked up the mirror, outlined her eyes carefully with 'kajal', drawing out their length with steady fingers, then hesitated, powdered her face, looked again in the mirror, and with panic decision put rouge on her cheeks, and painted her lips. Then she sat on the edge of the chair and waited.

After a time she shivered, and the fire from the brazier seemed to contain no warmth. She put on her new coat, though she did not like it hiding her new sari.

There was a sound of singing outside. Someone knocked on the door but she did not open it. She got up, walked to the bed and sat on it, then back again she went to the chair. She thought she was used to waiting, but knew now she was mistaken.

'Open the door,' called her cousin. 'I've brought you your dinner.'

'I'm not hungry,' she replied.

'Not hungry? How can you be?' and the laughter was to her as the sound of frost cracking on the pond in the garden.

She set her time now by the hour for dinner. How could she have expected him earlier? He could not come until after they had eaten, and were ready to retire. Would his mother and father ever feel the need of rest tonight, and know that time was dragging, and she was waiting? Nine years of waiting closed in upon her.

It was her heart and not the door against which the hesitant hand was knocking. She picked up the mirror for a brief glance at her face, and found it saddening. She opened the door.

His unfamiliar tall silhouette and the strange smell of him drew her fears forward from the crowd of her feelings, and she stepped back in silence, her eyes downcast after the first quick, searching look.

He walked awkwardly into the room, carrying a fibre suitcase which he put down as he shut the door.

The gas lamp hissed to bright light in the silence; then he started, 'How are . . .' cleared his throat, 'How are you?'

Her ears were holding the sound of this man's voice, trying to catch in it the familiar youthful notes she had heard nine years ago; then the strong weight of her upbringing levelled all her reactions to acceptance of this stranger who was her husband.

He took advantage of her lowered eyes to look at her. The red net sari with its golden flowers spread stiffly out from below the coat tight-buttoned across her chest and hips, its belt measuring her thickened waist. The powder was too light on her skin, the rouge too pink, and the mouth held tight in shyness smudged red by inexpert hands. She looked up and away, and her eyes were large, soft and timid supplicants.

His voice strained to hide his discomfort: 'I have brought a few things for you. I hope you like them.' He fumbled with the locks of the suitcase. 'I did not know what you would like and it was not the best time to buy anything. Would you like to take them out now?'

She slipped swiftly to her knees by the case, and with a child's eagerness began to unpack it, exclaiming with shy joy as she unwrapped each package. The two handbags and sewing-box she put aside after briefly examining them, but the gold watch she strapped on her wrist, and wore the necklace and earrings of cultured pearls more proudly than if they had been real.

Then she unfolded the coat that lay beneath the sheets of tissue paper.

She liked its bright colour, and the softness of the cloth.

'I wish I could have brought something better, but it was not possible. Why don't you put it on?'

She took off her coat and threw it across the back of the armchair in her eagerness to wear the one he had brought her.

'These loose coats look better with saris,' he said. He was trying to hide his uneasiness, talking to her as to a friend met after years.

She stood before him wearing his presents and her happiness as charms that lit her eyes and brought out the sweetness of her face through its masking paint.

'Thank you,' she said, 'thank you' – in English, though he had not spoken one word of it.

He felt a tender pity, which covered him and drove him to helpless anger against himself, his homecoming, his father, his mother, everyone.

'I must go now, Bano, to my room. I am tired.'

'Go? To your room?' Incredulous surprise forced the words from her; then her hurt was submerged in the shame of what people would say when they knew. Because she could not face her thoughts, she felt her mind paralysed.

He could not look at her eyes, which were alive and wounded; and he spoke quickly because he hated his words.

'I cannot stay, Bano. Please try to understand. It is not because I dislike you, but because I respect you. And there is no other woman, I swear. But we are like strangers. It's not your fault, it's all my fault. I'll do anything you wish me to do – it's better that I should tell you now than later. I kept putting off writing, because I couldn't explain in a letter, and indecision makes time pass quickly. I know how I've wronged you, but what can I do now?'

His voice faded, because it did not sound convincing any more. He felt his words fall into bottomless space, not of her silence but of her incomprehension. They went to her empty of meaning, the language of a strange world, though the sounds were from hers.

ATTIA HOSAIN

The lamp hissed and shed its bright light, and around and within her was dead darkness.

He could not defend himself against this silence, and turned to go. In his clumsy haste he knocked against the small table and the unlit night lamp fell on her coat, leaving an oily trail as it rolled on to the floor.

He cursed savagely then. 'I'm sorry,' he said, 'I am a clumsy fool.'

She did not move nor speak, and because he wanted to forget his words that had struck her to crumpled stillness he said with irrelevant banter, 'I didn't want you to wear this old coat anyway. It reminds me of . . . my landlady . . . no, of . . . Mrs Ram.'

At last she was able to cry.

Grace Paley

Distance

You would certainly be glad to meet me. I was the lady who appreciated youth. Yes, all that happy time, I was not like some. It did not go by me like a flitting dream. Tuesdays and Wednesdays was as gay as Saturday nights.

Have I suffered since? No sir, we've had as good times as this country gives: cars, renting in Jersey summers, TV the minute it first came out, everything grand for the kitchen. I have no complaints worth troubling the manager about.

Still, it is like a long hopeless homesickness my missing those young days. To me, they're like my own place that I have gone away from forever, and I have lived all the time since among great pleasures but in a foreign town. Well, OK. Farewell, certain years.

But that's why I have an understanding of that girl Ginny downstairs and her kids. They're runty, underdeveloped. No sun, no beef. Noodles, beans, cabbage. Well, my mother off the boat knew better than that.

Once upon a time, as they say, her house was the spit of mine. You could hear it up and down the air shaft, the singing from her kitchen, banjo playing in the parlor, she would admit it first, there was a tambourine in the bedroom. Her husband wasn't American. He had black hair – like Gypsies do.

And everything then was spotless, the kitchen was all inlay like broken-up bathroom tiles, pale lavender. Formica on all surfaces, everything bright. The shine of the pots and pans was turned to stun the eyes of company . . . you could see it, the mischievousness of that family home.

Of course, on account of misery now, she's always dirty. Crying crying crying. She would not let tap water touch her.

Five ladies on the block, old friends, nosy, me not included, got up a meeting and wrote a petition to Child Welfare. I already knew it was useless, as the requirement is more than dirt, drunkenness, and a little once-in-a-while whoring. That is probably something why the children in our city are in such a state. I've noticed it for years, though it's not my business. Mothers and fathers get up when they wish, half being snuggled in relief, go to bed in the afternoon with their rumpy bumpy sweethearts pumping away before 3 p.m. (So help me.) Child Welfare does not show its concern. No matter who writes them. People of influence, known in the district, even the district leader, my cousin Leonie, who put her all into electing the mayor, she doesn't get a reply if she sends in a note. So why should I, as I'm nothing but a Primary Day poll watcher?

Anyhow there are different kinds coming into this neighborhood, and I do not mean the colored people alone. I mean people like you and me, religious, clean, many of these have gone rotten. I go along with live and let live, but what of the children?

Ginny's husband ran off with a Puerto Rican girl who shaved between the legs. This is common knowledge and well known or I'd never say it. When Ginny heard that he was going around with this girl, she did it too, hoping to entice him back, but he got nauseated by her and that tipped the scales.

Men fall for terrible weirdos in a dumb way more and more as they get older; my old man, fond of me as he constantly was, often did. I never give it the courtesy of my attention. My advice to mothers and wives: Do not imitate the dimwit's girl friends. You will be damnfool-looking, what with our age and all. Have you heard the saying 'Old dough won't rise in a new oven'?

Well, you know it, I know it, even the punks and the queers that have wiggled their way into this building are in on the inside dope. John, my son, is a constant attendant now at that Ginny's poor grubby flat. Tired, who can blame him, of his Margaret's shiny face all pitted and potted by Jersey smog. My grandchildren, of which I have close to six, are pale, as the sun can't have a chance through the oil in Jersey. Even the leaves of the trees there won't turn a greenish green.

John! Look me in the eye once in a while! What a good little twig you were always, we did try to get you out with the boys and you did go when we asked you. After school when he was eight or so, we got him into a bunch of Cub Scouts, a very raw bunch with a jawful of curse words. All of them tough and wild, but at attention when the master came among them. Right turn! You would've thought the United States Marines was in charge they was that accurate in marching, and my husband on Tuesday nights taught them what he recalled from being a sergeant. Hup! two, three, four! I guess is what he knew. But John, good as his posture was, when he come home I give him a hug and a kiss and 'What'd you do today at Scouts, son? Have a parade, darling?'

'Oh no, Mother,' says he. 'Mrs McClennon was collecting money the whole time for the district-wide picnic, so I just got the crayons and I drew this here picture of Our Blessed Mother,' he says.

That's my John. And if you come with a Polaroid Land camera, you couldn't snap much clearer.

People have asked and it's none of their business: Why didn't the two of you (meaning Jack and me – both working) send the one boy you had left to college?

Well now to be honest, he would have had only grief in college. Truth: he was not bright. His father was not bright, and he inherited his father's brains. Our Michael was clever. But Michael is dead. We had it all talked over, his father and me, the conclusion we come to: a trade. My husband Jack was well established in the union from its early struggle, he was strong and loyal. John just floated in on the ease of recommendation and being related. We were wise. It's proved.

For now (this very minute) he's a successful man with a wonderful name in the building trade, and he has a small side business in cement plaques, his own beautiful home, and every kid of his dressed like the priest's nephew.

But don't think I'm the only one that seen Ginny and John when they were the pearls of this pitchy pigsty block. Oh, there were many, and they are still around holding the picture in the muck under their skulls, like crabs. And I am never surprised when they speak of it, when they try to make something of it, that nice-looking time, as though *I* was in charge of its passing.

'Ha,' Jack said about twenty times that year, 'she's a wild little bird. Our Johnny's dying . . . Watch her.'

OK. Wild enough, I guess. But no wilder than me when *I* was seventeen, as I never told him, that whole year, long ago, mashing the grass of Central Park with Anthony Aldo. Why I'd put my wildness up against any wildness of present day, though I didn't want Jack to know. For he was a simple man . . . Put in the hours of a wop, thank God pulled the overtime of a decent American. I didn't like to worry worry worry him. He was kindness itself, as they say.

He come home 6 p.m. I come home 6:15 p.m. from where

I was afternoon cashier. Put supper up. Seven o'clock, we ate it up and washed the dishes; 7:45 p.m. sharp, if there was no company present and the boy out visiting, he liked his pussy. Quick and very neat. By 8:15 he had showered every bit of it away. I give him his little whisky. He tried that blabbermouth *Journal-American* for news of the world. It was too much. Good night, Mr Raftery, my pal.

Leaving me, thank goodness, the cream of the TV and a cup of sweet wine till midnight. Though I liked the attentions as a man he daily give me as a woman, it hardly seemed to tire me as it exhausted him. I could stay with the Late Show not fluttering an eyelid till the very end of the last commercial. My wildness as a girl is my own life's business, no one else's.

Now: As a token for friendship under God, John'd given Ginny his high school GO pin, though he was already a working man. He couldn't of given her his union card (that never got customary), though he did take her to a famous dinner in honor of Klaus Schnauer: thirty-five years at Camillo, the only heinie they ever let into that American local; he was a disgusting fat-bottomed Nazi so help me, he could've turned you into a pink Commie, his ass, excuse me, was that fat. Well, as usual for that young-hearted gang, Saturday night went on and on, it give a terrible jolt to Sunday morning, and John staggered in to breakfast, not shaved or anything. (A man, husband, son, or lodger should be shaved at breakfast.) 'Mother,' he said, 'I am going to ask Virginia to marry me.'

'I told you so,' said my husband and dropped the funnies on his bacon.

'You are?' I said.

'I am, and if God is good, she'll have me.'

'No blasphemy intended,' I said, 'but He'll have to be off in the old country fishing if she says yes.'

'Mother!' said John. He is a nice boy, loyal to friends and good.

'She'll go out with anyone at all,' I said.

'Oh, Mother!' said John, meaning they weren't engaged, and she could do what she wanted.

'Go out is nothing,' I said. 'I seen her only last Friday night with Pete, his arm around her, going into Phelan's.'

'Pete's like that, Mother,' meaning it was no fault of hers.

'Then what of last Saturday night, you had to go to the show yourself as if there wasn't no one else in the Borough of Manhattan to take to a movie, and when you was gone I seen her buy two Cokes at Carlo's and head straight to the third floor to John Kameron's . . .'

'So? So?'

'. . . and come out at 11 p.m. and *his* arm was around her.'

'So?'

'. . . and his hand was well under her sweater.'

'That's not so, Mother.'

'It *is* so, and tell me, young man, how you'll feel married to a girl that every wild boy on the block has been leaning his thumbs on her titties like she was a Carvel dairy counter, tell me that?'

'Dolly!' says Jack. 'You went too far.'

John just looked at me as red and dumb as a baby's knees.

'I haven't gone far enough into the facts, and I'm not ready to come out yet, and you listen to me, Johnny Raftery, you're somebody's jackass, I'll tell you, you look out that front window and I bet you if you got yourself your dad's spyglass you would see some track of your little lady. I think there are evenings she don't get out of the back of that trailer truck parked over there and it's no trouble at all for Pete or Kameron's half-witted kid to get his way of her. Listen Johnny, there isn't a grown-up woman who was sitting on the stoop last Sunday when it was so damn windy that doesn't know that Ginny don't wear underpants.'

'Oh, Dolly,' says my husband, and plops his head into his hands.

'I'm going, Mother, that's libel, I'll have her sue you for

libel,' dopey John starts to holler out of his tomato-red face. 'I'm going and I'll ask her and I love her and I don't care what you say. Truth or lies, I don't care.'

'And if you go, Johnny,' I said, calm as a dead fish, my eyes rolling up to pray and be heeded, 'this is what I must do,' and I took a kitchen knife, a bit blunt, and plunged it at least an eighth of an inch in the fat of my heart. I guess that the heart of a middle-aged lady is jammed in deeper than an eighth of an inch, for I am here to tell the tale. But some blood did come soon, to my son's staring; it touched my nightie and spread out on my bathrobe, and it was as red on my apron as a picture in an Italian church. John fell down on his knees and hid his head in my lap. He cried, 'Mother, Mother, you've hurt yourself.' My husband didn't say a word to me. He kept his madness in his teeth, but he told me later, Face it: the feelings in his heart was cracked.

I met Ginny the next morning in Carlo's store. She didn't look at me. Then she did. Then she said, 'It's a nice day, Mrs Raftery.'

'Mm,' I said. (It was.) 'How can you tell the kind of day it is?' (I don't know what I meant by that.)

'What's wrong, Mrs Raftery?' she said.

'Hah! wrong?' I asked.

'Well, you know, I mean you act mad at me, you don't seem to like me this morning.' She made a little laugh.

'I do. I like you a great deal,' I said, outwitting her. 'It's you, you know, you don't like Johnny. You don't.'

'What?' she said, her head popping up to catch sight of that reply.

'Don't don't don't,' I said. 'Don't don't!' I hollered, giving Ginny's arm a tug. 'Let's get out of here. Ginny, you don't like John. You'd let him court you, squeeze you, and he's very good, he wouldn't press you further.'

'You ought to mind your business,' says Ginny very soft, me being the elder (but with tears).

'My son is my business.'

'No,' she says, 'he's his own.'

'My son is my business. I have one son left, and he's my business.'

'No,' she says. 'He's his own.'

MY SON IS MY BUSINESS. BY LOVE AND DUTY.

'Oh no,' she says. Soft because I am the older one, but very strong. (I've noticed it. All of a sudden they look at you, and then it comes to them, young people, they are bound to outlast you, so they temper up their icy steel and stare into about an inch away from you a lot. Have you noticed it?)

At home, I said, 'Jack now, the boy needs guidance. Do you want him to spend the rest of his life in bed with an orphan on welfare?'

'Oh,' said Jack. 'She's an orphan, is she? It's just her mother that's dead. What has one thing to do with another? You're a pushy damn woman, Dolly. I don't know what use you are . . .'

What came next often happens in a family, causing sorrow at the time. Looking back, it's a speck compared to life.

For: Following this conversation, Jack didn't deal with me at all, and he broke his many years' after-supper habits and took long walks. That's what killed him, I think, for he was a habitual person.

And: Alongside him on one of these walks was seen a skinny crosstown lady, known to many people over by Tompkins Square – wears a giant Ukrainian cross in and out of the tub, to keep from going down the drain, I guess.

'In that case, the hell with you' is what I said. 'I don't care. Get yourself a cold-water flat on Avenue D.'

'Why not? I'll go. OK,' said Jack. I think he figured a couple of weeks' vacation with his little cuntski and her color television would cool his requirements.

'Stay off the block,' I said, 'you slippery relic. I'll send your shirts by the diaper-service man.'

'Mother,' said poor John, when he noticed his dad's

absence, 'what's happening to you? The way you talk. To Dad. It's the wine, Mother. I know it.'

'You're a bloated beer guzzler!' I said quietly. (People that drink beer are envious against the ones in favor of wine. Though my Dad was a mick in cotton socks, in his house, we had a choice.)

'No, Mother, I mean you're not clear sometimes.'

'Crazy, you mean, son. Huh? Split personality?'

'Something's wrong!' he said. 'Don't you want Dad back?' He was nervous to his fingernails.

'Mind your business, he'll be back, it's happened before, Mr Two-Weeks-Old.'

'What?' he said, horrified.

'You're blind as a bat, Mr Just Born. Where was you three Christmases ago?'

'What! But Mother! Didn't you feel terrible? Terrible! How'd you stand for him acting that way? Dad!'

'Now quit it John, you're a damnfool kid. Sure I don't want to look at his dumb face being pleased. That'd kill.'

'Mother, it's not right.'

'Phoo, go to work and mind your business, sonny boy.'

'It is my business,' he said, 'and don't call me sonny.'

About two months later, John came home with Margaret, both of them blistered from Lake Hopatcong at ninety-four degrees. I will be fair. She was not yet ruined by Jersey air, and she was not too terrible looking, at least to the eye of a clean-minded boy.

'This is Margaret,' he says. 'She's from Monmouth, Jersey.'

'Just come over on the *Queen Mary*, dear?' I asked for the joke in it.

'I have to get her home for supper. Her father's strict.'

'Sure,' I said, 'have a Coke first.'

'Oh, thank you so much,' says Margaret. 'Thank you, thank you, thank you, Mrs Raftery.'

'Has she blood in her?' hollered Jack after his shower. He

199

had come home by then, skinny and dissatisfied. Is there satisfaction anywhere in getting old?

John didn't inquire an OK of his dad or me, nor answer to nobody. Yes or No. He was that age that couldn't live without a wife. He had to use this Margaret.

It was his time to go forward like we all did once. And he has. Number One: She is kept plugged up with babies. Number Two: As people nowadays need a house, he has bought one and tangled it around in Latin bushes. Nobody but the principal at Holy Redeemer High knows what the little tags on the twigs say. Every evening after hard work you can find him with a hose scrubbing down his lawn. His oldest kid is now fourteen and useless. The littlest one is four, and she reminds me of me with the flashiest eyes and a little tongue sharpened to a scrappy point.

'How come you never named one for *me*, Margaret?' I asked her straight in her face.

'Oh,' she said, 'there's only the two girls, Teresa, for my mother, and Cathleen, for my best sister. The very next'll be for you.'

'What? Next! Are you trying to kill my son?' I asked her. 'Why he has to be working nights as it is. You don't look well, you know. You ought to see a smart Jewish doctor and get your tubes tied up.'

'Oh,' she said, 'never!'

I have to tease a little to grapple any sort of a reply out of her. But mostly it doesn't work. It is something like I am a crazy construction worker in conversation with fresh cement. Can there be more in the world like her? Don't answer. Time will pass in spite of her slow wits.

In fact it has, for here we are in the present, which is happening now, and I am a famous widow babysitter for whoever thinks I am unbalanced but within reason. I am a grand storybook reader to the little ones. I read like an actress, Joan Crawford or Maureen O'Sullivan, my voice is deeper than it was. So I do make a little extra for needs, though my Johnny sees to the luxuries I must have. I won't move away to strangers. This is my family street, and I don't need to.

And of course as friendship never ends, Johnny comes twice a week for his entertainment to Ginny. Ginny and I do not talk a word, though we often pass. She knows I am right as well as victorious. She's had it unusually lovely (most people don't) – a chance to be some years with a young fellow like Blackie that gave her great rattling shivers, top to bottom, though it was all cut off before youth ended. And as for my Johnny, he now absolutely has her as originally planned and desired, and she depends on him in all things. She requires him. Her children lean on him. They climb up his knees to his shoulder. They cry out the window for him, *John, John*, if his dumb Margaret keeps him home.

It's a pity to have become so right and Jack's off stalking the innocent angels.

I wait on the stoop steps to see John on summer nights, as he hasn't enough time to visit me and Ginny both, and I need the sight of him, though I don't know why. I like the street anyway, and the hot night when the ice-cream truck brings all the dirty kids and the big nifty boys with their hunting-around eyes. I put a touch of burgundy on my strawberry ice-cream cone as my father said we could on Sunday, which drives these sozzle-headed ladies up the brown brick wall, so help me Mary.

Now, some serious questions, so far unasked:

What the devil is it all about, the noisiness and the speediness, when it's no distance at all? How come John had to put all them courtesy calls into Margaret on his lifelong trip to Ginny? Also, Jack, what was his real nature? Was he for or against? And that Anthony, what *did* he have in mind as I knuckled under again and again (and I know I was the starter)? He did not get me pregnant as in books it happens at once. How come the French priest said to me, crying tears and against his order, 'Oh no, Dolly, if you are *enceinte* (meaning pregnant), he will certainly marry you, poor child, now smile, poor child, for that is the Church's promise to infants born.' To which, how come, tough and cheery as I used to be, all I could say before going off to live and die was: 'No, Father, he doesn't love me.'

Dorothy Richardson

Seen from Paradise

'Just to let you know we are coming down on April 2nd. I can hardly believe it, though we've begun our terrific packing. Piles of books this time, besides all the rest. And we're bringing a tub plant, something Jim's brother knows all about and says blooms beautifully, to put at the side of the front door.'

Five days. Then events; crowding. Beginning with the setting down of the tub plant. Alien. Flouting the old grey cottage. Beginning of its gradual transformation. Each step of which, in turn, whenever I come down, I shall be expected to applaud.

All this I might have foreseen. But if ever I had looked ahead, even from one instant to the next, my winter would not have brought fulfilment of that autumn moment.

Soon after dinner. After dinner made late by my getting lost, gathering those mushrooms for London, on the cliff tops; drawn on and on by the gleaming circlets till misty twilight was there and night coming. Groping, I found at last the walled meadow; felt my way to its gate and the path towards the cliffside. Got somehow down, and home, triumphant. To find them distraught. Jim, I saw, could have shaken me for disturbing, by my alarming absence, the intensity of his evening vision of all he was leaving.

It was then, for the first time and by way of apology for his only partly jocular scolding, that he confessed *fear* of being out on the cliffs after dark and assured me the natives also felt afraid. Sunk in unaccountable happiness, I found no words. For a moment Jim was silent, reading my mood. Then, in the tone of one abandoning a hopeless case, he murmured into the tangle of twine engaging his hands: 'Don't forget you are in *Cornwall*.'

Cornwall. Cornwall. All through the spring, summer, autumn, he and I, whenever a region apart, we were outdoors by ourselves, had consciously shared the spell whose touch had first reached us when we got out on to the platform at the symbolically named St Erth.

Soon after dinner, the indoor evening enclosed us. Jim and Sylvia sitting collapsed, embodiments of departure, weary with packing. Nothing left to us of Cornwell but tomorrow's early grey, inaccessible in the bustle of getting off. Suddenly I knew I must be out again, alone, if only for a moment, in the Cornish night.

I got away unnoticed.

When my feet touched the mud of the lane, I felt again the timeless bliss sustaining me during my mushrooming on the cliff tops. As I went up the dark lane its power deepened. Suddenly brought me that thought of staying on alone in the cottage and sent me, to my own surprise, skipping into the air. All I then knew was that the muddy roadway, the misty darkness, the voices of the sea, the melancholy beloved hooting of the headland foghorn could be my own for the endless deeps of winter.

When I went indoors with my plan, they were incredulous. But presently Sylvia, though longing for London and puzzled by my odd scheme, acclaimed, in the deeps of her smile, the strange adventure, and even Jim, while still producing objections, was privately aware of their uselessness. And when at last he assured me that as far as they were concerned I was more than welcome to the cottage, if only to keep the place aired and dry, he was secretly giving, emerged from surprise, a moment to envy of my coming solitude. And when at last he heaved himself up from his chair to get on with the jobs still in hand, he clearly revealed, by his deliberately averted glance, his resentful awareness of my blissful longing for their departure, from which longing, at that very moment, I was distracted by the renewal of my sense of the relative helplessness of men, of their dependence, however employed, upon all kinds of service, matters that for them were mysteries without magic. So that if he had turned to me instead of saying, by his manner, so cleary that I could hear his very words: 'Well, so much for your interest in me and my work,' he would have seen, not my pity, but a fellow feeling. For to me, too, housekeeping was a repellent mystery.

The next morning, as soon as the sounds of their departure had died away, I went, passing the open door of the sound filled little room where we had breakfasted, incredulously into the vacant sitting room. Subsided into the nearest chair and sat drinking in the stillness and discovering, bit by bit, the meaning of the moment in the lane. First, the all penetrating relief of knowing the world retreated to the immeasurable distance where, until the arrival of Sylvia's letter, it had remained. Then the surprise of discovering the disappearance of all desire to get out into the open. Until that moment I had never recognized, within the daily longing to wander amidst outdoor beauty, the powerful presence of the need to escape perpetual confrontation. From now on, the outdoor beauty would be all about me in the house, day and night, unobstructed.

Then a momentary panic. I remembered the tradespeople, Sylvia's daily palaverings at the front door. Each nothing less, in this leisurely countryside, than a social occasion. From all this Jim and I, absorbed in our writing, had been exempt. My winter was shattered. Until I remembered the blessedly roomy covered porch where, whenever we were going out for the day, Sylvia would leave messages. There, the postman could drop letters, the milkman his bottles, the village store its goods ordered by written list, the laundress her packages. Payments could confidently be left on the porch shelf. The yells of the swiftly perambulating fishmonger I would ignore. Beyond an occasional visit to the post office, in twilight, at teatime when there is nobody about, I need exchange no word with a living soul.

It must have been almost at once after this realization of my security that I found myself gazing at my vanished world with a kind of affection I had never known before. Deep, inclusive. There they were, all my friends indistinguishable. Equally valuable and beloved, and as they began to fade, this strange new warmth moved on, across the world to its furthest inhabitants. My first voyage.

While still I was gazing, rejoicing in this newly revealed capacity of my own being, I saw, clear in the foreground, detached, and as if standing in space, the figures of just these two men. Incredibly together. My thoughts ran back across the years of friendship with each of them. Recalled my gradual gathering of their respective points of view. And their successive removal from my centre of interest.

On that morning I credited the selection of just those two to stand, clear of all the rest and restored to something of their original attractiveness, to the blissful expansion of my own being. And when I heard from Sylvia that indeed they had met and talked together, the psychic adventure of seeing them seemed less important than the revelation of my new relationship to all the world.

The memory of that morning, forgotten during my winter's work, comes back to me now because so soon I must be out in the world again? When once more I am in the midst of humanity, will that first morning's revelations fade away, or will they have given me the beginning of a new design for living?

Universal Ivory Tower?

Ivory Tower, the innermost sanctuary, sole reservoir for the tide ceaselessly flowing from beyond the spheres. Once this centre is reached, one's world is transformed. Will it remain transformed? At a price. The price of keeping the reservoir always available. That, not supplications, is the meaning of 'pray without ceasing'.

Universal ivory tower, the doorway to freedom? And to unity. Even for lovers? Even during the time while they believe themselves all-in-all to each other? For what then possesses them, in and through each other, and seeming to emanate from themselves alone, is what everyone is seeking? Cynics make game of this time, labelling it illusion. Wistful poets mourn its swift passing. But what *matters* is the illumination coming during this time of being in love. Even when the lovers are mistaken in each other and fall apart, the revelation remains, indestructible. Yes. This is true. And those who are together for life could retain consciousness of it if only, save in times of greeting and farewell, or upon special occasions when something urgent must be decided in haste, they would avoid confrontation, if only they would remain, as they were at the altar and at the wedding feast, side by side. They don't. Appalling, it is, to summon to mind the spectacle of all the married couples in the world sitting opposite each other; at table, at the fireside, each, for the other, obstructive, not only of the view, whether from window, or across a room, but also of thought wherein they may meet, or disagree, and, if disagreeing can do so far less destructively than when they clash in mutually visible opposition. On social occasions, too, the same mistake: sturdily supported by the ridiculous dogma of the impossibility of allowing husband and wife to be side by side.

Comically tragic it is to see, in a restaurant, a young couple out for an evening's enjoyment unconsciously destroying exactly what they came out to seek by sitting opposed, each, for the other summarizing dailiness. He, all too often, registering discomfort while she, for the benefit of onlookers, keeps up a would-be animated flow of talk designed to show that all is well and the outing a success. Side by side, each could relax and share a common spectacle, share, too, the sense of togetherness that is at its strongest when surrounded, *on neutral territory*, by fellow creatures.

If I could get this truth about confrontation home even to a few, especially to those serving life sentences, I should not have lived in vain. They would pass it on to others.

Only five more days in solitude that not for one instant has been loneliness. Fresh realization, from moment to moment, all the time. Everything available, all past experience seen, while I sat writing, for the first time as near, clear, permanent reality. An empty mind as I sat in the evenings by the fireside doing nothing, not needing to read or to think, just looking and seeing, taking in afresh the marvellousness of there being anything anywhere. Knowing, when I went to bed, alone in the empty house that was reported to be haunted, that I should sleep the night through, dreamlessly, waking only when the early light, gleaming through the small casements, gave me again the joy of the squat jars of geranium bloom, brilliant against the pale canary yellow of the little curtains. Summer in the wintry dawn.

Now, for the first time, I begin to be qualified to meet the world? To share, even when surrounded, exactly when surrounded, the rich deeps of solitude?

'Just to let you know we'll be coming down on the 2nd.' Five more days. Five whole days. But what is this on the other side? 'Do you think you could persuade old George to let us have a small beer barrel for the tub plant? An old one would do. If he had it ready, we could pick it up as we pass in the wagonette.'

So this is the end, today, now, this minute. The remaining days swept away by a preoccupation.

Damn the tub plant!

Yet even now, now that I have said farewell, I am not distressed. Something remains, has become a part of me, for ever.

For ever with me is that meeting with old George. There he stands, sunlit, in his doorway, a sturdy lifetime of experience, listening to my plea with eyes withdrawn, after the first moment, upon reality; the cautious, meditative gaze that townspeople so easily mistake for bucolic slowness in the uptake. Rich, and nourishing, when George had heard the whole of my appeal, came his gently protesting discourse, addressed to the universe, upon the subject of barls, precious reservoirs growing with age ever richer and more enriching.

'Aw, naw, me-dear, they barls don't belong to be scatted.'

Inspired, in the midst of my disappointment, by the possession of a small region of knowledge, happy in the sense of having made my return journey into the world hand in hand with this gentle old wiseacre, I went gladly on to the village shop to acquire one o' they little barls they use for lard and such. Whenever I behold the plant set in its crudely smooth enclosure I shall substitute, in imagination, one of old George's sacred reservoirs.

Rebecca West

The Salt of the Earth

I

Alice Pemberton had not expected to enjoy the motor-drive home, since because of it, the previous afternoon, she had received a bitter hurt. She had gone into the drawing-room to tell her mother that one of the young men who had been coming in for tennis so much of late, was very pleased indeed to give her a lift to Camelheath. With her invariable consideration she had been careful to mention the proposal nonchalantly, though she knew she would enjoy the drive through the spring countryside, and would find the society of the obviously admiring young man just such a gratification as a woman of forty needs from time to time. There could be no getting away from the fact that this meant her leaving her mother two days earlier than had been planned, and she was never one to take family duties lightly. But before she could well get the sentence out of her mouth there had flashed into her mother's eyes a look which nobody in the world could mistake for anything but an expression of intense, almost hilarious relief.

'It ought to be lovely for you!' Mrs Anglesey had exclaimed. 'You'll go through the New Forest, I expect. It'll be at its best with all the trees coming out.'

'Very well, mother dear,' Alice had said quietly, and had gone out of the dark drawing-room into the sunlit garden. Though she was reassured by the sight of the young man in white flannels, plainly eager to hear her decision, she could hardly still the trembling of her upper lip.

'Not, my dear, that I shan't be terribly sorry to lose you!' her mother had called after her, but a second too late, a semitone too high pitched.

That night she lay awake for quite a long time wondering why it was that her mother had always had such a curious attitude to her. It was not that she did not care for her. Alice knew that quite well. When she had had diphtheria as a girl at school, when she had been operated on for appendicitis, the extremely passionate quality of her mother's anguish and relief had been as recognizable as the brilliance of lightning. Nevertheless she could not help seeing that in the ordinary intercourse of life Mrs Anglesey felt her as a burden. She had sometimes suspected that her mother had hurried on her marriage to Jimmy not only because as she had so often said at the time, long engagements dragged young romance past its proper time of ripening, but because she wanted her out of the house; and she had had to do more than suspect, she had often to record in black and white on the pages of her diary, that when her mother came to stay with her her visits were apt to be far briefer than those she paid to Madge or Leo.

'Of course there may be some reason for it,' Alice pondered, determined to be broad-minded and generous. 'I am the eldest of the three, I was born very soon after she married. Perhaps I came too soon, before she was reconciled to giving up all her pleasures for her babies, and she may have felt a grudge against me that she has never lived down.'

But she could not help thinking that her mother ought to have lived it down if she had any sense of gratitude. For neither Madge nor Leo had done anything like as much for their mother as she had, and she had been willing to make even greater sacrifices, had they been accepted. Though she and Jimmy had loved each other so much, she had been quite willing to face a long engagement, simply because she hated to imagine what home would be like without her. Since her father's death she had done what she could to replace his influence. She had kept Madge and Leo from getting out of hand as fatherless children notoriously do, she had tried to prevent her mother from giving way to that strain of feckless-ness and untidiness which her most fervent admirers had to admit existed alongside her charm and vividness. Well, all that hadn't been appreciated. Alice remembered, and it was as if a pin had stuck into her, how Mrs Anglesey had grown gay and gayer as the wedding-day approached, and at the actual ceremony had shone with a radiance quite unlike the melancholy conventionally ascribed to the bride's mother. She rolled over in bed, rubbing her face angrily against the sheets.

Anyway, even if her mother had not valued her properly then, she ought to have learned to do so, in the last few years of her age and mellowness. Hadn't she noticed what her daughter had done for her during this visit? Alice had put out of doors the horrible gipsyish old dressing-gowny tea-gowns her mother had loved to shuffle about in for the evenings, and had bought her some nice old-lady dresses from quite a good shop, in the proper colours, dove-grey and dark brown. She had gone over the housekeeping books and saved pounds by changing several of the shops, and had put an end to the custom by which cook had brought in the menu-book last thing at night and launched out into what proved simply to be shockingly familiar gossip. One can't get on those terms with one's servants. She had hired a car, too, and taken her mother round calling on all the nice people with whom she had lost touch, and when her mother had insisted on calling on the Duchess, and had settled down to chat as if they were two old cronies, she had been firm and just taken her home, for it does not do to presume on one's acquaintance with people like that. It had all been a lot of trouble, too, particularly when she was still feeling so weak. But it had all gone for nothing. And so, too, she suspected, had all she had done for Madge and Leo. They hardly ever seemed to realize any of her kindnesses to them, and sometimes they were quite rude. And Leo's wife, Evie, was almost worse.

But perhaps this was the price she had to pay for her perfect marriage. At least Jimmy adored her. 'My dear husband!' she sighed, and presently went off to sleep, but not, as it appeared, to rest. For there began to hover about her a terror which she had met before in her sleep, and she stood helpless while it circled closer and closer, unable to move hand or foot, able only to shriek. Able to shriek, it appeared, not only in her dream, for she opened her eyes and found her mother leaning over her and trying to shake her, although she herself was shaking so that there was very little strength in her hands.

'Oh, mother darling!' said Alice. 'These wretched nightmares! I wish I didn't have them so often!'

Mrs Anglesey sat back, still shaking, her grey hair wild about her.

'Oh, my poor little girl,' she gasped. 'My poor little girl! What can it be that frightens you so?'

The immediate preludes to the motor-drive, therefore, were not auspicious. Alice had a headache when she woke in the morning, and on the young man's arrival her mother proved uncommonly tiresome. She insisted on getting up to say goodbye to her daughter, and when she presented herself on the front lawn Alice realized that a ruby velveteen morning gown, adorned with moulting marabout of a fawn shade that owed more to time than to the dyer, had somehow got back from the dustbin to which she thought she had sent it. The young man was very nice about it, even affecting interest when Mrs Anglesey insisted on telling him the story of the time when she met Edward the Seventh at Monte Carlo; and he dissembled what must have been his emotions when, after he had started his engine, a shriek from her made him stop again.

'Alice! Have you remembered to send them a telegram to say you're coming?'

'No. I don't want to. It'll be a lovely surprise for Jimmy. And I like walking in on servants unexpectedly. It does them good.'

The engine birred again. There was another shriek. ' – and Alice!'

'Oh, mother dear!'

'Be sure you look in the kitchen for the copper pan. It's no use your laughing, my dear, it might be that – ' she had her arm over the side of the car and they had to let her go on talking – 'you know, Mr – Mr? – Mr Acland, is it? – my daughter came here for a little sea air after she's been terribly ill, and my doctor says that though he didn't see her during one of the attacks he thinks it sounds like irritant poisoning. Anything gastric he says wouldn't have been cured so soon. And we can't account for it any way except that I say it is one of the copper pans I gave her for her wedding that they've forgotten to have re-coppered. That's dreadfully dangerous, you know. The Duchess's sister Jane died of it somewhere abroad. So I tell Alice she must look most carefully when she gets home. Oh, my dear Mr Acland, you don't know how ill she was, yellow as a guinea, and such vomiting and diarrhoea . . .'

These are not words one wants shouted to the winds as one drives off, looking one's best, beside a young man of twenty-three who believes one to be very nearly his contemporary, for a journey through the springtime. But the day went very well indeed. They got out of the town very soon and cut up through pinewoods to the heathy hills, presently turning and looking their last on the Channel, where immense pillars of light and darkness marched and countermarched on a beaten silver floor against a backcloth of distant storm. Not long after they were in the New Forest, where the new grass blades were springing up like green fire through the dark, tough matting of heather, and in the same plantations the black ashes affirmed it was still winter, the elms went no farther than to show a few purple flowers, the oaks made their recurring confusion between spring and autumn and were ablaze with red young leaves, and the birches and hawthorns were comfortably emerald.

Up there, as the morning got along, they had their lunch, sitting by a stream that reflected a bank of primroses. Mr Acland told Alice many things. Helping in his father's factory seemed rather grim after Oxford. It was terribly hard work, and no chance of success, only the hope of staving off failure. Life was awfully difficult just now, particularly if you were young. When, for example, was he likely to be able to afford to marry? And he would like to marry. Not that he knew anybody at the moment that he wanted to marry. There had been somebody . . . but that had proved to be a mistake. He supposed he wasn't quite like other people, but he wanted something more than mere prettiness. He wanted ideas . . . broadmindedness . . . sympathy . . .

He kept his eyes on Alice as he spoke, and that was very natural, for she was very nearly a perfect specimen of her type, and time had done almost nothing to spoil her. A touch of silver gave her golden hair a peculiar etherealized burnish, and the oval of her chin was still firm. She had neither crowsfeet nor lines round her mouth, perhaps because she habitually wore an expression of child-like wonder, which kept her blue-grey eyes wide open and her lips parted. She did in actual fact look under thirty, and what was more than that, she looked benevolent, candid, trustworthy, all in terms of grace. Her acts of kindness, her own resolutions of honesty, her Spartan guardianship of secrets, would all, one felt confident, be transacted so that the whole of life would take a more romantic form for evermore. It was no wonder that Mr Acland felt the liveliest satisfaction at her appearance.

His own, however, did not satisfy her nearly so well. She realized this when, speaking as earnestly as he had done, and encouraging him to seek for the perfect mate by relating her own story, she fixed her eyes on his face. Proudly yet modestly she described how she had lived all her life in Camelheath, and admitted that many people might pity her for this, since it would be idle to deny that it was quite the dullest town that could be found within fifty miles of London, but she claimed that nobody in the world could have lived a richer and fuller life than she had, thanks to the circumstance that when she was nineteen the leading solicitor in the town had sent for his nephew to come and be his junior partner, and that the boy had immediately fallen in love with her. 'We have been married nineteen years, and we are as much in love as ever,' she said. The sound of her own words made Jimmy's face appear before her, and she realized with an almost shuddering intensity how much she would rather be looking at him than at Mr Acland. This was no vague, sentimental preference. There was some particular feature in Jimmy's face that gave her deep and delicious pleasure; yet she could not think what it was. Academically, she acknowledged, Mr Acland's broad-browed fairness was more likely to earn points than Jimmy's retiring, quickly-smiling darkness, but that was irrelevant to the intense joy he gave her by this quality which, just for the moment, though she would have liked to tell the boy about it, she could not name.

After she had told her story they got back into the car, feeling very warm and intimate but a little solemn and silent; and about half-past three they stopped in front of the Georgian house at Camelheath which was her home.

'It's a very pretty house,' said Mr Acland.

'We've done a great deal to it,' said Alice.

She rang. Though she always carried a key she hardly ever used it, for she liked to keep Ethel on the alert about door-opening; and this technique had evidently paid, for Ethel confronted them before a minute had passed.

'Why, it's the mistress! And looking so well, too! Why, I never did expect to see you looking so well, ever again mum! Well, the master will be pleased . . .'

Cook, who had been waddling upstairs when the door opened, leaned over the banisters and joined in.

'Well, mum, it's no need to ask if you're feeling better! I didn't never see anybody so far gone come right up again! You're the proper picture of health, now, you are, mum . . .'

She beamed at them while they ran on, regretting that Mr Pemberton wouldn't be able to run over from his office that very minute, because old Mr Bates up at Stickyback Farm had died three days ago, and he had had to go to his funeral this afternoon, assuring her that Mr Pemberton had missed her ever so, that when Ethel had taken him up his blacks for him to change into after lunch he had said, 'Well, thank goodness, we'll be having your mistress with us very soon.' Of course the servants adored her. Well, so they might. She knew she had an almost perfect manner with subordinates, and she really took trouble over training them and thinking out devices for ridding them of their little faults. She would never need to part with her servants, if it was not for the curious vein of madness running through all women of that class, which invariably came out sooner or later in some wild attack of causeless rage. Well, there was some ground for hoping that these two were superior to the rest of their kind. Cook had been with her eighteen months, Ethel nearly three years. Perhaps at last all her kindly efforts were going to be given their reward.

Graciously smiling, she dismissed them and took Mr Acland into the drawing-room. But he would not stay for tea. He had to admit, with some nervous laughter and blushes, that his home was not quite in the direction he had led her to suppose: that, in fact, he had made quite a preposterous detour to drop her at Camelheath, and that he would have to keep quite good time for the rest of his drive to get back for dinner.

'But it's been wonderful to see where you live,' he said, looking round with admiration. Alice was leaning on the Adam mantelpiece, her brilliant fairness and her quiet, good beige suit harmonizing with the pale golden marble. On the fine Chippendale furniture, polished till amber light seemed to well up from the depths of the wood, were bowls of daffodils and early tulips; and between the mellow green brocade curtains a garden tidy to the last leaf showed spring flowers against the definite fine-grained darkness of hoed earth, a quaintly planned rose-garden here and there ruddy with new shoots, and orchard boughs rising frosted with blossom above black yew hedges.

'It's lovely, of course. But can you find people fit to be your friends in this little town?'

'I don't ask for very much, you know,' said Alice bravely, 'and I'm the centre of quite a little world here. Do you see that house over the fields, standing among the elms? My sister, Mrs Walter Fletcher, lives there.'

'It looks as if it was a lovely house, too.'

'It might be. But poor Madge is a funny girl. She isn't a very good manager.' She paused and sighed. 'Then, as you drive out of town, you'll pass a big modern villa just by a fork in the road. That's where my little brother lives. At least he isn't little at all now, in fact he's the local doctor, as our father was before him. But I always think of him as my little brother. I had so much to do with him as a baby, you see, and then I haven't been able to see so much of him in later years. He made a marriage that from some points of view hasn't been a success.' She looked into the distance for a minute and then said simply, 'You know, I used to mind terribly not having any children. But I realize that if I had I wouldn't have been able to do a whole lot of things for others that badly needed doing.'

'I'm sure that's true,' said Mr Acland gravely, 'there aren't enough people like you to go round.'

Soon after that he went. Alice was quite glad, for it would have been an anti-climax for him to have stayed any longer now that they had established this peculiarly deep and reticent sympathy. She walked out with him through the front garden, pausing sometimes to show him her collection of old-fashioned English herbs. 'They have such lovely names,' she said, 'rosemary . . . thyme . . . musk . . . herb-of-grace . . . and dear old lavender. They give one the feeling of an age I believe I would have liked better than this horrid, hustling present day.'

When they said goodbye he held her hand a minute longer than was necessary. 'I wish you'd promise me not to do too many things for other people,' he said. 'I expect that's how you got ill.'

'I'll try and be more sensible,' she smiled.

As soon as she got back to the house she started on a tour of inspection. There was a pile of visiting-cards on the tray on the hall table – odd how many people had called while she was away – and she lifted them to see if there was much dust underneath. But there was none there, or anywhere in the drawing-room, nor in the dining-room, nor in the little library. Everywhere the flowers were fresh, and the water in the vases had been changed that morning, the ash trays had been emptied and polished, and the oak floors shone like brown glass. She went upstairs, running her hand along the fluting of the banisters. When she reached the landing she paused and examined her fingers, but they were still pink and clean.

There was nothing wrong in her bedroom, either. The billows of glazed chintz, biscuit-coloured and sprigged with rosebuds, had evidently just been put up again after a visit to the cleaner's. The silver toilet set on the dressing-table caught the afternoon sun with its brightness; and on the top of the tall-boy the pot-pourri bowl of blue and white porcelain shone with the proper clean milky radiance. She felt a great relief at getting back to her own house, so airy and light and spacious, so austerely empty of anything that was not carefully chosen and fine and mellow, after her mother's cluttered rooms. But she did not linger any longer, though this was perhaps her favourite room in the house, but opened the door into her husband's dressing-room. Perhaps Ethel had let herself be careless there.

Everything was all right there, too, however. There were too many books on the table beside the bed; its Sheraton legs quivered under the strain if one added the weight of a finger tip. She took an armful and put them back on the shelves on the wall, marvelling at the kind of book her quiet Jimmy liked to read: crude, violent tales about tramps, sailors before the mast, trappers of wild animals. But there was nothing else in the room that she could have wished different. The brushes and combs lay in front of his swinging mirror, gleaming and symmetrical; even the sock and handkerchief drawer was in perfect order; and the photograph frames along the mantelpiece almost gave her what she wanted, for it seemed impossible that Ethel could have got them quite as bright as this without neglecting some of her other duties. But as she turned away, her eye was caught by something about the largest photograph, the one standing in the middle of the mantelpiece, which showed her as a bride looking with wide eyes and parted lips over her sheaf of lilies. There was a hair running half across it, under the glass. She took up the frame and slipped out the photograph and then paused in surprise. There was no hair on the glass; but the photograph had been torn almost in two.

'Ethel!' she said angrily, and stretched her hand towards the bell. But she perceived that this damage must have been done long ago. Somebody had tried their best to repair it by pasting the torn edges to a piece of paper beneath, and had made a very neat job of it. It had only become visible now because the paste had shrunk and hardened with age and the torn edges were gaping again. One of Ethel's predecessors must have done it during the frenzies of spring cleaning. 'It must have been Lilian Hall,' thought Alice bitterly. She could remember the names of all her many hated servants. What a pack they were! One could not trust any of them. She peered eagerly into her husband's wardrobe, for she knew that her careful supervision of his valeting had given him such confidence that he never looked at his clothes or shoes. But the suits hung sleekly pressed and completely buttoned from the hangers, and down at the bottom black shoes looked inky, brown shoes glowed with their cornelian tints.

When she saw the grey tweeds she felt a little startled, for he always wore them at the office, until she remembered he had had to change to go to a funeral. The sight of his everyday suit brought him vividly before her, with his dark, thoroughly pleasant but not excessive good looks, his slouch that seemed not so much slackness as a modest retreat from notice, the curious thrilling sense of expectation which, in spite of his quietness, he still gave her after their nineteen years of marriage. She put out her hand and stroked the suit affectionately, and then paused, puzzled because she had felt through the tweed something hard of an odd shape. It was lying along the bottom of his right hand inside breast pocket, and when she fished it out she saw that it was a cylindrical tube of very thick glass fitted with a screw-top, and two-thirds full of white powder.

'Why is Jimmy carrying medicine about with him? Can he be imagining he's ill again?' She wondered not for the first time, why she should be the only perfectly normal person, who never said she was ill except when she was ill, in a family of hypochondriacs. Then her heart contracted. 'Perhaps he really is ill!' She remembered what her mother had suggested, that there might be a faulty cooking vessel in the kitchen which was tainting the food with mineral poison, and she hoped that poor Jimmy had not been keeping from her the news that he had had an attack like hers. To see what the medicine might be, she put her finger in the white powder, and sucked it; but though the haunting bitterness of its taste reminded her of something, she could not put a name to it. But she recognized the container. Old Dr Godstone, who had looked after the local practice during the period after her father had died and before her brother had been ready to take it over, had used these funny glass containers for some of his drugs. How like Jimmy to go on using something made up by that silly old man, which had probably lost whatever virtues it ever had through the lapse of time, instead of going along to Leo and having something really up to date made up! What would Jimmy do without her?

She went down the stairs humming with satisfaction and looked down on the top of Ethel's head in the hall, as she bent over her mistress's suitcase. Then it flashed over her why the house was so tidy. Mrs Anglesey had rung up after all and warned them she was coming back. That had happened once before, shortly after Ethel had first come to her. She had come back and found the house a whirlwind of plate-powder and blacking-brushes with the girl's attempts to catch up with her neglected work. What a talking-to she had given her! The silly girl had cried her eyes out, and would probably have left if her mother hadn't been so ill. Of course she had greatly improved since then, and no doubt she had allowed less to fall in arrears this time, but only some such warning would account for the exquisite order she had found everywhere.

'Ethel!' she called, in a coolly humorous tone.

The girl's sleek head cocked up. 'Yes, mum.'

'The house is beautifully tidy.'

'I'm so glad you found it right, mum.'

'So tidy,' said Alice, who had got down to the hall and was standing with her head lowered so that she could look searchingly into Ethel's doe eyes, while a whimsical little smile played round her lips, 'that I was wondering if Mrs Anglesey hadn't telephoned this morning to warn you I was coming back.'

The girl grew pale and caught her breath for a second, then banged the suitcase down on the floor. 'No, she didn't,' she said. 'The house has been this way all the time you've been away, and would have stayed so if you'd been away twice as long. And if you don't believe me you can call up the Post Office and see if there's been any but local calls put through here all day.'

'Oh, very well, very well,' said Alice, 'but such things have been known to happen, haven't they, before now?'

The girl's eyes blazed. She picked up the suitcase and went up the stairs with it. As she went by her resentment was as tangible as a hot wind.

'What tempers they all have!' thought Alice. 'And how tiresome it is just when I've got home! I wonder if anyone realizes just how much it costs me to run this house in self-restraint and patience.' She sighed as it occurred to her that her own household was only one of her responsibilities, and looked at her wrist-watch. It was improbable that Jimmy would be in before five, she might just as well go over and see how Madge and Leo were getting on, and what new problems she would have to cope with in their households. 'Ah, if I only keep my health!' she said, looking at herself very gravely in the glass over the hall table. It often struck her that there was something terrifying in the way the happiness of so many people, Jimmy, Madge, Walter, and their two children, Leo, Evie, and their four, all depended on her physically fragile self.

She liked the little walk across the fields to Madge's house; every corner of the district was dear to her, for she was one of those people who feel that they live in the nicest house in the nicest town in the nicest county of the nicest country. But she was not so happy when she was inside Madge's garden. If it looked as wild as this in the spring, what would it be like in autumn? She knew Walter had turned off one of the gardeners, but it shouldn't have been necessary to do that, considering his income, if only Madge had been a better manager. It was really impossible to guess what she did with all her money. And if one did have to turn away a gardener, surely one tried to repair the damage by taking on as much of his work as possible. But she wasn't in the least surprised to find Madge lying on the sofa in the drawing-room, wearing an invalidish kind of tea-gown that suggested she had been sticking in the house all day. She looked a very bad pasty colour. It was really dreadful, the way she was letting herself go.

But she jumped up and kissed her sister with quite a show of animation. 'Why, Alice, how marvellous you look! But I thought you weren't coming back till Friday?'

'That's what I had planned, but a young man gave me a lift in his car,' answered Alice. 'We had such a lovely drive across the New Forest. It's been the most glorious day. Haven't you been out at all, dear?'

'As it happens, I haven't.'

'My dear, you ought to make some effort to get over this tendency to lie about. It isn't good for you. You're a most dreadful colour . . .'

'Am I?' asked Madge, with a curious, distressed urgency. She sat up on her cushions and stared at herself in a mirror on the other side of the room.

'Yes, you are,' said Alice, 'most earthy and unwholesome. And it's all because you don't take enough exercise. Look at me!' She laid a finger against her perfect cheek. 'I'm out in all weathers. Really, dear, you must be careful. You know you're five years younger than me, and you look at least five years older.'

'I dare say you're right,' said Madge listlessly. 'But you, dear? Are you quite better? You haven't had any more of those terrible attacks?'

'Not a trace of them. Mother's doctor thought they might have come from some pan in the kitchen that we hadn't had re-coppered. I'm going to look. I certainly hadn't a suspicion of a recurrence while I was away. But I did have another of those awful nightmares, you know. I suppose it's all the worry that weighs down on me.'

'What worry?' asked Madge, rather petulantly.

Alice smiled to herself, but the smile was a little sad. Didn't Madge really know even now how much of her happiness she owed to her sister's readiness to take on what most people would have pushed away as unnecessary worries? How Alice worked over her when she was a girl, always saying to her just as they went into the ballroom, 'Now do hold yourself properly and try to hide those dreadful elbows,' and keeping near her to see that she was behaving properly and saying the right things to her partners, and on the way home telling her all the things she had done wrong! And then, since Madge's marriage to Walter, Alice had been on hand day in, day out, always ready to point out faults in her housekeeping, to explain just why her parties had not been successful, to suggest where she was going wrong in bringing up her children. There was no use pretending it had always been an easy task. Madge had a childish intolerance of criticism, she sometimes became quite rude.

'Well, Madge,' Alice began quietly, but Madge was asking, 'How did you leave mother?'

'Oh, mother's all right,' said Alice indulgently, 'it's funny how she's quite happy muddling along.'

'I don't see that she does much muddling,' said Madge. 'She knows how she likes to live, and she lives that way.'

'Oh, my dear!' exclaimed Alice. 'I call it a terrible muddle. Just think what I found her doing ...' But Madge cut in quickly, 'Here are the children coming in from their walk, and please, please, don't encourage Betty!'

'My dear, I think you're so wrong about Betty,' Alice started to explain, but the children were with them. Little Godfrey ran straight to his mother; there was really something very morbid and effeminate about the way he always clung to her, and he ought to have been told to be polite and run and kiss his aunt instead of staring at her with great vacant eyes. But Betty went at once to Alice, who held out her arms. The child had a touch of her own brilliant fairness and neatness and decision, which was urgently needed in this dingy, feckless household. It was really very strange, the way that Madge did not seem to appreciate having such an attractive little girl. She supposed that it was just such an unreasonable aversion, probably springing from some odd pre-natal cause, as her own mother felt towards her. Every now and then she gave Betty a little smile, to show that there was a special understanding between them; but really she regretted having done it before long, for the poor child began to make confidences to her, which seemed to exasperate Madge. When Betty said that she had been sure her aunt would get better, because she had prayed for her every night, Madge had been visibly annoyed; and when Betty carried on the conversation along these lines to the point of describing a lecture on Indian missions that had been given at their local school and expressing a hope that she herself might become a missionary some day, Madge called sharply, 'Annie, Annie!'

The nursemaid hurried in from the hall.

'Take the children straight up to the nursery,' Madge told her, and leaned back on the cushions with her eyes shut until the din of protest had died, and she was alone with her sister again. 'I asked you not to encourage Betty,' she said. 'I really don't see why you should come here and make my family talk the idiom of very old volumes of *The Quiver.*'

'My dear, I never heard such nonsense,' Alice objected. 'If modern ideas have come to such a pass that a little girl of ten can't show a nice healthy interest in religion . . .'

'Betty's interest in religion isn't nice or healthy,' said Madge. 'It's sheer priggishness and exhibitionism.'

'If you used shorter words and didn't try to be so scientific, and looked after your children in an old-fashioned way, it might be better. Must you have that untidy girl from the village as a nursemaid? I refused to let her come in and help Ethel last winter, she's so slatternly.'

'We know she's not ideal. But we can't afford anyone better.'

'But, my dear, why can't you? Your money seems just to run through your fingers. It isn't fair to Walter, and it's simply cruel to the children. They ought to have a nice, well-trained woman to look after them and teach them pretty manners.'

She waited for any defence that might be forthcoming, but Madge had fallen into one of her sulky silences. 'Well,' said Alice at last, 'you're a funny set, you new-fashioned mothers, I must say. Goodness knows what I shall find when I get to Leo's.'

'Oh, are you going to Leo's?' said Madge. 'I'll go down the avenue with you if you like.' She was on her feet at once and moving towards the door, while Alice thought in amazement, 'Why, I believe she's trying to get me out of the house, and I haven't been here for much more than half an hour! How queer and . . . petty!'

But she tried to conceal her feelings as they walked under the trees to the high road. 'Nobody can say I am tactless,' she thought, as she passed by the patches of rough grass and weeds without pointing them out to her sister. 'And I'm not saying anything about how absurd it is that she should be wearing those trailing things that she has to hold up round her when she gets a breath of fresh air, instead of being out and about in sensible country clothes. I'll just give her a word about pulling herself together when we part.' But when they came to the gate she forgot, for Madge let her skirts fall and put both her arms round her giving her a hug as if they were children again.

'Dear Alice, I'm so glad you are better,' she said, and stood with her head on one side for a minute admiring her. 'I love to see you looking so young and pretty. It was horrid when you were ill. You ought always to be well and happy.'

'You're crushing my coat,' said Alice; but she was pleased. 'I think she is really grateful, though she's so odd and ungracious,' she said to herself as she hurried along to Leo's house. 'Well, it's encouraging.'

She received no such encouragement when she arrived there. The front door was open, and when she passed into the hall she saw Colin, the eldest boy, walking up the staircase in the undisciplined manner of the bookish young, taking an immense time to mount from step to step because he had his nose deep in an open book.

'Colin!' she called.

He turned round, but did not answer the greeting. For a minute he stared blankly at her, his black forelock falling over his brows – heaven knew why Evie let her children go about with their hair that length – and his mouth stupidly open. Then a look of consternation spread over his face, he slammed the open book, and without saying a word rushed upstairs two steps at a time.

'Well, of all the manners!' breathed Alice. She heard her brother's short, dry, tired cough from the surgery, farther down the passage, and made a step in that direction. 'Leo really ought to be told,' she thought furiously. But just then her sister-in-law came to the top of the stairs. She stared down on Alice incredulously, turned and whispered, 'Hush!' as if she were quelling a tumult in the shadows behind her, and then ran downstairs saying, 'Well, Alice, this is a surprise! We thought you weren't to be with us till Friday!'

How hopelessly odd she was, how neurotic and unstable, the very last person to be a doctor's wife. She was trembling and breathless as if she had had a severe shock instead of merely receiving a visit from a sister-in-law. It was no wonder the children were such unattractive little savages.

'A young man gave me a lift in his motor-car,' said Alice, trying to pass things off lightly, 'and I thought I'd come along and see how you all were. How are you, Evie? That's right. And Leo? No symptoms, I hope?'

'None,' said Evie, 'absolutely none.' She said everything

with such odd over-emphasis that it really made one feel uncomfortable.

'Can I see him?' said Alice, moving towards the surgery.

'No, you can't,' said Evie, stepping between her and the surgery door. 'He's out. He's gone to Cadeford for a consultation.'

There was a minute's silence.

'Has he, Evie?' asked Alice, raising her eyebrows and smiling.

Again there came the sound of Leo's high, dry, tired cough.

'I'll come some other day,' said Alice, turning to the front door, 'when I'm not in the way.'

Evie put out a weak, shaking hand. 'It's only that he's so busy . . .'

'Oh, my dear, I understand,' said Alice. 'It's a wife's duty to protect her husband. And anyway you of all people must know by this time that I'm not one of those people that bear grudges.'

With a frank smile she held out her hand and after Evie had gripped and released it she let it rest for a minute on a half-inch of gaping seam in the other's jumper. 'I wish you'd let me send you my little sewing-woman one day. Let me ring up and find out what day would be convenient. It would be a real pleasure if you'd let me treat you to that. I always think one feels much calmer and happier when one's really neat and tidy.'

She found herself walking back to her house at a swinging pace. 'I mustn't be angry with her,' she kept on telling herself. 'I know there's nothing the matter with the woman but jealousy, and it's a shame that Leo's children should be brought up as ill-mannered little gutter-snipes, but I must remember that she can't help being what she is. It's only by chance that I was born what I am instead of like her.' When a turn of the road brought her house in sight tears of relief stood in her eyes. There, in her beautiful, orderly spacious rooms, she could shut out all these awful people who loved quarrelling and unkindness. Already the afternoon sun was low over the fields, and it would soon be time to turn on the lights. She liked to think of that, because it had occurred to her once, when she had driven home later and seen from far off the rosy glow of her curtained windows, how fortunate, how right it was that her house could send brightness shining out into the dark, but that the dark could not come into her house and dim the brightness. In one's own home one was safe. She would take off her suit the minute she got in and put on a soft, lacy dressing-gown and put eau-de-Cologne on her forehead, and lie down on the couch in her bedroom till Jimmy came.

But when she got home she was waylaid by the cook. 'Might I speak to you, mum?'

She followed her into the big, clean, airy, blue-and-white kitchen. 'Well?' she said, looking round. 'I'm sure you've nothing to grumble about in your kitchen, Cook! It's really a picture. Everything you could possibly want . . .'

'Yes, indeed, mum,' said Cook. 'But I was going to tell you we'd forgotten to say Mr Robert Norman's coming to dinner with the master, and I wanted to ask you if I should cook something special for you, or if you'd have what they do.'

'What are you giving them?'

'Artichoke soup, cod, saddle of mutton, and apple dumpling, and welsh rarebit.'

'Oh, Cook,' said Alice, 'what a dreadful dinner! So dull and so heavy! After all the trouble I've taken working out menus with you, you really shouldn't give the master dinners like that just because you think I'm going to be out of the way.'

'I wouldn't do no such thing,' answered Cook, with her colour rising, 'the master's eaten full as dainty every night you been away as when you was here. But Mr Robert Norman likes to eat when he eats, and it was for him the master ordered this very dinner. I ain't nothing to do with it, 'cept cook it best I can.'

'I can't think he really wanted this awful dinner,' said Alice. 'Are you sure you haven't made a mistake? Such things have been known to happen, you know, Cook. We're none of us perfect. Do you remember when just after you came you sent up a rice pudding at a dinner party when I ordered ice pudding? That was funny. Fortunately they were all very nice about it. Oh, don't be offended, Cook. We all make mistakes sometimes.'

'We do, mum,' said Cook. 'And shall I cook you anything separate?'

'Well, I certainly won't be able to eat much of this terrible meal,' smiled Alice. 'But I'll try to get along on the cod and some of the apples out of the dumpling. And then before I go to bed I'll have my usual glass of hot chocolate malted milk.'

'I've got a new brand of that for you,' said Cook. '"The Devon Dairymaid", instead of Harrison & Cooper's. The man at the stores told me he had it, and I ordered a small tin to try.'

'Oh, Cook, why did you do that? Haven't you a tin of the old sort left?'

'No, mum. It was all finished when you left. But it was twice you complained that the old kind tasted bitter.'

'Yes, but I've tried this new kind when I was staying with Mrs Anglesey, and it's horrid. It's just as dark as the other, but it has hardly any chocolate flavour, and you know I can only get down the malted milk if I don't taste it. I do think it's a pity you did that without asking me.'

'Well, I'll get a tin of the old in the morning.'

'Yes, but there's the new tin wasted, and every penny counts nowadays. And there's tonight. I'll have to do without one of the very few things I enjoy. But send it up just the same. Now do remember not to do this sort of thing. The times when you should show initiative you never do, giving people the same dreadful dinners I've taught you not to do, and then you go and make a perfectly unnecessary purchase like this. It's heartbreaking, Cook.' She repeated, 'Yes, it's simply heartbreaking'; but Cook made no answer, so she moved towards the door, but was plucked back by a recollection.

'Oh, by the way, Cook, are you sure that there's none of the copper pans that need re-coppering?'

'Quite sure, mum. We had the man to look at them only a few months ago. And anyway I'm cooking more and more in the fireproof and the aluminium.'

'That can't be it, then. You know, Mrs Anglesey's doctor thought that my attacks might have been not gastric at all, but due to irritant poisoning. And the only way we could think that I could have been poisoned was through some of the copper vessels having worn out. I can't think of any other way, can you, Cook?'

'No, mum, I can't. If you was a lady with a nagging tongue, always finding fault with everything, and making trouble where there's only kindness meant, then I suppose we might be all wanting to drop poison in your food. But you aren't like that, are you, mum?'

Alice's heart nearly stopped. Cook's face was bland, but her tone was unmistakably insolent. What was the reason for this madness that afflicted one and all of the servant class?

'We'd better talk about this tomorrow, Cook,' she said quietly, and left the kitchen. She supposed that they would both be going now, Ethel as well as Cook. How could they be so causelessly malevolent as to do this when she had just come home? The tears were rising in her eyes and she was going blindly towards the staircase when she heard an exclamation, and turned to see that the front door had opened and Jimmy was standing on the step outside, paralysed with amazement in the act of pulling off his gloves.

She ran to him and stretched her arms up his tallness. 'Yes, I'm back two whole days too early! But a nice young man gave me a lift in his car!' Under her lips his face felt worn and cold; but clients' funerals were always trying. 'Oh, my dear, I'm so much better!'

'I'm glad of that,' said Jimmy. 'I'm very glad of that.'

'And, oh, I'm so pleased you've come in!' she cried. 'It's been so horrid ever since I got back. Madge was horrid to me except for a little bit at the end, and Evie was horrid, and Colin was a hateful little beast, and Ethel was horrid, and now Cook's been horrid. Why does nobody but me want to be happy and live in peace?'

Jimmy put his arm round her shoulder and led her into the house, looking down on her tenderly as one might on a crippled child. 'Poor little Alice,' he said, 'Poor little Alice.'

II

Ethel had lit the log-fire in the drawing-room, and it spat at them playfully while they crouched on the rug, Jimmy stretching out one hand to the warmth while Alice rubbed the other.

'It'll be a glorious blaze in a minute,' said Alice, 'and just as well, for you're simply icy, my darling. Was it too dreadful at the funeral?'

'No, not really,' said Jimmy. 'It wasn't too cold, or too harrowing, even. They'd all been expecting the old chap to go for ages so nobody felt it as a great shock.'

'I like the younger son best, I hope he stays on at the farm, he's an awfully nice boy. Oh, Jimmy, the young man who brought me home was so nice. And it was miles out of his way really. He's coming to see us some day, you will like him. He was so sweet and patient with Mother, too. Just think, she would not let us get off this morning until she'd told him the whole of that interminable story about how she met King Edward at Monte Carlo.'

'But perhaps he liked hearing it.'

'Oh, my dear, who could? Who cares about such things

nowadays. Besides, it's rather vulgar, I always think. But, darling, I do appreciate the way you turn a blind eye to my family's failings. I know perfectly well they're awful . . .'

'But, Alice, I don't think your family's awful.'

'You chivalrous darling, you know it is. Anyway Madge and Evie were pretty awful this afternoon, I can tell you.'

'What did they do?'

'Oh, Madge was lying on the sofa looking horribly pasty and unwholesome. She hadn't put her foot outside the house all day. I can't understand why she's letting herself go. And then she's so silly about Betty. Just because the child's got a natural leaning to religion . . .'

'But, Alice, it's Madge's foot and Madge's house. If she doesn't want to put the one outside the other, surely it's her business. And surely Betty's her child and her business too?'

'But, Jimmy dear, Madge is my sister. You haven't any family feeling. You don't understand that I can't watch my sister doing everything wrong and just let her do it.'

'Why not? She's thirty-five, darling. Time she learned to save her own soul.'

'Nonsense, dear. You'd never have any civilization at all if you didn't have the people who knew best teaching all the others what to do.'

'Oh, Alice, dear!'

'Well, it's true, darling. And that's why I won't give up going to Leo's house, however rude that woman is. Do you know what she did this evening? She looked me straight in the face and told me that Leo was out, when I could hear him coughing in the surgery! Did you ever hear of a wife being so jealous of her husband's sister? But I'm not going to give up. I've got a duty to that household. I must see the children get some sort of upbringing. That Colin's a perfect little savage.'

Jimmy had got up and was standing above her, lighting his pipe. 'Alice, Colin belongs to Leo and Evie, not to you.'

'But, darling, you don't understand! If they can't look

after him properly then I must do what I can,' she answered absently. She loved the look of his face, lit red by the flame.

He sat down in the arm-chair and beckoned her to come and sit on his knee. 'Alice, I wish you'd promise me something. It would really do a lot to make me happy. Will you do it?'

'I'll do anything for you, darling.'

'Then promise me to leave Madge and Walter, and Leo and Evie alone for a bit. Don't visit them unless they ask you. Don't try to manage their affairs.'

Alice stood up. 'Jimmy, how absurd you are!' she exclaimed. 'I've never heard you say anything so silly before! Anyone would think I was tactless or interfering.'

'That's what I want you to promise.'

She stared at him with eyes made immense by tears. 'Jimmy, you don't think I'm tactless and interfering, do you? Because I couldn't bear to think you so completely misunderstood my character! As for being tactless, that is absurd, because if there is one good quality that I've got, it's tact. I've always been able to handle people without hurting their feelings. And as for interfering, I simply loathe it. But after all Madge and Leo are my sister and brother, and the trouble is that since they were babies they've depended on me for everything, and they'd never get anywhere if I didn't push them.' She suddenly dropped on her knees and looked up into his face with an expression of panic. 'They don't think I'm tactless and interfering, do they? Because I couldn't bear that, it would be so ungrateful of them! And you know I've thought of them, all my life long, far more than I've thought of myself.'

Sobs began to shake her. 'Oh, you poor child!' said Jimmy, and drew her close to him. 'I know you have. But people are funny after they've grown up and married and got children. They like to be left alone.'

'But they couldn't think that,' said Alice, the tears running down her cheeks, 'unless they'd stopped loving me.'

'My dear, I'm sure they haven't. But I want you to make that promise all the same. Just humour them. Just let them be silly. To save your nerves.'

'I'd rather do what was right than save my nerves.'

'To please me, then,' said Jimmy. He took her by the shoulders and smiled into her eyes, his dark, secret smile. 'I might beat you if you didn't,' he told her gravely.

He always made her laugh when he said that. 'Silly!' she giggled, and he crushed her suddenly in his arms. 'I promise!' she whispered in his ear, and disentangled herself just as Ethel brought in tea. 'But all the same,' she said, to cover her embarrassment because she knew her hair was rumpled, 'I think they're preposterous if they are offended.'

For tea there was a whole jarful of strawberry jam, which neither of them liked very much, and only a little cherry jam, which they both liked so well that the household supply rarely lasted thus late into the spring. It might have been thought there was enough of this for two, but she knew how thick he liked to pile it on his buttered toast, so she gave it all to him, and took the precaution of spreading it for him and putting it on his plate, so that he had no chance to be unselfish. Then, when the tea had been cleared away, she went and sat on his knee again and they were both silent, looking into the blazing wood.

'Lovely your hair is,' he said at last. 'You're a lovely child, and capable of being noble, even about cherry jam.'

She leaned farther back, putting her face close to his. 'Yet you haven't kissed me properly yet,' she said.

'Haven't I?'

'No. You let me kiss you in the hall. But you haven't kissed me.'

He murmured something under his breath and bent his lips towards her. But she twisted out of his grasp.

'Why did you say that under your breath?'

'What did I say?'

'You know perfectly well what you said. You said, "Forgive me". Why should I forgive you? Oh, Jimmy, what have you been doing?'

'Nothing. I didn't mean anything. They were just words that passed through my mind. Something I've been reading.'

'Jimmy, really? Is that really true? You haven't been unfaithful to me?'

He shook his head. 'No. I couldn't have done that, even if I'd wanted to. I've thought of you continually nearly all the time you've been away. No husband ever was haunted more steadily by the presence of his absent wife.'

Her storm of suspicion weakened. 'Is that true?' she asked piteously. 'Are you sure? But then what did you want me to forgive you for?'

'I wanted you to forgive me for being me,' he said, 'and having to be what I am, and do what I have done.' A smile passed over his lips. 'Just as you might ask me to forgive you for being you.'

She laughed happily at the idea, and settled down in his arms again, to receive his embrace. After his mouth had left hers, she nodded her head wisely. 'Yes, you love me. But how tired you are.'

He muttered, lying quite relaxed, his head against her breast. 'Yes, that's just it. I love you. But I'm so tired that I don't know what to do . . . I don't know how to carry on . . .'

'My poor darling, there's nothing worrying you in your business, is there?'

'Nothing.' She could hardly hear his voice, he was evidently just dropping off to sleep.

'Well, everything else will be all right now I'm home.'

'I hope so . . . I hope so . . .' She saw his hand drowsily groping for the table beside the chair, to touch wood.

They sat thus, with the twilight deepening on them to darkness, the firelight showing redder and more comforting. Sometimes they sighed in contentment, sometimes one or the other began to murmur a phrase of endearment, but did not finish it, sometimes they slept. Then all of a sudden, the room was flooded with light and Ethel was saying, 'It's seven o'clock, and time you were dressing, because Mr Norman do come early and no mistake. And I'd like you to have a look at the table, mum, to see if you think I did it right.'

She spoke with the benignity of conscious pride, which they understood when they stood in the dining-room and saw the shining glory she had made.

'I put the tall daffies at the corner,' Ethel told them expansively. 'Nobody else done a table that way, that I ever see, but it gives you the good of them without you having to crane your necks to see who you're eating opposite. And I put the little dwarf daffies in the middle.'

'My word, you've made a lovely thing of it, Ethel,' said Jimmy. 'The flowers aren't so many that the table looks crowded, but it's a grand show.'

Alice said, 'Wait a minute,' moved a fork a little to the left, leaned over and shifted the linen centrepiece under the dwarf daffodils a fraction of an inch, then moved back and surveyed the table with great satisfaction. 'Yes, that's very nice.'

Jimmy sighed, very deeply. He seemed to be terribly over-tired.

Ethel, blossoming under the warmth of praise, continued, 'There's so many daffodils out now that even old Wray can't be stingy about bringing them up to the house, though he'd do anything to keep all his flowers to hisself in the garden.'

Alice said stiffly, 'Well, Ethel, we've all of us so many faults that I don't think it becomes any of us to make fun of others.'

There was a minute's silence, before Ethel swung round and went out of the room. 'I say, I don't think you need have said that,' said Jimmy. 'She didn't mean to be ill-natured. She just said it as you or I might have said it.' He had dropped into a chair and looked very white and lined.

'Nonsense, darling,' said Alice, 'you can't have servants talking against each other. But, oh, Jimmy, you do look tired. I wish this old man wasn't coming.'

'Oh, I like old Norman. We get on awfully well together. He's been in a lot while you've been away. The nurse who looks after his imbecile child isn't well, and Mrs Norman has to take charge in the evenings a good deal. So he's been glad to come along and have something to eat, and play a bit of two-handed bridge.'

'Funny darlings you must have been together,' said Alice. 'Let's go and dress.'

It was quite a successful dinner, Alice thought. She put on the new turquoise dress she had bought when she was staying with her mother, and the old man's eyes had brightened when he saw her. He was a gentleman farmer, the wealthiest and most important of his kind in the district, and there was some seignorial dignity about him, as well as the ashes of romantic charm, for, till he had been sobered by the tragic issue of his marriage, he had been a famous beau and blood. Even now that he was silver-haired, he made every woman he spoke to feel a little better-looking than she really was, and Alice found herself glowing as she entertained him, and forgetting to be sorry that she and Jimmy were not alone. But Mr Norman seemed to tire very soon. His frosty grey eyes stopped sparkling and grew heavy, he talked less and less, and though they had started bridge he rose and left at twenty minutes to ten.

'What a handsome old thing he is, in his weather-beaten way,' said Alice, when Jimmy came back from seeing him out. 'But does he always leave so early?'

Jimmy went over to the fire and kicked a log down with his heel. 'No, I've known him stay quite late.'

'I expect that dreadful heavy dinner made him sleepy,' said Alice. 'I was sure when I heard what you'd ordered that it was a mistake.'

Jimmy sat down in an armchair, and stared into the fire. 'No, I don't think it was the dinner. But I think it was a pity you tried to teach him those new Culbertson rules. He's an old man, and he'd probably been out on horseback since eight o'clock this morning, and he just wanted to fiddle round with the cards a bit.'

'Oh, my dear, he can't have found that a strain! And anyway, what's the use of doing anything if you don't do it well? Still I probably was wrong. But you forget, when you've been away, what clods the best of these people are.'

'Yes, clods,' said Jimmy, 'without brains, without feelings, without sensitiveness. I think it was a pity too that you told him he ought to take his child to that brain surgeon at Geneva.'

'Well, why shouldn't I? He's a wonderful man. Mother knows somebody who told her about the most marvellous cure . . .'

'I dare say,' said Jimmy, 'but you see Norman and his wife took the child there six years ago, and it wasn't any good.'

'But why didn't he tell me so? What an extraordinary thing of him to do, to let me go on talking about it and never say a thing!'

'I expect he likes so little hearing the child talked about that when people start he just lets them say what they have to say and finish, and doesn't prolong it by getting up an argument.'

'Well, if he feels like that even when people are trying to help him, I can't help it,' said Alice, 'but I must say I'm disappointed to think the old man's so ungracious.'

'And I think it was a pity, too,' said Jimmy, 'that you told him so much of the ways you've reformed me since we were married, the way I naturally forget everything and lose everything unless you look after me. You see, he's thinking of handing over all his business to me, because he isn't satisfied with the firm of solicitors at Rosford that have handled his affairs up till now. The old partners are too old, and the young partners are too young, and he thinks I'm about right.'

'Well, my dear, nothing I said can have made much

difference. He can't have taken it as seriously as all that. And I did say I'd got you over all those things.'

'Oh, I don't think he thought I really do lose and forget things more than most people,' said Jimmy, 'but I think he thought that a man whose wife talked about him like that couldn't be very good stuff.'

'What a funny, old-fashioned point of view!' laughed Alice. 'But I wish you'd dropped me a hint of all this. I might have said a few things that would have just turned the scales.'

'I know. I was afraid of that,' said Jimmy. 'I think he might not have liked having his mind made up for him.'

'If he's such a hopeless old crotchet as that,' said Alice, 'I wonder you want to have anything to do with him.'

'Well, for one thing, I really do want some new business,' said Jimmy. 'It's odd how people don't come to me. It's almost as if one or other of us were unpopular in the county. And for another thing, I'm fond of old Norman, and I'd like him to feel confidence in me for his own sake. It's worrying for an old man to have a wife thirty years younger than himself, with a big estate and the responsibility of the child, and not feel that he's put some reliable person to look after her. I wanted to do that for him.'

'Well, my dear, it's certain to come all right,' said Alice. 'We must just have him to dinner again, and I shall be specially nice to him. Are you coming to bed now, dear?'

'No, dear,' said Jimmy, 'not at once. I want to stay down here for five minutes and think something out.'

He looked so boyish and pathetic, as he lay back in the chair with his long legs stretching out in front of him and his dark hair rumpled, and his perplexed eyes staring into the fire, that she had to bend over and kiss him as she passed. 'Poor little boy!' she murmured in his ear. 'You're sure you've got no special business worries? You will tell me if you have, won't you? If you've got into a muddle, it's quite likely I shall be able to think of some way out.'

'Thank you, dear,' said Jimmy, 'there's nothing special. It's only that I'm living under a strain, and I've got to make up my mind to bear that strain.'

'But what strain, darling?'

'Oh, just these difficult times, these difficult times.'

She kissed the top of his head. 'Poor little overwrought fellow!' she crooned, then straightened herself. 'Don't be too long coming up to bed.'

She enjoyed undressing in her own lovely room after having been away so long. Humming to herself she kicked off her satin shoes and peeled off her stockings, and stood on the rug in front of the fire, digging her bare toes into the clean, smooth, clipped lamb's pelt, as she cast her several skins of silk. She liked the mountainous softness of her bed, with its fluffy apricot blankets and honey-coloured taffeta quilt, and the secret, sacred look the hangings gave the shadowed pillows, and the rosy, lacy nightgown they had spread out for her. In her mind's eye she saw her gaunt, voluble, wild-haired mother pacing her utilitarian room where there was a mahogany bed and a big round table with a reading lamp and many books on it, and she shuddered. 'Will I ever get old?' she thought, 'and stop matching my lovely room? I suppose I will some day, and quite soon too, for I am not young. It will be awful. But Jimmy will be nice to me, he will somehow spare me the worst of it. He always tries to spare me things, he is always kind. I thought he was a little fault-finding this evening, but that was only because he was tired. Oh, I am a lucky woman, I ought to be very kind to other people out of gratitude.' Grave with this reflexion she went into the bathroom, and as she lay in the warm waters a way she could be kind occurred to her. It was such a good plan that she longed to work it out at once, and a pricking urge to activity swept through her body, so that she had to jump out of the bath almost at once and rub herself with hot towels. Then she heard Jimmy go into the bedroom, and she flung on her dressing-gown and hurried to tell him the news.

'Jimmy,' she said, sitting down on the long stool in front of the dressing-table and brushing her hair with long, vigorous strokes, because her inspiration had filled her with vigour. 'I've had an idea.'

He had opened the dressing-room door, but he turned. 'Well, it suits you, darling,' he said, and came and stood by her, smiling as he watched her glowing face in the mirror, the flash of her arm as she passed the brush to and fro, and the changing lights in her hair.

'Listen,' she explained, 'I've been thinking over Madge. She can't go on as she's doing. I can't stand by and see my sister turning into a dowdy, middle-aged frump years before her time. Darling, do you realize she's a whole five years younger than I am? I must do something about it, and to-morrow morning I will. I'm going straight to Walter, and I'm going to suggest that he sends Madge for a month to that wonderful sanatorium near Dresden where they did Mrs Lennox so much good. It's just what she wants. They give you massage and baths, and above all they won't let you be soft. They get you out of bed at seven o'clock and make you do exercises in the pinewoods in a bathing dress, no matter how cold it is. She'll come back a different person. And while she's away I'll take on Betty and Godfrey – I am sure I could bring out Betty quite a lot, they don't understand her – and maybe I could look into the housekeeping books and see where the waste is, why there's always this air of pinching and scraping where there's ample money. Don't you think it's a grand idea?'

Jimmy sat down beside her on the stool. He took the hairbrush from her and laid it down on the dressing-table, then gripped both her hands with his. 'Alice,' he said. 'Have you forgotten the promise you gave me this evening, in front of the fire? Didn't you give me your word you wouldn't interfere with Madge and Walter, or Leo and Evie any more?'

'But, heavens alive, this isn't interference!'

'My darling, what else is it?'

'Oh, it may be interference, strictly speaking, but you must admit that sometimes one just has to interfere. If Madge fell down in the road and there was a car coming along, surely you'd let me drag her out of the way?'

'Alice, won't you stop doing this thing if I tell you I'd rather you didn't?'

'No, I don't think I will. I hate the way you've suddenly started objecting to everything I do that's kind. And anyway I don't think it would be fair to Madge not to do it.'

'Then,' said Jimmy, 'I'll have to tell you a whole lot of things that we all rather wanted to keep from you.' He got up and walked to the fire and stood on the hearth, looking down on her intently. 'Alice, you're all wrong about Madge and Walter. If you went to Walter tomorrow and told him that Madge ought to go to a sanatorium in Dresden, it would be monstrously cruel of you. Because he couldn't afford it.'

'But, darling, it wouldn't cost much more than a hundred pounds.'

'Walter hasn't got a hundred pounds.'

'What do you mean, Jimmy? You must be mad. You know perfectly well they've at least three thousand pounds a year.'

'They had, Alice. They haven't now. We live in bad times, and the worst of it is we've come straight to them out of times that were too good. About six years ago, when prices were rocketing, Walter sold out all his safe stuff, his gilt-edged, and bought things like steel and oil. They aren't worth a tenth of what they were. I tell you Walter hasn't got a hundred pounds. He owes quite a number of hundred pounds to the banks and the income-tax people.'

'But, Jimmy, Walter must have been atrociously reckless. I do think when he had a wife and children he ought to have been more careful. I do think someone ought to speak to him . . .'

'Anyone who spoke to him would be a meddling fool that likes to kick a man when he's down. The whole world did what he did. It seemed the only sensible thing to do at the time. I'm sorry, Alice, but there isn't a single way of looking at the situation which affords one the slightest justification for feeling superior to Walter.'

'Well, goodness knows, one wouldn't want that. Oh, I am sorry for them. But I do hope Madge is doing everything she can . . .'

'She's doing marvels. I've been over all the books. There isn't a woman living who could have been pluckier and more sensible. Madge is all right.'

'I'm glad. Dear little Madge. But what I don't understand is why they didn't tell me? It seems a little cold and inconsiderate, when they know how fond I am of them. I can't help feeling just a weeny bit hurt . . .'

'They're hurt themselves, Alice. Walter's a proud man, and he cares for his family. He wanted to give them the best of everything, and leave them to carry on the life his stock have always lived, in the house where they've been for a couple of centuries. Now he can't give them anything but the bare necessities, they may not be able to go on living in that house. They're struggling nobly, but they may be beaten yet. While they're struggling they don't want anyone to talk to them about the tragedy, to suggest that if they had acted differently it needn't have happened, that they aren't taking it as sensibly as they might, that this and that little treat they give themselves when they're at breaking-point is an unjustifiable extravagance. That would just put the lid on their torture.'

'Yes, but I obviously wouldn't be that someone. I only would have tried to help. Well, I am sorry!' She sighed and took up her hairbrush again.

Jimmy came back and sat beside her. He put his arm round her body, and kissed her ear, and she rested her cheek against his. He whispered to her and she said, 'What, darling?' but then recoiled from him with annoyance, exclaiming. 'No, of course I won't speak about it to them. I wouldn't care to, since they haven't chosen to tell me themselves.'

'That's a good girl,' said Jimmy.

Alice went on brushing her hair, and presently she smiled at the dark face she saw smiling at her in the mirror. 'Aren't we lucky to have no worries?' she said. 'Really, we couldn't be more at peace with ourselves and the world. But I suppose that's partly our own doing. We might have had lots of worries if we'd given way to them. I think I shall say something to Madge, you know. That's what she's doing, giving way to her troubles. Just because Walter's lost some money and she has to be careful, she needn't lie about on sofas looking dowdy and listless – Jimmy, Jimmy, what are you doing? Let go my wrist!'

'Alice, won't you please take it from me that there isn't any necessity to say anything at all to Madge, that she's one of the finest women who ever lived, and that she doesn't need any advice at all?'

'No, I can't take it from you, because I can see with my own eyes, and – Jimmy, you're hurting!'

He got up and went back to his place on the hearthrug, and looked down on her again with that queer, intent look.

'Jimmy, what's the matter with you? Your eyes are blazing! And you haven't said you're sorry!'

He did not seem to hear. 'Alice,' he said, 'have you ever read a fairy story where the princess lived in a beautiful palace, with a beautiful garden, and was warned by her fairy godmother that she could enjoy all this happiness for ever only if she didn't pick one particular flower, or eat one particular fruit? If she ignores that prohibition, she loses the whole thing. Out palace, out garden, out princess. It's quite an important story. You'll even find it in the Bible. And you sometimes find it coming true in real life.'

'Jimmy, what are you talking about?'

'The point is that the fairy godmother's perfectly right, though there's no reason on the surface to show that she is. When the princess picks that flower or eats that fruit, the whole thing really does fall to pieces. If I ask you to take me as a fairy godmother, and ask you not to speak to Madge about being listless, will you remember and grant me this favour? Do it, do it, darling. Let's pretend we're people in a fairytale.'

Alice turned her back on him and stared into the mirror, and presently saw him reflected just behind her. 'Well,' she began, but he said, 'No. You needn't make any promise or half-promise. I can see from your face that you'd speak to Madge, if I went down on my knees, if the heavens opened. You couldn't possibly give up such a good opportunity of ordering somebody about, of making them feel inferior to you, of making their destiny seem so that if it worked out well they'd have to thank you for it, and not themselves.'

'Jimmy!'

'Now listen. Madge doesn't lie on sofas and look dowdy because she's a sloven. She does it because she's ill. So ill that it's an effort for her to walk, to put on her clothes.'

'Jimmy, you're dreaming! Madge has always made a fuss about little ailments, but she's as strong as a horse.'

'Alice, Leo arranged for her to see a specialist six months ago, and I sneaked up to town to go with them. He said there wasn't any doubt. She's got pernicious anaemia.'

'Oh, my dear, I know all about that. There's a wonderful new treatment for pernicious anaemia. I'll soon see to it that . . .'

'Alice, there isn't anything you can see to. There is a wonderful new treatment for pernicious anaemia, which cures everybody except two or three people out of every hundred. And the trouble is that Madge seems to be one of those two or three people. She's persevering with the treatment, and the tide may turn at any moment, but up till now she's been getting worse and worse. Do you understand? She's very, very ill.'

Alice stood up. Her hairbrush slipped from her hand to the floor. 'Oh, poor little Madge! My poor little Madge!' she whispered.

Jimmy gathered her into his arms. 'I knew you'd feel

pretty bad when you heard that,' he said. 'I've always known you really cared for her a lot. Cry if you want to, dear.'

But she swallowed her tears and drew away from him briskly, saying, 'But we ought to do something! What can we do for her?'

'Heaven's alive, why should we have to do anything? Why must you always try to be omnipotent, and shove things about? Tragic things happen sometimes that we just have to submit to. We can't do anything in this particular case except stand by and be sorry for little Madge, and hope that the tide will turn, and give her as many presents and treats as we can. And above all we mustn't ever talk of it again. We mustn't even think of it, in case it shows in our talk, because Walter doesn't know.'

'Walter doesn't know! But that's absurd. He ought to be told.'

'Dear, he's having a hard struggle. Madge doesn't want him to be worried by knowing that she's dangerously ill. Particularly when the danger might pass and he'd have had the worry all for nothing. Besides, it's Madge's husband, and it's Madge's secret, and it's for Madge to decide whether he shall be told.'

'But, really, Jimmy, I think you're wrong. Walter ought to be told. It's only fair to him. You know how irritable he is. I've often heard him say things to her lately that he wouldn't have said if he'd known how ill she was.'

'Alice, I think I'll kill you if you don't promise not to tell Walter.'

'Jimmy! What a queer, exaggerated thing to say! What's the matter with you tonight, Jimmy? I've never known you like this.'

'Stop staring into that mirror. Put down that hairbrush. Turn round and look at me.'

She wriggled round on the stool, her lip quivering. 'It was your face I was looking at in the mirror, Jimmy.'

'Listen,' he said, 'because I'm going to tell you the truth . . .'

'Don't tell me anything tonight. I'm tired and you're tired . . .'

'I'm going to tell you the truth about yourself, and I'm going to do it now, because it may be too late tomorrow. Alice, you're the salt of the earth. In all the twenty years I've known you I've never seen you fail once in honesty or courage or generosity. You wouldn't tell a lie if you were to gain a million pounds by it. You'd hold your hand in the fire to save a person or a principle you valued. You'd give away your last crust to anyone you felt as kin. I know perfectly well that now you've learned Madge is hard up you'll cover her with presents, even if it means you have to go without things yourself. And besides that, you've got a kind of touching, childish quality – a kind of – a kind of . . .'

'Jimmy, what's the matter with you? Why, you're almost crying! What's the . . .'

'Well, we'll leave that. The point is that nobody likes having salt rubbed into their wounds, even if it is the salt of the earth.'

He bent over her like a boxer, peering at a recumbent adversary to see how his blow had told; but her blue gaze returned his steadily. 'I'm afraid I'm not clever enough for all this,' she said. 'I haven't the vaguest notion of what you're driving at.'

'I'm trying to tell you that you hurt people. You hurt them continually and intolerably. You find out everybody's vulnerable point and you shoot arrows at it, sharp, venomed arrows. They stick, and from time to time you give them a twist.'

'Jimmy . . .'

'I know why you want to talk to Walter. You'll point out to him that he's been sharp to Madge several times lately, and that she's probably a dying woman. That'll harrow him. It'll add remorse to the agony he'll be filled with by the dread of losing her. It'll turn a simple, honourable grief to something shameful and humiliating. But it'll do worse than that. Walter's a man who lives on his temper. He can't find his way in action unless he lets himself go. When something happens he's quite incapable of thinking it out quietly. He has to swear and storm and stamp about, and at the end of all the fuss some definite plan has crystallized in his mind, and he can get on with it. Madge doesn't care when he snaps at her, she knows perfectly well that at the bottom of his heart he hasn't a thought except for her and the children. But if you pretend to him that what he did in temper was of deadly importance, then you break his mainspring. He'll go about cowed and broken, he won't be able to stand up to life. That's the worst of you, Alice. You find out what people live by, and you kill it.'

Alice said gravely, 'Jimmy, I don't understand this. Are you telling me that Madge and Walter have been talking against me? I've sometimes thought Madge wasn't quite loyal.'

'Oh, stop talking nonsense.'

'But you're being rude!'

'No loyalty can live near you. You are disloyalty itself. Of course we talk against you behind your back. We have to protect ourselves. You're out to kill your nearest and dearest. No, sit still. I've got a whole lot more to tell you. Do you want to know the real reason why you aren't welcome in Leo's house? You think it's because Evie's jealous of you. That is the most utter rubbish. The trouble about Evie, if there is any trouble about Evie, is that she's overtrained. She's had every instinctive naughtiness like jealousy educated out of her. If she thought your brother was fonder of you than of her she'd set her teeth and invite you to lunch, tea, and dinner, at her house for every day in the week. But she knows that Leo can't bear you. Oh, he loves you, as we all do, because we know that apart from this devilish cruelty you're an angel, and because you've got this queer power of seeming a pitiful child that one can't help loving. But you frighten

Leo. You see, he came back from the war after he'd been gassed, and forgot it. He felt splendid, and he married Evie, and they had four children. Then he had to remember he'd been gassed. He had that attack of pneumonia, and that slow recovery. And every day when he was getting better you went and saw him, and you sat and looked at him with those round eyes and asked, with an air of prudence and helpfulness that meant damn-all, "But what are you going to do, Leo, if you have a breakdown and have to give up your practice?"'

'Well,' said Alice, 'if a sister can't express her concern when her only brother's ill, I really don't know what we're coming to.'

'Darling, don't you see what you were doing? You were up to your murderous tricks again. You were killing the thing by which he lived. He knows his number's up. He knows that one winter's day he'll get pneumonia, and then he'll die. And he doesn't want to die. He doesn't want to leave Evie. He adores her wit and her carelessness and her funny offhand way of treating everything as if it were a joke. People do, you know. Leo and Evie have a lot more friends than we have, you know. He doesn't want to leave his children either. And especially he doesn't want to leave Evie and the children deadly hard-up as he knows he will. So the only way he can get on from day to day is to forget that he's ill and going to die. But every time you come near him you remind him of it. "How's the cough to-day?" you say. "Oh, Leo, you ought to be careful." My God, if you knew how often Evie's telephoned me, "He's feeling low today, for God's sake keep her away . . ."'

'Jimmy,' said Alice, 'are you admitting to me that behind my back you've entered into a conspiracy against me with that woman?'

'But don't you understand that I'm telling you something real and true that you've got to listen to? This is something that you've done and mustn't go on doing. You've tortured Leo. Don't you realize that's why the eldest boy hates you so? Colin adores his father and he knows that every time you go to the house you leave him fit to cut his throat with depression. Naturally he gets black in the face when he sees you. But you're wrong when you hate him just as you're wrong when you like that abominable little pest Betty. She's becoming practically what they call a problem child. Just about her age children often start imitating some particular person in their surroundings, and somewhere in Betty's surroundings she seems to have found somebody who is an aggressive prig and public nuisance, who spends the whole of her forcible personality in proving everybody else her inferior. I can't think who it can be, of course. But anyway, she's almost driving the family mad. Will you try and realize in future when you try to stir up trouble against Colin that you do it because the boy comes between you and somebody you're trying to hurt, and when you encourage Betty it's because you scent she's going to be as cruel as yourself?'

Alice turned round on the stool and began to brush her hair again. 'You're simply being rude,' she said icily. 'I think you'd better sleep in the dressing-room tonight.'

'Oh, for God's sake listen to me and try to understand! Don't you realize that there's something wrong in this household and that we've got to alter it? Hasn't it struck you as odd that we've got no friends? People come here to formal dinner-parties and they ask us back, but they keep at arm's length. They're afraid of us. They're afraid of you. Look how you got old Norman on the hip tonight. Look how we can't keep our servants. And look how your own mother had to pack up and leave the town where she was born because she couldn't bear your tongue . . .'

'Oh, Jimmy, Jimmy, you mustn't say that!'

'It's true. You couldn't bear to admit her qualities, that she was brilliant and erratic and a marvellous story-teller. You built up a pretence that she was silly and untidy and garrulous. Didn't you tell me today what a shame it was that she'd made the young man who brought you here listen to the story of how she met Edward VII at Monte Carlo? Well, you're no fool. You ought to see that that's one of the funniest stories in the world, that she tells it superbly, and that the whelp, whoever he was, was damn lucky to have the chance of hearing it. But you don't see that because you want to make her out senile and worthless. Well, she knew that perfectly. She went to Madge and Leo crying and said that she hated leaving them, but that you made her feel she ought to be either in her coffin or in a home for the aged . . .'

'Stop, Jimmy, stop! I know that's true!' She was crying now, with the deep, painful, interminable sobs of a child, with their overtone of rebellion against wrong.

'Oh, my poor little girl, don't cry!' He had taken her into his arms, he was pulling out his big handkerchief. 'You don't know how I've hated saying all this.'

'But it's true about mother. I know that it's true about mother. She was so horrid to me.'

'Horrid to you? But she was crazy with anxiety when – when you were ill, and she wrote again and again saying how much she wanted you to come down and have your convalescence with her. Don't think she doesn't love you. We all love you – only . . .'

'No. No. She doesn't love me. She was horrid to me last night. I did everything I could to be nice to her, I helped her in all sorts of little ways. But when I told her that I was going home two days earlier than I had meant, she was glad. She gave an awful look of relief that I'll never forget.' She rubbed her weeping face against his coat-collar, but raised it to accuse him with miserable puzzled eyes. 'Of course mother's always been horrid about me underneath, and of course we haven't any friends. People have always loved being nasty to me all my life. The girls at school gave me a most horrible time. And I've always minded it so because I do so like people to like me.' Sobs choked her. 'That young man – who brought me home in his car – he liked me.'

'I'm glad of that,' said Jimmy. 'Poor little Alice, I'm glad of that.'

For a minute her memory blotted out this hot room full of quarrelling, and built round her the fresh morning on the moors, with its background of sooty branches and sharp green buds, its music of birds singing high in blue, shower-washed space, its foreground of forget-me-nots bending all one way under a glassy grey current. She remembered how gravely the boy's eyes had rested on her face, how gravely he had said goodbye. Then her face was contorted with a fresh spasm of weeping. 'People are always so nice to me at first,' she murmured, 'but afterwards when I get to know them something hateful happens to them and they turn round and are cruel to me. But what I can't understand is why quite suddenly you've taken sides with them against me.'

He gently pushed her away from him and took her face between his hands. 'Alice, is that really all that I've been saying has meant to you? Haven't I made you feel the slightest suspicion that maybe you do things to people which they think horrid?'

'You've been talking a terrible lot of nonsense,' said Alice. 'What's the use of pretending that a dreadful boy like Colin, who sticks out his underlip when he sees you and looks awful and hasn't any manners, is a nice child, and that a charming little girl like Betty, who's always polite and clean and well-behaved, is for some obscure reason a little horror? And as for the rest, I think I understand only too well, thank you. For one thing it's perfectly plain that you've been listening to Evie. She's apparently made some wonderful story out of the simple fact that, being fond of my only brother, I've guessed that there's something wrong with his health, and shown a very natural anxiety. And as for Madge, I can see she's been disloyal. But sisters often are, and I never thought poor Madge was perfect, and I won't let it make a bit of difference. What worries me is that you should have listened to all these people when they were being spiteful about me.'

'But, Alice, hasn't what I've said made any difference to you at all? Don't you feel that you've been doing some things that maybe, after what you've heard, you'd better stop doing?'

'No, I don't,' said Alice. 'It seems to me that what you've been attacking me about, thanks to all this nonsense you've been listening to, is just what you have to do when you're one of a family. I can't suddenly pretend that I haven't got any relations. Why, they'd be the first to be hurt. If I stopped going round to Evie's and helping her to clear up the messes she's always getting into, there'd be no end to her complaints.'

'Sometimes,' said Jimmy, 'you don't strike me as a grown-up, wicked person at all. You strike me as a child who for some extraordinary reason wants to be punished, and who goes on behaving worse and worse so that she'll compel somebody or other to punish her. Do you really mean to go on just the same?'

'Yes, I think so. If there's anything particularly you object to, I might . . .'

'Do you mean, for instance, to speak to Walter about Madge?'

She sat down on the stool again, and stretched behind her for the hairbrush with an enchanting gesture. 'As a matter of fact, I do.'

'Alice!'

'You see, I must.' She squared her jaw and looked like an exquisitely beautiful, tear-stained little bull-dog.

'Why?'

'I happen to know something about Walter that makes it necessary.'

'What's that?'

'Walter hasn't always been the husband to Madge that he ought to be.'

'You mean he's been unfaithful to her? Ah, that little blonde slut at Cadeford.'

'And he'd better be warned that this is no time for that sort of thing.'

Jimmy whistled. 'You could have a whole lot of fun out of that, couldn't you?' he said. 'You might even get poor Walter into such a state of dither that he confessed everything to Madge, and that would kill her outright. She doesn't understand that sort of thing, God bless her. Really, this is a find of yours, Alice. With your peculiar gift there's no end to what you might be able to make of it.'

He slid to the floor at her feet so suddenly, and in so limp a heap that she thought he had fainted, and was about to scream when he gripped her knees, laid his head on her lap, and spoke softly, 'Alice, remember what I said to you. About the unreasonable requests in the fairytale, and how the threats came true. That if the flower was eaten, the fruit plucked, the castle falls to pieces. I'm going to make another of those unreasonable requests.'

'My dear, I'm tired. This is my first night home, and I'd hoped for something rather different. What is it?'

He raised his head and his eyes implored her. 'Let me sell the business. Let's sell this house. Let's go abroad. Let's stop bothering about Madge and Walter, and Leo and Evie, and just be ourselves. We wouldn't be rich, but with what Father left me, we'd have enough for comfort. Please, Alice. Please.'

'Jimmy, I can't fathom you tonight. Do you really mean this?'

'I mean it more seriously than I've ever meant anything in my life.'

'You seriously mean that for no reason you want us to sell all our beautiful things and give up my family and my friends, and wander about as if we'd done something awful and had to live abroad? Jimmy, I really think you're mad.'

His head dropped back in her lap. It felt as heavy as a lump of lead, as if he were asleep. Then he looked up, and she saw with a kind of faint disgust, for she hated emotional displays in men, that the tears were thick on his lashes. 'Forgive me,

Alice,' he said. 'I think I've been mad, too, all evening. I've said cruel things to you, and they were useless as well as cruel. However, that's all over. You're a wonderful woman, Alice. You've got me right back where I was before you went away. As I was during your illness and before it. Perfectly sane.' He jumped lightly to his feet and gave her a loud, almost a smacking kiss on the cheek. 'Well, I'll go and undress now. The time's over for talk.'

'I'm glad you're sensible again,' she said, 'and if I've irritated you by sticking to my point about Walter, do forgive me. But, you see, I am so fond of Madge.'

'And just how fond I am of Madge,' he answered, 'is one of the things that you will probably never know.'

The dressing-room door closed softly behind him. She sighed with relief that the scene was over, and went on with her hair, putting down her brush and using her comb. But she had to admit that she felt shattered by this curious breakdown of Jimmy's, this appearance of frenzy and unreason in a character that had seemed till now wholly free from them. When a coal fell from the fire, she started; and when behind the swaying red taffeta curtains there was a tap on one of the windows, she swung round and said aloud, 'What's that?', and again there opened around her an image of a lost paradise, of forgone security and peace, the sense of that blue cold noon on the clean heath. Then she remembered that the ivy had not yet been pruned this year, and that its dark arms often stretched as far as the window-panes, and she turned about again. But she felt uneasy and tearful, and was glad when Jimmy came in again, slim and well-made in the dark blue silk dressing-gown she had given him for Christmas, which he would wear only seldom, because he said it was too dandified for ordinary occasions.

He came and stood beside her, and she stopped combing her hair while she studied his reflexion, and she uttered a faint exclamation of dismay.

'Anything the matter?' said Jimmy.

257

REBECCA WEST

'No. Only when I was in the New Forest with that young man this morning, I looked at him and thought he was very good-looking, but that he hadn't something in his face which you have, and which I specially love . . .'

'Yes?'

'And now I see what it is. It's your mouth.'

'Well?'

'And yet your mouth's cruel. Your lips are full, but you hold them so that they're thin – it's a cruel mouth.'

'Is it?' He bent down close to the glass. 'It may be. It's hard to tell about oneself. I think I hate it when I have to be cruel, but maybe I don't. Probably one never gets into a position when one's forced to do something unless one really wants to do it.'

'Jimmy . . .' she threw her comb down on the dressing-table. 'I wish you wouldn't go on being so horrible and hateful and queer. I know I seem not to have any nerves, but I have, really. I'm frightened of lots of things. I have those nightmares, you know.'

'What are your nightmares about?' he asked. 'You've never told me what they actually were about.'

'Why, I am standing in a room – now I come to think of it, it's this room – and something awful comes nearer and nearer to me, circling round me, drawing in on me, and I know that in the end it's going to destroy me utterly.'

'And you can't stop it?'

'No. The funny thing is – now, that's something else I never remembered before after I'd woken up – I could perfectly well stop this awful horror coming at me. Only for some reason I can't. I have to go on doing the very thing that brings it nearer.'

Jimmy turned away from the mirror. 'God, what a life this is,' he said, 'full of presciences that don't do us any good, full of self-consciousness that tortures us by telling us just what sort of hole we're in but never how to get out of it. It's nothing to cling on to, really.'

'Jimmy, you're being odd again,' she said. 'Please don't. I can't stand it, my first night home.' There ran before her mind's eye pictures of everything which had happened to her during this day which had risen so early to its peak, which was falling, in spite of all she could do, to such a dark, perplexing decline, and the memory of her first, slow, satisfied inspection of her home made her exclaim: 'Oh, Jimmy, I found two things in your room that interested me.'

He was at one of the windows now, staring out into the night between the red curtains, but now he strolled back to her. 'What were they?'

'Well, you know that big photograph of me in my wedding dress? Just think, it's been torn nearly the whole way across!'

'No!'

'Yes, really. Whoever did it tried to cover it up by gumming the edges together, but now the gum's got old and it's cracked, and the tear shows again. I thought at first it was a hair under the glass. It must have been that dreadfully clumsy housemaid we once had, called Lilian, Hall.'

'I wonder if it was?'

'It would be Lilian, she ruined everything she touched. Then the other thing was the tube of white powder in your pocket.'

'You found that too?'

'Yes. What is it?'

He dug down into his dressing-gown pocket and showed it to her on the palm of his hand.

'Yes, that's the thing,' she said. 'It looks like one of old Dr Godstone's phials.'

'That's just what it is,' he said. 'Once in his dispensary I picked it up, years ago, and he told me what it was. Then long after when he died and I was going through his effects I saw it and remembered the name on the label, and I slipped it in my pocket, though I never thought I'd need it then. Yet I suppose I must have known I would, really, or I would never have taken it.'

'Well, there's no label on it now. What's it for?' said Alice.
'It's just something that sends people to sleep.'

'But if you want anything of that sort, why don't you go down to Leo and get him to give you whatever's most thoroughly up to date? You know what old Dr Godstone was. This is probably something that was used in the Ark.'

'Oh, don't be too harsh on the old man. There's nothing wrong with this. It works quite all right if you give it in the right dose. If you give too little it's no good; and if you give too much that's bad, too. But if you give the right dose, there's no more trouble.'

'Well, I suppose that's all right, provided you know the right dose.'

'I do now,' he said. He sighed deeply and stood for a second or two rolling it backwards and forwards on his palm, as though he would not be sorry to drop it; but he kept his eyes on it all the time. 'I only found that out ten days ago. Saturday before last I felt restless all the morning . . .'

'Oh, darling, I ought never to have left you,' said Alice, 'but I wrote you every Monday, Wednesday, and Friday, so you must have had a letter from me that morning.'

'I had,' said Jimmy. 'Well, in the afternoon I got out the car and drove right across England to Bathwick. I'd never been there before in my life, I don't know anybody there. When I found myself driving past the Public Library I stopped and walked in, just as if I was a good Bathwick ratepayer, and consulted a book on drugs. And I got the proper dose.'

'Well, it seems a casual way of taking medicine,' said Alice, 'but I suppose you'll be careful. Come in, Ethel.'

But it was Cook who came in with a glass and a steaming jug on a tray. She put it down on the dressing-table with a clatter, and her body was solid as màsonry with grimness.

'Seeing as how there was unpleasantness about the new brand of chocolate,' she said, ignoring Alice's absent smile, 'I came up myself to explain that this is the old brand which I got through sending my sister's girl special down to the stores.'

'Good gracious, is Minnie back from her place in London? I'm afraid they'll never keep her anywhere you know, she's so untidy . . .'

'She's home on her holidays, while the family's gone to Italy,' said Cook with quiet triumph and shut the door with a bang.

'What's all that about?' asked Jimmy. He was still rolling the phial of powder backwards and forwards across his palm, and looking at it as if it were a jewel.

'Oh, a fuss about nothing. She's a rude woman, and she'll have to go. It's only that she bought another brand of chocolate malted milk,' said Alice, filling her glass from the jug, 'and I like this. The sort she got was mawkish stuff, I could taste the malted milk through the chocolate, and I hate that. This is very strong, you can't taste anything but the chocolate.'

'So if you hadn't made a row with Cook, you'd be drinking something with a milder flavour tonight?' said Jimmy. 'By God, that's funny.'

'Why?' asked Alice, and raised the glass to her lips. But she set it down again, because Jimmy was holding up his finger and jerking his head towards the door. 'What's the matter?'

'Why has Cook gone down the passage to the spare rooms instead of going upstairs to her bedroom?'

'Has she?'

'Yes, I heard her.'

'What an extraordinary thing. But these women,' she tiptoed to the door, opened it softly, and stood for a minute on the darkened landing, peering down the passage and listening. But she heard nothing save the creaks and stirrings that are the voice of an old house at night, and presently she heard Cook's ponderous tread across the ceiling above her. She went back into the bedroom and said, 'Jimmy, you're dreaming,' and sat down at her dressing-table and drank her chocolate.

Jimmy did not answer her, and she turned and looked at him over the rim of her glass. He was standing on the rug in front of the fire, his hands shoved so deeply into the pockets of his dressing-gown that his shoulders were hunched up, and his tallness looked rangy and wolfish. He was watching her with eyes that stared like a fever patient's, and his teeth pulled in his lower lip and let it go, again and again, as if he were enduring agony.

'But you look so ill,' she said, and set down her glass.

'Drink up that chocolate!' he told her, and she obeyed, then turned to him, her brows knit in annoyance, her lips parted, waiting for an explanation. But he said nothing, only came towards her and took the empty glass out of her hand with so curt a movement that she cried out in protest. It was a movement of a quality utterly unexpected in him, quite unlike any gestures she had ever seen him make throughout all the years they had been together. So might a burglar have snatched a ring from her finger. She stared at his back as he hurried out of the room, and put her hands to her head, trying to puzzle it out, when she heard the bathroom taps running.

'But what are you doing?' she asked as he came in with the clean glass in his hand and put it down, on the tray beside her, and poured into it what chocolate was left in the jug. 'What are you doing?' she repeated, as he poured the chocolate back again out of the glass into the jug.

Her own voice sounded far away in her ears, but his voice sounded farther away as he answered, 'Just taking precautions that probably won't be successful, but I really don't care much about that.'

She wanted to ask him to repeat what he had said, and say it more intelligibly, but then she thought she would rather tell him that she felt very ill. Sweat had come out on her forehead, snakes seemed to be sliding through her bowels, she wished she could either sit in a chair with a back to it or lie down, she was afraid she was going to slip down on the floor. She found it, however, difficult to speak. But Jimmy had seen for himself what was happening. She felt his hands slip under her armpits, and knew that he was carrying her over to the bed. With a great effort, for her lids were now very heavy, she opened her eyes and tried to see his face, and though everything shimmered glassy and wavered about her, she was sure that he was looking sorry for her, and as he laid her down and drew the blankets over her, she caught the words, heard indistinctly as through the surf of a tremendous sea, 'Poor little Alice'. She rolled over, cooling her damp forehead against the fresh linen pillow-slip, and moaning, because she knew that it meant something, if she could but collect her wits and think what it was, that now the taste of chocolate had gone, her mouth was full of a haunting bitterness. But she was too tired, she could only mutter that she wanted some water.

Notes on the Authors

Djuna Barnes (1892–1982) was born in an artists' colony
north of New York and educated by her parents. In the early
1900s she studied art and by 1913 was a regular columnist for
the *Brooklyn Daily Eagle*, illustrating her own work, also
contributing to other newspapers. In 1915 she published her
first poems, *The Book of Repulsive Verse*. After separating
from her husband in 1919 she travelled to Paris with letters
of introduction to Ezra Pound and James Joyce. Here she
became a stylish figure of expatriate life, at the centre of the
Modernist movement and began a ten-year relationship with
the silverpoint artist Thelma Wood. When this ended in 1931,
she was helped by Peggy Guggenheim and wrote her novel
Nightwood in its aftermath. Published by T. S. Eliot in 1936,
with his own introduction, it immediately became a cult
success, as did her last major work, *The Antiphon* (1958), a
dramatic poem inspired by her association with Eliot. This
enigmatic figure, whose circle included Natalie Barney, Kay
Boyle, Gertrude Stein and Antonia White, became a Green-
wich Village recluse in 1940. Virago publishes Djuna Barnes'
Smoke and Other Early Stories (1985), from which 'The Jest
of Jests' is taken and a collection of her articles, *I Could
Never Be Lonely Without a Husband* (1985).

Jane Bowles (1917–1973) was born in New York and began
writing at the age of fifteen. In 1938 she married the composer
and writer Paul Bowles and they spent the first year of their
marriage in the famous Brooklyn Heights boarding house in
New York, also tenanted by W. H. Auden, Benjamin Britten
and Carson McCullers. They then spent many nomadic years,
in Europe, Central America, Mexico and Ceylon, before

settling in Tangiers in 1947. One of the most celebrated figures of the 1940s, Jane Bowles was a writer's writer, described by her friend Truman Capote as 'a modern legend'. Her literary output was small, her career ending abruptly in 1957 when, aged forty, she suffered a cerebral haemorrhage which made reading and writing impossible. After a long illness she died in Malaga, Spain. *Everything is Nice: The Collected Stories* (1989), from which 'Plain Pleasures' is taken, features three previously uncollected tales. Jane Bowles' other work includes a remarkable play, *In the Summerhouse* and her only novel, *Two Serious Ladies* (1943), also published by Virago.

Leonora Carrington was born in 1917. She spent her childhood in a Lancashire mansion and was educated at convent schools and in Florence. When her family acceded to her desire to paint, she went to an influential school in the same year as the first Surrealist exhibition in London. Soon afterwards she met Max Ernst, a leader of the movement. She was nineteen, he was forty-six and married. They eloped, first to Paris and then to the South of France, where both painted and she started to write. In 1939 Ernst was arrested as an enemy alien. She procured his release, but when he was imprisoned the following year, she descended into madness and was subjected to horrific treatment in a Madrid asylum. Rescued, she met her first husband, a Mexican diplomat, with whom she went to New York. Separated amicably, she married a Hungarian photographer, with whom she had two sons and they settled in Mexico City. Disillusioned by savage reaction to student unrest in 1968, she left with her sons. One of the most talented writers and artists in Surrealism, she now divides her time between Chicago and Mexico City. Virago publishes her novel *The Hearing Trumpet* (1976), *The House of Fear* (1988) and *The Seventh Horse* (1978), which includes 'As They Rode Along the Edge'.

Willa Cather (1873–1947) was born in Virginia. When she was eight her father bought a Nebraskan ranch and the family moved from the ordered life of Old Virginian society to the Western prairies, then a frontier land of immigrant people. This pioneer life was to colour her later work. She graduated from the University of Nebraska, becoming a teacher and journalist, for six years working for and later editing *McClure's Magazine*. Her first collection of stories, *The Troll Garden*, appeared in 1905. In 1912 she gave up journalism to produce the novels, short stories, poetry and essays which established her reputation as one of the great American writers of this century. Her twelve novels (all of which are published by Virago) include *My Antonia* (1918), *The Professor's House* (1925) and *Death Comes for the Archbishop* (1927). Virago also publishes *The Short Stories of Willa Cather* (1989), selected and introduced by Hermione Lee and Hermione Lee's biography, *Willa Cather: A Life Saved Up* (1989).

Colette (1873–1954) was born Sidonie Gabrielle Colette, in a Burgundy village and educated locally. At twenty, she was brought to Paris by her first husband, Henri Gauthier-Villars, 'Willy', who pseudonymously published – and profited from – her first novels: The *Claudine* series (1900–03). Through him, Colette came to know Proust, Ravel, Debussy and Fauré, among others. After she divorced Willy, she spent six years on the stage and began an affair with the Marquise de Belbeuf (Missy). This ended when she married Henri de Jouvenal, with whom she had a daughter. As 'Colette', she established herself as a major talent with *Chéri* (1920) and *La Fin de Chéri* (1926). In 1935 she married Maurice Koudelet, with whom she lived until her death. One of the most admired French writers, Colette published over fifty books. She was also a drama critic, fashion columnist, feature writer and women's page editor. The first woman President of the Académie Goncourt, Colette was also the first French woman to be granted a State funeral. 'The Secret Woman' is taken from her collection of stories, *The Other Woman* (1971).

Nell Dunn was born in London in 1936 and educated at a convent, which she left at fourteen. She came to fame with the publication of *Up the Junction* (1963), the series of South London stories which opens with 'Out with the Girls'. Awarded the John Llewelyn Rhys Memorial Prize and filmed for television and cinema, it became a controversial success, as did her bestselling novel *Poor Cow* (1967, also published by Virago), which was also filmed. Her other work includes a children's book; a collection of interviews, *Talking to Women* (1965); *I Want* (1972; co-written with Adrien Henri and staged ten years later) and, most recently, *Grandmothers* (1991). Her acclaimed play *Steaming* (1981), was followed by *The Little Heroine* (1988) and *Babe* (1993). She has also written the television film: *Every Breath You Take* (1987). Nell Dunn has three sons and divides her time between London and Wiltshire, accompanied by two Jack Russells.

Penelope Gilliatt was born in London in 1932 and brought up in Northumberland where she was privately tutored. She attended Queen's College, London and Bennington College, Vermont, and has studied music theory, piano, harpsichord and clavichord. From 1961 to 1967 she was the film critic of the *Observer* and, for one year, exchanged roles with Kenneth Tynan, becoming theatre critic. In 1967 she became film critic for the *New Yorker*, for which she has written for twenty-five years, contributing profiles and stories. She has published several collections of short stories. The first, *What's It Like Out?* (1968), includes 'Living on the Box' which she adapted for television, and was followed by *Nobody's Business* (1972, also published by Virago). Her most recent collection is *Lingo* (1990). She has written five novels, including *A Woman of Singular Occupation* (1988) and was the author of the award-winning screenplay, *Sunday Bloody Sunday* (1971), which was nominated for an Oscar. Her other dramatic work includes films for television, plays and a libretto for the English National Opera. Her latest work of non-fiction is *To Wit* (1990), a celebration of comedy. Penelope Gilliatt is a Fellow of the Royal Society of Literature and has received a grant in recognition of her work from the American Academy of Arts and Letters. Based in London, she frequently spends time in New York and has one daughter.

Attia Hosain was born in Lucknow, UP, India, in 1913. She combined an English liberal education with that of a traditional Muslim household where she was taught Persian, Urdu and Arabic, and was the first woman to graduate from the feudal 'Taluqdari' families into which she was born. Influenced, in the 1930s, by the nationalist movement and the Progressive Writers' Group in India, she became a journalist, broadcaster and writer of short stories. In 1947, the year of Indian Independence and partition, she came to England with her husband and two children. Presenting her own women's programme on the BBC Eastern service, among others, for many years, she also appeared on television and the West End stage. Her collection of short stories, *Phoenix Fled*, appeared in 1953; her novel, *Sunlight on a Broken Column*, was published in 1961. Attia Hosain divides her time between London and India.

Jessie Kesson was born Jessie Grant McDonald in Inverness in 1915. Living in Elgin with her beloved mother (she never knew her father), her early days were spent dodging the Cruelty Inspector and the rent man, before she was sent to an orphanage in Skene, Aberdeenshire. She entered service as a teenager, settling on a farm in 1934, with her husband Johnnie. Her early years inspired her novels: *The White Bird Passes* (1958, and a prize-winning film in 1980); *Glitter of Mica* (1936); *Another Time, Another Place* (1983, also a prize-winning film in that year); and her collection of short stories, *Where the Apple Ripens* (1985), from which 'Until Such Times' is taken. All are published by Virago. Until recently, even while writing fiction and plays for radio and television, Jessie Kesson, has always done other work – as a cinema cleaner, an artist's model and, for nearly twenty years, as a social worker in London and Glasgow. Now a great grandmother and the proud recipient of a 'scarlet goon' (conferred by the Universities of Dundee and Aberdeen), she lives in London with Johnnie.

Rosamond Lehmann (1901–1990) was born in Buckinghamshire, a daughter of R. C. Lehmann. One sister was the actress Beatrix Lehmann; her brother was the writer John Lehmann. Educated privately, she was a scholar at Girton College, Cambridge. Her first novel, *Dusty Answer*, an esteemed success, was written while she was in her early twenties. In 1928 she married the Honourable Wogan Philipps, with whom she had a son and daughter. Her other novels include *Invitation to the Waltz* (1932) and its sequel *The Weather in the Streets* (1936), which were filmed by the BBC in 1983. During the war Rosamond Lehmann contributed short stories, including 'A Dream of Winter', to John Lehmann's *New Writing*; these form *The Gypsy's Baby* (1946). Her autobiography, *The Swan in the Evening*, appeared in 1967. A Vice President of International PEN and of the College of Psychic Studies, and a Fellow of the Royal Society of Literature, Rosamond Lehmann was made a Commander of the British Empire in 1982. Virago publishes all her work, with the exception of *Dusty Answer* and *The Echoing Grove*.

Tillie Olsen was born in Nebraska in 1912 and has lived in San Francisco for most of her life. The necessity of raising and supporting four children through 'everyday jobs' silenced her for twenty years. Public libraries were her college. Her publications include *Tell Me a Riddle*, whose title novella won an O. Henry Award as the best American story of 1961, and in which 'I Stand Here Ironing' appears; *Yonnondio: From the Thirties* (1974, Virago 1980); *Silences* (1978, also published by Virago); and *Mother to Daughter, Daughter to Mother* (1984). Among the colleges where Tillie Olsen has taught or been writer-in-residence are Amhurst College, Standford University, MIT and Kenyon College. She is the recipient of five Honorary Degrees; grants from the National Endowment for the Arts and the Ford Foundation; Radcliffe Institute and Guggenheim Fellowships; and an award from the National Institute of Arts and Letters. In 1980, when the British Post Office issued commemorative stamps for Emily and Charlotte Brontë, George Eliot and Elizabeth Gaskell, they selected Tillie Olsen for a special award as 'the American woman writer best exemplifying in our time their ideals and literary excellence'.

Grace Paley was born in the poor quarter of Lower East Side Manhattan in 1922, the child of Russian Jewish parents. She grew up a creature of two cultures – her father teaching her Yiddish and Russian, the people around her providing raw material for her future work. She had little formal education and began to write in the 1950s. Her first volume of short stories was *The Little Disturbances of Man* (1959); *Enormous Changes at the Last Minute*, which features 'Distance', followed in 1974, and *Later the Same Day*, in 1985. These collections and her poems *Begin Again* (1993) are published by Virago. Grace Paley has never published a novel: 'Art is too long and life is too short,' she has said. She has a son and daughter and has taught literature at Columbia College, Syracuse University and Sarah Lawrence College, New York, but her most important distraction from writing is politics. A pacifist, she has devoted enormous energy to anti-war campaigns, especially during the Vietnam war, and nuclear disarmament. She lives in Vermont and New York City.

Dorothy Richardson (1873–1957), a daughter of an impoverished gentleman, was obliged to earn her own living from the age of seventeen and worked as a governess, in Hanover, London and finally in the country. Following the break up of the family after her mother's suicide in 1895, she began a new life in London, working as a secretary-assistant to a dental practice, while writing magazine articles. Her friends were the socialist and avant-garde intellectuals of the day and she was encouraged by H. G. Wells, among others. In 1917 she married the artist Alan Odle and they divided their time between London and Cornwall. Journalism became her livelihood, but the sequence of novels *Pilgrimage* (published in four volumes by Virago), was Dorothy Richardson's vocation from 1912 onwards. With its innovative use of the 'stream of consciousness' technique, she was hailed as the greatest woman genius of her time. 'Seen from Paradise' appears in *Journey to Paradise* (Virago, 1989), a volume of stories and sketches, selected and introduced by Trudi Tate.

Elizabeth Taylor (1912–1975) was born Elizabeth Coles in Reading, Berkshire, and educated at the Abbey School in Reading. She then worked as a governess and in a library and, at the age of twenty-four, married a businessman with whom she had a son and daughter. Much of her married life was spent in the village of Penn, Buckinghamshire. Elizabeth Taylor published twelve novels: her first, *At Mrs Lippincote's* (1945), was written during the war while her husband was in the RAF; *Angel* (1957) was selected by the Book Marketing Council as one of the 'Best Novels of our Time' (1984); her last novel, *Blaming*, written while she was dying of cancer, was published posthumously in 1976. Her short stories were published widely in magazines such as the *New Yorker* and *Harper's Bazaar*, and collected in four volumes, of which the best known is perhaps *The Devastating Boys* (1972), in which 'Flesh' appears. All of Elizabeth Taylor's novels and short stories are published by Virago. Her friends included Elizabeth Bowen, Ivy Compton-Burnett and Robert Liddell; one of her many contemporary admirers, the American writer

Anne Tyler, has written: 'Like Jane Austen, like Barbara Pym, like Elizabeth Bowen – soul-sisters all – Elizabeth Taylor made it her business to explore the quirky underside of so-called civilization . . . when you're reading [her work] there's always an element of self-congratulation. Oh, what you've caught.'

Sylvia Townsend Warner (1893–1978) was born in Harrow, the daughter of the Head of the Modern Side of Harrow. As a student of music, she became interested in the fifteenth and sixteenth centuries, spending ten years as one of the four editors of the ten-volume compilation, *Tudor Church Music*. A volume of verse, *The Espalier*, appeared in 1925. She found immediate recognition with the novels *Lolly Willowes* (1926), nominated for the Prix Femina; *Mr Fortune's Maggot* (1928); and *The True Heart* (1928); and established a transatlantic reputation with the stories she contributed to the *New Yorker* for over forty years. In the 1930s Sylvia Townsend Warner was a member of the Executive Committee of the Association of Writers for Intellectual Liberty and, in 1937, as a representative for the Congress of Madrid, witnessed the Spanish Civil War firsthand. A writer of formidable imaginative power, she published seven novels (six of which appear in the Modern Classics series), four volumes of poetry, a volume of essays, an acclaimed biography of T. H. White, and eight volumes of short stories. 'An Act of Reparation' appears in her *Selected Stories* (1989). Sylvia Townsend Warner spent most of her adult life with Valentine Ackland in Dorset.

Rebecca West (1892–1983) was born Cicily Isabel Fairfield in London, adopting her pen name from Ibsen's drama *Rosmersholm*. She appeared in print as a journalist and political writer as early as 1911, in *The Freewoman* and was soon deeply involved in feminism and social reform. Her novels include *The Return of the Soldier* (1918), *The Thinking Reed* (1936), *The Fountain Overflows* (1956) and *The Birds*

Fall Down (1966). 'The Salt of the Earth' appears in her collection of four novellas, *The Harsh Voice* (1935). Among Rebecca West's other notable works are a biography of St Augustine, her two-volume magnum opus, *Black Lamb and Grey Falcon* (1937) and *The Meaning of Treason* (1949) drawn from her reports of the Nuremberg trials. Her only child, Anthony West, is the son of H. G. Wells. In 1930 she married Henry Maxwell Andrews, the banker. A writer who dominated the world of letters for over seventy years, Rebecca West was created a Dame Commander of the British Empire in 1959. Virago publishes twelve books of her fiction and non-fiction.

Edith Wharton (1862–1937) was born in New York. In 1885 she married a Boston socialite, Edward Robbins Wharton. They lived on Rhode Island, frequently travelling to Europe, where she became a good friend of Henry James. Her first novel, *The Valley of Decision*, appeared in 1902. She went on to publish an average of more than a book a year for the rest of her life, finding her first critical and popular success with *The House of Mirth* (1905). Her husband's mental health steadily declined and in 1910, when they had settled in France, the unhappy marriage finally collapsed, ending in divorce in 1913. Edith Wharton was awarded the Cross of the Légion d'Honneur and the Order of Leopold for her work during the First World War, during which period her writing was largely abandoned. Afterwards, she moved north of Paris and wintered on the Riviera. With *The Age of Innocence* (1920), she was the first woman to win the Pulitzer Prize; she was also the first woman to receive a Doctorate of Letters from Yale University. One of America's greatest novelists, Edith Wharton became a member of the American Academy of Arts and Letters in 1930. Virago publishes eleven of her works of fiction, including *Roman Fever* (1964), which features 'Souls Belated'.

NOTES ON THE AUTHORS

Antonia White (1899–1980) was born in London and educated at a Roehampton convent, St Paul's Girls' School and RADA. She joined W. S. Crawford as a copywriter in 1924, became Assistant Editor of *Life and Letters* in 1928, theatre critic of *Time and Tide* in 1934, and was the Fashion Editor of the *Daily Mail* and then the *Sunday Pictorial*. During the Second World War she worked at the BBC and the Foreign Office Political Intelligence Department. *Frost in May*, which was later to launch the Modern Classics series in 1978, appeared in 1933 and was followed by *The Lost Traveller* (1950), *The Sugar House* (1952) and *Beyond the Glass* (1954). This famous quartet of novels, filmed by the BBC in 1982, charted with extraordinary precision the growth to maturity of a Catholic girl. Antonia White also published a collection of short stories, *Strangers* (1954), an account of her reconversion to Catholicism, *The Hound and the Falcon* (1965), and *Minka and Curdy* (1957), her tribute to her cats. All these works, together with her early autobiography, *As Once in May*, and her two-volume *Diaries*, edited by Susan Chitty, the eldest of her two daughters, are published by Virago.